Praise for

CARLA NEGGERS

"Carla Neggers is one of the most distinctive, talented writers of our genre."
—Debbie Macomber

"Neggers delivers a colorful, well-spun story that shines with sincere emotion."
—*Publishers Weekly* on *The Carriage House*

"Tension-filled story line that grips the audience from start to finish."
—*Midwest Book Review* on *The Waterfall*

"Suspense, romance and the rocky Maine coast—what more can a reader ask for? *The Harbor* has it all. Carla Neggers writes a story so vivid you can smell the salt air and feel the mist on your skin."
—*New York Times* bestselling author Tess Gerritsen

"A well-defined, well-told story combines with well-written characters to make this an exciting read. Readers will enjoy it from beginning to end."
—*Romantic Times BOOKclub* on *The Waterfall*

"Neggers's brisk pacing and colorful characterizations sweep the reader toward a dramatic and ultimately satisfying denouement."
—*Publishers Weekly* on *The Cabin*

Also by CARLA NEGGERS

DARK SKY
THE RAPIDS
NIGHT'S LANDING
COLD RIDGE
THE HARBOR
STONEBROOK COTTAGE
THE CABIN
THE CARRIAGE HOUSE
THE WATERFALL
ON FIRE
KISS THE MOON
CLAIM THE CROWN

CARLA NEGGERS
BREAKWATER

ISBN 0-7783-2237-8

BREAKWATER

Copyright © 2006 by Carla Neggers.

All rights reserved. Except for use in any review, the reproduction or utilization of this work in whole or in part in any form by any electronic, mechanical or other means, now known or hereafter invented, including xerography, photocopying and recording, or in any information storage or retrieval system, is forbidden without the written permission of the publisher, MIRA Books, 225 Duncan Mill Road, Don Mills, Ontario, Canada M3B 3K9.

www.MIRABooks.com

Printed in U.S.A.

1

Quinn Harlowe gave up trying to concentrate and tapped a few keys on her iBook, saving the file she'd been working on.

Defeated by an alphabet book, she thought, smiling at the little boy who'd crawled, book in hand, onto his mother's lap at the next table. He made a face and turned his head away from her. His mother, flaxen-haired and smartly dressed, didn't seem to notice and kept reading.

She was only on B. There was a lot of the alphabet to go.

Quinn took a sip of her espresso. The draft of the workshop she was giving at the FBI Academy next month would have to wait. She didn't mind. It was just one o'clock on a perfect early-April Monday afternoon, and she was her own boss. She could work tonight, if necessary. Why *not* blow off an hour?

Thinking it would be cooler today, she'd worn a

lightweight black cashmere sweater that now was too warm. At least she'd pinned up her hair, almost as black as her sweater, and had worn minimal makeup.

Four tiny, rickety tables, each with two chairs, and a row of big flowerpots filled with pansies passed for a patio at the small coffee shop just down the street from her office. Despite the gorgeous weather, she and the mother and son were the only ones outside, and the other two tables were empty.

Washington, Quinn thought, was never more appealing than in early spring.

She suppressed an urge to head off to Potomac Park and see the cherry trees—that would take the entire afternoon. Even native Beltway types like herself couldn't resist the brief, incredible display of delicate pink blossoms on the more than three thousand Japanese cherry trees that lined the Tidal Basin in Potomac Park. The annual National Cherry Blossom Festival, which attracted tourists from all over the world, was winding down. In a matter of even just a day or two, the blossoms would be gone.

The mother was on the letter D. What would D be for? Quinn smiled—duck. Had to be.

Dinosaur.

She took a bite of her croissant, the bittersweet chocolate center soft but not melted. An indulgence. She'd have a salad for dinner.

"Quinn—Quinn!"

Startled, she looked up, crumbs falling onto her iBook as she tried to see who'd called her.

"Quinn!"

Alicia Miller ran across the street, heading for the small patio. Instead of going around to the opening by the coffee shop's entrance, she pushed her way between two of the oversize flowerpots, banging her knees.

"I need your help—*please*."

Quinn immediately got to her feet. "Of course, Alicia." She kept her voice calm. "Come on, sit down. Tell me what's going on."

Gulping in a breath, Alicia stumbled over an empty chair and made her way to Quinn's table. "I can't—you have to help me." She seemed to have trouble getting out the words. "I don't know what else to do."

"Alicia—my God. What's wrong?"

Tears had pasted strands of her fine dark blond hair to her cheeks. Her face was unnaturally flushed. Her eyes—almond-shaped, a pretty, deep turquoise—were red-rimmed and glassy, darting anxiously around her.

The young woman at the next table shut the alphabet book and grabbed her son around his middle, poised to run.

Quinn tried to reassure her. "It's okay—Alicia's a friend."

But the woman, obviously not reassured, dropped the book on the table and lifted her son, his bottom planted on her hip as she swept up her slouchy, expensive tote bag and kicked the brake release on his stroller, pushing it in front of her toward the opening at the end of the flowerpots.

The little boy pointed at the table. "My book!"

"I'll get you another."

He screeched with displeasure, but his mother didn't break her stride until she reached the sidewalk. She dumped the boy in the stroller, hoisted the tote bag higher onto her shoulder and was off.

Alicia didn't seem to notice the impact she'd had on the mother and son. She couldn't have gone to work today. Not in this shape, Quinn thought, concerned about her friend. They'd known each other since their days together at the University of Virginia, keeping loosely in touch after Alicia returned home to Chicago to work. A year ago, Alicia had headed back East, taking a job at the U.S. Department of Justice, where Quinn was an analyst. Not a great move for their friendship. Quinn's departure from DOJ in January hadn't helped as much as she'd hoped it might. She'd let Alicia borrow her cottage on the Chesapeake Bay for the last five weekends in a row, but not once had her friend invited her to join her, even for an afternoon.

Quinn suspected Alicia must have come straight from the cottage. She smelled like saltwater and sweat and wore a blue cotton sweater, jeans and sport sandals that looked as if they'd been wet recently.

Of Quinn's friends and former colleagues, Alicia Miller was least likely to make a scene.

"Please. I need to…" She grabbed Quinn's lower arm, her fingers stiff and clawlike as she struggled to stay focused on what she was saying. "I need to talk to you."

Quinn touched her friend's cold hand. "Okay, we can talk. Let's sit down—"

She squinted, shutting her eyes. "I can't think."

"What can I do to help?"

Her eyes flew open. "Nothing! No one can do anything now. The osprey…" She screwed up her face, fresh tears leaking out of the corners of her eyes. "I saw an osprey tear apart a duckling. I think it was last weekend. It was horrible. The poor little baby."

"I'm sorry. They're birds of prey, so that sort of thing happens, but it's not pleasant to witness." Quinn kept her voice calm. "Can I get you a cup of coffee, anything?"

"You're working…"

Quinn reached over to her table and flipped her iBook shut. "Not really. It's a beautiful day. I've been resisting heading over to the Tidal Basin to see the cherry blossoms. They won't last much longer."

Alicia mumbled something unintelligible. She couldn't seem to stand still or stop fidgeting. This was beyond a touch of burnout and the stress of her job getting to her—today she appeared to be on the verge of a total meltdown. She jerked her hand back from Quinn's forearm. "I can't…I don't know what to do."

"About what? The osprey? Alicia…" Quinn hesitated, not wanting to say the wrong thing. "Why don't we go back to my office? We can talk there."

Her friend didn't seem to hear her. "The osprey, the osprey. Quinn, the osprey." Stabbing stiff fingers into her hair, Alicia gulped in three rapid breaths, fresh tears spilling down her raw cheeks. "The osprey will kill me."

She stiffened her arms as if she was trying to keep herself from shattering into little pieces. Her movements were uncoordinated, jerky. In recent months she'd been openly restless, looking, she said, for more to life than her work, her next promotion, success—she just didn't know what. Weekends on the bay were supposed to help her figure that out.

"Alicia, at least let me take you to your office. Someone there can help—"

"No!" She backed up a step, hitting Quinn's table, startling herself. "I can't—I can't think."

Alicia pushed at the air, as if she was trying to bat away something flying at her. Had the osprey preying on a duckling so traumatized her? Quinn reached for her briefcase, her cell phone zipped inside. If necessary, she'd call 911.

"No one knows I'm here, seeing you. I didn't tell anyone." Alicia lowered her voice to a conspiratorial whisper, but she couldn't seem to stop herself from moving. "Not a soul."

Quinn felt a surge of helplessness. "Alicia, what's wrong. Just relax—"

"Don't tell anyone about me." Her eyes seemed to clear, and her entire body stiffened. She took in a sharp breath. "*Please* don't tell anyone."

"Okay."

"Promise me." But she didn't wait for an answer, and whispered, "I'm not myself. I—I know I'm not."

Ivan Andropov, the Russian immigrant who owned the café, came out onto the tiny patio in his white chef's apron, holding up a cell phone in one hand. "What's going on? I'm calling the police—"

Alicia gasped and bolted, knocking over a chair, pushing her way between two flowerpots.

Quinn waved a hand at Ivan as she climbed over the flowerpots, her three-inch high heels not as suited to mad dashes as Alicia's sport sandals. "Don't call the police, Ivan. She's a friend." She ran onto the sidewalk, but Alicia was already to the corner. "Alicia! Hold up. Nobody's calling the police."

She didn't even glance back. At the intersection, a shiny black sedan pulled alongside her. It resembled half the cars in D.C.

The back door on the driver's side opened.

Alicia jumped inside, and the door shut immediately, the window's tinted glass hiding her from view as the car sped up the street.

Quinn kicked off her shoes and ran, but when she reached the corner, the car was out of sight. She hadn't caught a single number of its license plate or so much as a glimpse of the driver.

Who had opened the back door?

If Alicia hadn't told anyone she was here, how had the car managed to find her? Had she hired one for the day? But hiring a car seemed beyond her abilities. Physically, emotionally, she didn't seem to be in a state to do much of anything on her own.

Quinn returned to the café, her iBook and briefcase on the table where she'd left them. She picked up the abandoned alphabet book and brought it over to Ivan, frowning at her in the coffee-shop doorway, his arms crossed tightly on his chest. He was in his early forties, round-faced and congenial, but he didn't like scenes.

He took the alphabet book and grunted. "They'll never be back."

"Did you call the police?"

He shook his head. "I don't like police. This friend…" Ivan seemed to exaggerate his Russian accent. "She's crazy?"

"No. I know it looked that way just now, but no, she's not crazy. We haven't been that close lately—since I left Justice."

His eyes widened. "She's a lawyer?"

"Yes, but she hasn't been in a courtroom since law school. I'm sure she didn't go in to work today, not looking the way she did just now." *And acting,* Quinn thought. "She's been borrowing my cottage for weekends. She said she was a little burned out at work."

"A little?"

"Maybe more than I realized."

Quinn felt her hair coming out of its pins, but didn't care. She had left behind the pressure-cooker atmosphere of working at Justice because she'd wanted more normalcy to her life. The flexibility of self-employment. A more gentle pace to her days, or at least a pace she could control herself instead of one foisted upon her.

While most of her friends had applauded her departure from DOJ, Alicia regarded it as a personal affront, a betrayal not only of friendship but of shared ambition, despite their different jobs and interests.

"I never imagined…" Quinn didn't know what else to say. "I swear, Ivan, what happened just now isn't like Alicia at all."

"Drugs," he pronounced, dropping his arms to his sides. "She's on drugs."

Quinn didn't argue with him.

2

Wedged on the floor of the Lincoln Town Car's back seat, Alicia Miller twitched and sobbed, no real words coming out, at least none that Steve Eisenhardt could distinguish. He was in back with her, trying not to show the Nazis up front how upset he was. He worked at the Justice Department with Alicia—he was her friend. If he'd had his way, he'd have been more than a friend. Lately, though, he hadn't had his way about much of anything.

Yet even now, after he'd betrayed her to the goons up front, Steve found himself wanting to save her. He'd never felt so helpless. His shit parents, his yawner years at law school, his panic over passing the bar—nothing in his past came close to rivaling the mess he was in now.

He'd made his deal with the devil. Now the devil had come for his due.

Alicia kicked his shins in spasms she couldn't

seem to control. She'd worsened noticeably in the five minutes since she'd gotten in the car. She was more anxious, more incoherent. In her normal state of mind, she'd be horrified to see herself this way. She was a poised, cool beauty, a smart attorney, the adored daughter of Chicago doctors. He had never stood a chance with her. He'd come on board at DOJ two months ago, another ambitious lawyer with inherited money and political connections. Alicia would confide in him, advise him about toning down his "arrogance" and grace him with her friendship, but she would never consider him as a potential love interest. He wasn't bad-looking—but not a stud, either. By Washington standards, he was pretty ordinary. Alicia Miller, however, wasn't interested in ordinary.

And now her attitude had gotten her into serious trouble.

Steve leaned forward over the front seat. "If something happens to her and the cops check this car, you bastards better have the number of a good lawyer." He thought he sounded relatively calm, although his voice was slightly more high-pitched than normal. "Her DNA's all over the place back here."

No answer from the two goons in front. He didn't know who they worked for. He had ideas, but he didn't want details. The driver looked like an SS guard. The other one was straight off a Hitler Youth poster—he couldn't have been more than twenty. They both had buzz cuts, fullback shoulders, square jaws, lots of attitude and no sense of humor. None. Steve dealt with tension through humor. Not these bastards.

The SS guard pulled to the side of Pennsylvania Avenue and turned around to face Steve. He didn't know the guy's name. He didn't *want* to know. The bastard's yellow-looking eyes by themselves were enough to scare the hell out of the dead.

"Get out. Go back to your desk. You know nothing."

"Damn right."

Not even a glimmer of a smile. "We'll be in touch."

"I've done my part. You can't keep—"

The Hitler Youth kid joined the driver in glaring into the back seat. "Out, now."

Steve didn't argue. He didn't ask what would happen to Alicia. He'd received a call on his cell phone during lunch instructing him to be on Pennsylvania Avenue in ten minutes. The "or else" was implied. He hadn't been threatened with maiming or death. Not yet. So far, the only threat was an end to his career, public humiliation, arrest and possible jail time.

The bastards had pictures of him and a prominent congressman's fifteen-year-old daughter.

Complying with his instructions, Steve had raced to the appointed place, arriving in less than ten minutes. The Lincoln picked him up and whisked him off toward Dupont Circle. Alicia was wandering around D.C., and his job was to get her in the car. She trusted him. If she saw him, she'd cooperate.

They were right, of course, which he found only marginally comforting. If he was going to be blackmailed by Nazi goons, he wanted them to be smart Nazi goons, ones who wouldn't get caught and expose him. He would do their bidding and hope they went away once they'd run out of dirty work for him.

When he'd spotted Quinn Harlowe, he had experienced a moment of panic. Quinn was a historian, not an attorney, but the Harlowes were notorious for noticing *every* damn thing. Probing, questioning, launching headfirst into danger. Quinn said she wasn't like her forebears, but that was denial. Hadn't she quit a secure job and gone out on her own at thirty-two? Wouldn't it occur to her that she might need a few more years of salaried work under her belt, that she might just screw up and lose her shirt.

As far as Steve was concerned, courageous people made cowards like him look bad, and often got them in trouble.

He had to admit the situation he was in right now was his own fault. He'd been stupid and weak.

Fortunately, the car's tinted windows prevented Quinn or anyone from seeing into the back seat, and the Nazis, experts in defensive driving, had moved fast.

But Steve knew he'd die with the image burned into his brain of Alicia's look of relief turning to horror when she saw the two men in the front seat and realized he'd betrayed her.

The sedan stopped just long enough for him to

hit the pavement, then pulled back onto Pennsylvania Avenue, becoming just another Lincoln Town Car on D.C.'s jam-packed streets, Washington's notorious traffic even worse during cherry-blossom season. The annual two weeks of insanity would be over soon. With any luck, Steve thought, so would his month of nightmares.

He adjusted his suit coat and tie and took out a folded handkerchief, mopping his brow. Nothing he could do about his saturated shirt. He'd been sweating like a pig since the call to come meet these guys. Fortunately, he hadn't had time to eat. Otherwise he'd have barfed up his lunch by now.

He slowed his pace as he approached the imposing neoclassical headquarters of the United States Department of Justice, a massive building that occupied the entire block between Pennsylvania Avenue and Constitution Avenue. His excitement at finding out he'd be working under Deputy Assistant Attorney General Gerard Lattimore himself had faded in his two months on the job. Now he had not only betrayed Alicia, his only real friend at DOJ, but also the hundreds of superb, honorable DOJ employees who'd be tarnished by what he'd done.

But he was an aberration. Duplicitous, reprehensible. Scum. He'd known what he was doing, both with the congressman's underage daughter and with Alicia. The kind of risks he took were never for anything noble or remotely worthy. With the congressman's daughter—sexual gratification. With

Alicia—saving his own skin. At least with his sexual escapades he could rationalize his behavior by deluding himself into believing he was the only one who got hurt.

But after seeing Alicia stuffed in the back seat of the Nazis' car, whimpering and twitching, he no longer could deceive himself.

The goons can't have any reason to want her dead.

Steve arrived at his cubicle. Who the hell was he kidding? These bastards were true believers. He had no doubt they'd kill anyone who got in their way. Alicia. Him. He didn't know how Alicia had run afoul of them—he didn't want to know. But, clearly she had.

A message from Quinn Harlowe was on his voice mail. His heart pounded as he listened to her tight, controlled voice, asking him to call her as soon as possible.

He checked his cell phone. She'd left a message there, too. He used it to return her call.

She picked up on the first ring. "Steve, thanks for getting back to me. I know you and Alicia have become friends—have you seen her this afternoon by any chance?"

"I haven't seen her at all today. As far as I know, she didn't come in to work. I thought she was still at your cottage. What's going on?"

"I saw her about a half hour ago. I was having coffee down the street from my office, and she stopped by. She was upset about something and wanted to talk to me about it, but she ran off before I could find out what was wrong."

"Why did she run off?"

"The owner of the coffee shop misread the situation and threatened to call the police."

Steve felt a fresh rush of sweat on his brow. *The police.* "He didn't go through with it?"

"No."

Quinn wasn't one to get ahead of herself, no matter her sense of urgency. And she was loyal to Alicia. Their friendship might be strained, even on its last legs, but Quinn would never reveal compromising details regarding Alicia's condition without more to go on.

"Alicia hasn't been herself for the past few weeks," Steve said. "She's burned out. Everyone says it hasn't been the same around here since you left—not that it's your fault she's on edge. What do you want me to do?"

"I'll stop by her apartment and see if she's there. I don't want to make matters worse. She took off before I could get much of anything out of her, at least anything that made any sense."

Good, Steve thought. Quinn was dismissing or at least couldn't put together whatever Alicia had told her. He cleared his throat, wishing he could get the squeak out of his voice. "I'm sorry she was that upset."

"Me, too. If she shows up there, or if she calls, will you let me know?"

"Absolutely." His wet shirt felt cold now. "If there's anything else I can do, call me. I'm just here toiling in the trenches."

He didn't get even a chuckle out of Quinn. She

thanked him, promised to be in touch if there was news and hung up.

Steve slumped in his chair and blinked back tears. *Hell*. What a scumbag he was. He had met Quinn a few times at get-togethers after work with his colleagues, her former colleagues. She had a sense of humor and although she was very good at what she did, she wasn't calculating and superambitious, common ailments among Washington types.

Wherever the Nazis were taking Alicia—whatever her transgressions were—he wished he could believe she'd be okay.

It's out of my hands.

His calendar alert dinged. Five minutes until his afternoon meeting. Steve couldn't even remember what it was about. Would Lattimore be there?

Swearing to himself, he opened up a bottle of water and drank it down without once coming up for air. He felt better, and got back to work on behalf of the American people.

3

Something was wrong.

Huck McCabe paused to do a few leg stretches, a couple miles into his midafternoon run. He'd come to the end of a narrow road, a short spoke off the loop road that encircled the small Chesapeake Bay village of Yorkville, Virginia. In his forty-eight hours there, Huck had discovered that getting around the picturesque village didn't take impressive navigational skills. It had a main street lined with cute shops and an old-fashioned diner. It had the waterfront with lots of modest cottages. It had a couple of marinas and a smattering of restaurants that each served its own private family recipe for crab cakes, and it had three bait-and-tackle shops that offered up everything a fisherman could possibly need for anything from a weekend to a lifetime on the Chesapeake.

There were no giant trophy houses in Yorkville.

Most of the houses—year-round or second home—were built in the 1940s and 1950s. If he ran the town for a day, Huck would outlaw chain-link fences. It seemed every house had one, and he thought they were damn ugly, the only real blot on the otherwise quaint town.

The cottage where Alicia Miller had spent the weekend was the second of two small, older cottages on the dead-end road. It had no fence. Its ground-level front porch was low enough not to need a balustrade, allowing an unimpeded view of the water from its clean white wicker chairs.

Huck had noticed there was no car in the short dirt driveway. Nor was there any sign of life inside, although he hadn't gone so far as to knock on the front or side doors or peek in the windows.

He finished his stretches. He could have skipped them, but they gave him an excuse to check out the area. The road dead-ended at a salt marsh. On the other side of the marsh, about three-quarters of a mile farther up the bay, was Breakwater, known locally as the Crawford compound, the hundred-acre waterfront estate owned by wealthy Washington entrepreneur Oliver Crawford. Crawford had made his fortune in real estate and bought Breakwater five years ago. Most locals expected him to renovate the pre-Civil War house and retire there.

They were wrong. Crawford changed his plans for his bayside property after he was kidnapped off his boat in the Caribbean last December. His own security people rescued him after fifteen days of captivity. He was kept under grueling conditions and constant fear of a bullet in the head. His kidnappers got away. Traumatized, determined to help other businessmen avoid such horrors, Crawford decided to start his own elite private security company. Never mind that he knew little to nothing about the private security industry. He set about converting his bayside country estate into Breakwater Security, bringing in the people and equipment he needed, building the right facilities, sparing no expense.

Huck was a new Breakwater Security hire.

Ostensibly.

As he looked out at the water, he decided he could do worse than Virginia in springtime. He noticed that some kind of bird had built a giant mess of a nest on a buoy out at the mouth of the small cove. An osprey nest, he thought. The Northern Neck, a tidewater peninsula tucked between the Potomac and the Rappahannock Rivers, was on the Atlantic Flyway, making it popular with bird-watchers.

A Californian, Huck was getting used to the lay of the gentle land with its rolling hills, creeks, marshes, nature preserves, historic sites and small towns. Washington and Lee country. Life was slower here. He could picture George Washington and Robert E. Lee as little boys, fishing the same rivers, praying in the same churches that were still scattered across the landscape.

Or not—Huck didn't know what Washington and Lee did as boys or if the places he'd seen on his way to Yorkville had existed in their day. History had never been his long suit.

He was better at catching fugitives.

It was, after all, a fugitive who had inadvertently led him to the Northern Neck in the first place.

But he shut off that line of thinking, as if it might betray him, and jogged back down to the loop road, passing the second cottage, a sister to the one where Alicia Miller had stayed. He kept his pace slow, following the wider, but still quiet, road along the water, feeling the humidity building in the midafternoon air.

He came to a small, old-fashioned motel with its own dock. A couple of old guys in baseball caps smoked cigarettes on two benches above the water, watching fishing boats tie up for the day.

At first, even Huck didn't recognized Diego Clemente, his partner and backup, also an undercover deputy U.S. marshal. Clemente—also a Californian—looked as if he'd been fishing the Chesapeake Bay his entire life. He hopped off his boat onto the rickety dock wearing a New York Yankees cap, a bright yellow anorak, cargo pants and beat-up boat shoes. His brown skin and black hair set off a killer smile and killer eyes. Women liked Diego, but he and Huck had both sworn off women until they were back home, their current assignment behind them.

Breakwater Security wasn't necessarily the legitimate security company it purported to be. Diego was posing as a guy from up North who'd taken a month off to fish and get over his recent divorce, a cover designed to explain why he kept to himself. Not that there was a hell of a lot to do in Yorkville, Virginia.

Locked in Diego's boat, Huck knew, were state-of-the-art communications equipment, tactical gear and weapons, including, no doubt, Clemente's favorite MP5. If things went bad at Breakwater Security, Huck knew he could count on Diego Clemente to help him kick ass and stay alive.

Huck pretended to pause to catch his breath, although it would take more than a five-mile run to really wind him. He worked his butt off on a regular basis to stay in shape.

Standing next to him, Diego tapped out a cigarette, then held up the pack to Huck. Huck shook his head. "Smoking'll kill you."

"So will women, and still the knowledge of my impending doom doesn't stop me," Diego replied.

In his regular life, Diego didn't smoke. He was a nuts-and-seeds type. He pulled a small lighter from his pocket. "Storm's brewing. You can feel it in the air, can't you?"

"It's East Coast air. I can't tell."

Diego lit his cigarette and inhaled, blowing out smoke. "I talked to Nate Winter." Winter was leading the investigation into Breakwater Security's activities. "I don't have many answers for you. Alicia Miller is an attorney at Justice. She works under Deputy Assistant AG Lattimore."

"Gerard Lattimore? Hell, Diego, he and Crawford—"

"Friends since they were roommates at Princeton twenty years ago."

"The cottage?"

"It's owned by a woman named Quinn Harlowe.

Expert in transnational crime. She worked under Lattimore until January. Now she's consulting. I heard she's teaching a class or something at the FBI Academy." Diego pointed toward the water, as if they were discussing fishing. "She helped get Alicia Miller her job at Justice."

"So they were friends before they worked together. Any word on Miller?"

Diego didn't answer.

That meant no.

Alicia Miller had turned up at Breakwater early that morning—just past dawn—and yelled incoherently at the front gate. A couple of Crawford's existing security guys took her back to her cottage. They told Huck, who never saw Alicia, the basics—her name, that she'd spent the weekend in the cottage across the marsh and didn't approve of Oliver Crawford turning his estate into a new private security firm.

Follow-up questions weren't invited. Since he had a role to play, Huck shrugged off the incident and spent the morning settling in at Breakwater. At lunch, he took off for the village and found Clemente. They relied on face-to-face communication. It had its risks, but given the technical expertise of the people they were investigating, Huck and Diego both agreed—and got their superiors to agree—that primitive communication methods were safest.

Like Huck, Diego didn't believe Alicia Miller had shown up at Breakwater at dawn just to make a protest, either. He promised to find out what he could about her. Huck had returned to Breakwater.

Now, he was back, talking to Diego for a second time—a risk, but a necessary one.

"The Breakwater guys said Miller calmed down and went back to D.C.," Huck said.

Diego took a token drag on his cigarette. "Maybe." He tossed the cigarette onto the pavement, grinding it out under one foot. "She doesn't fit the profile of the typical crack-of-dawn protester. How incoherent was she?"

"I don't know. Nobody's saying. What about her boss, Lattimore? What does he know about our investigation?"

"Nothing. He's out of the loop. Nobody knows about you who didn't know before this morning. You're not compromised. Whatever Alicia Miller was up to at Breakwater—we'll find out." Diego cracked a small smile. "Maybe she *was* protesting."

Not exactly reassured, Huck left Diego to his fisherman's life and resumed his slow jog around Yorkville.

Very few people were aware of the existence of the task force looking into a particularly violent group of vigilante mercenaries operating in the U.S. and abroad, breaking the law when they saw fit. Their ends justified their means. They were responsible for kidnappings, tortures, extortion, smuggling, illegal interrogations, breakouts and murder.

Definitely bad guys, Huck thought.

Only a handful of the members of the task force had been informed of his presence in Yorkville.

Very, very few people were aware that a federal agent was on the verge of penetrating the vigilantes.

Huck preferred it that way. The fewer people who knew about him, the safer he was. The law of averages. He wasn't handpicked by the vigilante task force—he'd pretty much stumbled into the job. He'd gone undercover in California to search for a violent fugitive wanted by state and federal authorities. In the process of finding his fugitive and taking him into custody, Huck had managed to infiltrate the vigilante network. That brought him to the attention of the Washington-based task force. They offered him the most dangerous, tricky and bizarre assignment of his law enforcement career.

His lucky day, Huck thought with mild sarcasm.

That was back in January. For four long months he'd worked hard to earn the trust of the paranoid, ideological vigilantes and hard-core thugs who'd cheerfully slit his throat if they knew who he really was.

A half mile up the loop road from Diego's motel, a black Breakwater Security SUV pulled alongside him. Vern Glover was at the wheel. Vern was Huck's main lifeline to the vigilantes network. Scrubbed, freckled and auburn-haired, Vern was already half-bald at thirty and never would be anyone's idea of good-looking. He was also one unpleasant individual.

He rolled down the passenger window. "Get in. Storm's about to hit. You don't want to get struck by lightning."

Huck grinned. "Lightning bolts would bounce off me."

Vern ignored him and rolled up the window. No sense of humor. Huck climbed into the passenger's seat. Vern's best buddy was Huck's now-incarcerated fugitive, due to go on trial for drug dealing, rape, armed robbery and attempted murder. Although Vern had no criminal record, Huck presumed that his new friend hadn't exactly led a clean and quiet life. Occasionally, Vern would bitch to him about the bastard who'd turned his buddy into the feds and how he was going to find out who it was and kill him.

But Vernon Glover saw himself as one of an elite cadre of mercenaries who would save the U.S. from its enemies within its borders and beyond. A tall order, but Vern seemed determined and confident—a scary thought as far as Huck was concerned, because it meant Vern and his cohorts either had plans or were completely delusional. Or both.

Thunder rumbled off to the west.

Vern turned around at the small motel, practically in front of Diego Clemente's truck with its New York plates, and drove out toward Quinn Harlowe's road, bypassing it since it was a dead end. Huck could see the cute waterfront cottage. Still no car, still no sign of life.

"That an osprey nest?" he asked, pointing to the buoy in the quiet cove, giving Vern a reason for him to be peering in that direction.

Vern made a face. "Yeah. It's protected. Birds have more rights these days than people."

Always the optimist, Vern was. Huck said nothing. He had the same feeling he'd had on his run. Something was wrong. He just couldn't pinpoint what.

4

Quinn rang the doorbell to Alicia's first-floor Georgetown apartment for a third time, but she instinctively knew her friend wasn't there. When Alicia moved to Washington, as far as she was concerned, only one address would do—somewhere, anywhere, in Georgetown. With a trust fund her grandfather, a prominent Chicago doctor, had established for her, she bought a small condo in a black-shuttered brick townhouse on a narrow street of the historic, prestigious neighborhood.

Quinn realized Alicia wouldn't be coming to her front door at all—let alone acting like herself again, explaining that the stress of her job had finally gotten to her and she'd simply freaked out that morning.

Quinn descended the steps down to the street, recalling her last visit to Alicia's just after New Year's, when she had broken the news that she was quitting her job at Justice and going out on her own. Alicia, adept at concealing her true feelings, had claimed she wasn't surprised and wished Quinn well, then let it be known through mutual friends that she viewed Quinn's departure as something of a betrayal and resented her ability to make the jump into working for herself.

Quinn noticed the flower boxes on the front windows, which last spring Alicia had planted with a mix of bright flowers but now were filled with dead leaves and stale, dry dirt. She loved her home. Jobs and men might come and go, she'd say, but she always had her refuge.

The neglected window boxes were just another sign, if a trivial one, of Alicia's mounting burnout. In law school, she'd ended up in treatment for depression. The medication she was given didn't agree with her, but therapy by itself did the trick, and she got better. The entire experience wasn't something she shared with many people, but Quinn had been there. Now, given Alicia's bizarre behavior earlier, Quinn wondered if her friend ought to seek treatment for whatever was going on with her—it might not be just some funk she could snap out of on her own. If she was suffering from depression or some other mental illness, she needed to see a doctor. Period.

But Quinn recognized she didn't have the expertise to make a diagnosis herself.

Debating what else she could do, she walked back down to M Street, Georgetown's main commercial street. After giving up on chasing the black

sedan, she'd stopped at her office, in case Alicia
had asked her driver to drop her off there, but no
luck. Now she wasn't at her apartment, either. And
Steve Eisenhardt, who worked with Alicia at Justice, hadn't called back with any news of her.

If she called the police, Quinn knew they'd ask if
Alicia had gotten into the black car voluntarily, and
she would have to say yes. Alicia hadn't screamed for
help. She'd been agitated and semicoherent, but
she'd somehow found her way from Yorkville to
Washington and Quinn's office, then her favorite coffee shop. If Alicia was having some kind of breakdown, she wouldn't want the police involved. And
Quinn wanted to help, not to make Alicia's life more
difficult.

She crushed the temptation to let her mind spin
ahead of the facts and took the Metro Connection
bus back to Dupont Circle, a few blocks from both
her office and her apartment. She loved being able
to walk to work in the morning, one of her favorite
perks of self-employment.

She was so preoccupied with the bizarre scene at
the coffee shop that she almost walked past the ivy-
covered 1896 Italianate brick headquarters of the
American Society for the Study of Plants and Animals. Her eccentric great-great-grandfather was one
of the founders, and her slightly-less-eccentric marine archaeologist parents were directors, their latest project, funded by a private grant, having taken
them to the Bering Sea for most of the past year.

During college and graduate school, Quinn had
worked on and off for the Society, and when she de-

cided to go out on her own, she negotiated use of a vacant second-floor office in exchange for modest rent and help with cataloguing the mountains of stray stuffed carcasses, drawings, journals, musty papers, old clothes and junk tucked in the building's attic, basement and closets, a task the Society's directors had meant to get to for decades. So far, she had filled more trash bags than Society treasure chests.

A cherry tree shaded the gracious building's front entrance, its pale pink blossoms fluttering onto the sidewalk in a humid breeze. Quinn mounted the steps, waving to Thelma Worthington through the glass-front door. Thelma had served as the Society's receptionist since John F. Kennedy was president, the only occupant of the White House to acknowledge its existence when he referred to it as one of the country's great institutions. Nowadays, its well-managed endowment more than its contemporary relevance kept the American Society for the Study of Plants and Animals operational.

Thelma buzzed her in. When she tugged open the heavy door, Quinn entered another world, one of tall ceilings, ornate moldings, crystal chandeliers, Persian rugs, curving staircases and a respect—an encouragement—of eccentricity and risk-taking. Glass-fronted cabinets lined the center hall. As a child, Quinn remembered displays of glass jars of pickled organs and stuffed wild rodents and raptors. A new director, however, had replaced them with graceful porcelain figurines of wildflowers and songbirds.

Thelma took off the gaudy purple reading glasses she'd picked up at a drugstore. Despite the warm spring weather, she wore a sage-green corduroy ankle-length skirt and an argyle sweater vest over a white turtleneck. She had short gray hair and a Miss Hathaway face. Every summer, she picked ten mountains to climb.

"Any luck finding your friend?"

Quinn sighed heavily, suddenly tired. "Afraid not. Nothing new?"

"I'm sorry, no."

Alicia had stopped by the Society first, apparently not as agitated as she was by the time she'd arrived at the coffee shop. Thelma thought nothing of telling her that Quinn was just down the street, but she'd already apologized for not having paid closer attention to Alicia's frazzled emotional state.

"Did she go up to my office?" Quinn asked. "I wonder if she might have left a note, anything that could help—"

"She didn't go any farther than where you're standing right now. I almost didn't recognize her. I've only met her once. She hasn't seen your new office, has she?"

"No. We haven't been that close lately."

Thelma's eyebrows arched, but she kept whatever questions she had about the friendship between the two younger women to herself. She leaned forward, glancing toward the stairs. "You have company. He got here about ten minutes ago. He said he'd wait for you. I don't know how he has time—"

"Who, Thelma?"

She made a face. "Deputy Assistant Attorney General Lattimore."

"*What?* You didn't let him into my office, did you? All I need is for him to catch me cleaning out files on buffalo bones—he'll never let me hear the end of it."

"Relax. He's in the library." Thelma lowered her voice. "He's even better looking in person than he is on television. If I liked lawyers..."

Quinn tried to smile. "Thelma, you are so bad. I'll go see what he wants."

Resisting the urge to run up the stairs, Quinn contemplated what she would say to Lattimore. Steve wouldn't have told him about Alicia, but Gerard Lattimore was the type—alert, always waiting for the next shoe to drop—to have guessed.

She found her former boss in a high-back leather chair in front of the massive stone fireplace in the walnut-paneled library at the top of the stairs. He looked as if he belonged there.

"All you need are a pipe and slippers," Quinn said.

He didn't smile as he rose, studying her. He had on an expensive dark gray suit and looked every inch the high-powered Department of Justice official he was, but Quinn could see the strain in his eyes. Although he was only forty-two, he seemed ten years older this afternoon. He was the newly divorced father of three preteens and a talented attorney with awesome responsibilities. On most days, he had the ego, ability and ambition to meet all his obligations.

He took her hand. "It's good to see you, Quinn."

She reminded herself that he didn't have to be there because of Alicia. It could be anything. She let her hand fall back to her side. "Mr. Lattimore—"

"Gerard. No more formalities." He glanced around the old library, largely unchanged since the late nineteenth century. "What a great room this is. This whole building is like stepping into a simpler past."

"I'm not sure it was that simple. We do tend to run into the errant skull around here."

He laughed stiffly. "Museum-quality animal skulls only, I hope." He sighed, shaking his head. "Ah, Quinn. We miss you in the department."

"Thanks. I'd hate to have spent three years there and not be missed. I can just hear it: *'Harlowe? Not a minute too soon did she get her arse out of here.'*" But when she saw that her stab at humor only elicited a tense smile from him and realized how awkward and phony the banter felt, she gave it up. "What can I do for you?"

His gray eyes settled on her. "Alicia Miller."

Quinn licked her lips. "What about her?"

"I'm worried about her. She spent the weekend at your cottage in Yorkville. She didn't come in today. She didn't call in sick. Steve Eisenhardt— you've met him, haven't you? He says he tried to reach her on her cell phone, but she hasn't answered or returned his calls." He studied her a moment. "Quinn?"

"I saw Alicia this afternoon. Around one o'clock."

He motioned for her to sit down, but they both remained standing. "Tell me," he said, his expression even tighter.

Quinn resisted the impulse to pace. How much should she tell him? She'd promised Alicia to be discreet, but never expected her to bolt the way she did. If she was in any trouble, Lattimore needed to know. He was in more of a position to help than Quinn was.

"Quinn," he said quietly, "I know Alicia hasn't been herself recently. I'm worried about her mental health. She left early on Friday. She was agitated, anxious. She couldn't sit still. I caught her crying, hyperventilating, before she left."

"I didn't realize how burned out she was until today."

"What happened?"

In that split second, Quinn decided to tell him everything, including as much of Alicia's ramblings as she could remember. He listened without interruption. When she finished, Quinn was relieved that at least someone else now knew what she knew and could help figure out what to do. "I didn't recognize the car that picked her up or see who was inside. If you think I should call the police—"

"And tell them what? There's no reason to think Alicia didn't want to get in that car."

"She was totally freaked out, Gerard. I don't know that she was capable of making a good decision."

"Let's hope the people who picked her up were friends who understand she's on the verge of a nervous breakdown and can help her. Do you think she'd been drinking? Was she on drugs?"

"She didn't seem drunk, no. On drugs—I just don't see it."

He sighed. "I'm sorry. I know she's been preoccupied the past few weeks. She's taken a few extra days here and there—to stay at your cottage, I presume."

"I gave her a key after your party at the Yorkville marina last month and told her she could come and go as she pleased. I had no plans to use the cottage until later this month. When she first arrived in Washington, she helped me work on the place. We're not as close as we once were..." Quinn wondered if she'd said too much. "I hoped the cottage might help to thaw things between us."

"I understand. I know it must be hard for you, worrying about her. Alicia can be very distant at times, but she's smart and capable—she'll find her way through her problems. I'll see what I can do on my end."

"Alicia came to me for help. She never said what it was she wanted. Maybe there was nothing specific, but now..." Quinn shrugged helplessly. "I don't know what to do."

"You're a good friend to Alicia, Quinn, but sometimes—" He took in a breath. "Sometimes there's just not a damn thing we can do to help even a friend."

"I've got time. I'll drive down to Yorkville and see if she's at the cottage. I don't have a phone there—I can't call and see if she's there." She thought a moment, liking this idea. "I can ask the neighbors what they know."

"Why not call them?"

"I tried earlier. They're not home. Anyway, I don't want them to feel obligated to find Alicia. If she's there and needs help—maybe I can do something. I can take work with me if she turns up fine in the meantime."

"Let's hope she does." Lattimore walked out into the hall, his footsteps silent on the thick Persian runner, also original to the building. "Going to show me your office?"

"It's just down the hall—it's in the Octagon Room." Quinn could hear how stiff she sounded. "Gerard—"

"Maybe another time." He rubbed the back of his neck in a rare display of awkwardness. "If you ever heard anything, knew anything, that would put me in a bad light, you'd tell me, wouldn't you? Rumors, people's agendas. Whatever."

She frowned. "Why? Is there something going on that I should know about? Does it affect Alicia—"

"No, nothing like that. Sometimes the vultures get to me. That's all." He gave her a fake smile. "Comes with the territory."

Quinn followed him downstairs. By the time he reached Thelma's desk, he was loose and smiling, and when he said goodbye, the starchy, lawyer-hating receptionist couldn't maintain her neutral expression.

Outside on the steps, Quinn smiled at her for-

mer boss. "You charmed Thelma. That's not easy
to do."

"Thelma? Oh, the receptionist." He grinned.
"Doesn't like lawyers, does she?"

An answer wasn't necessary. Quinn had no illusions about Gerard Lattimore. He didn't like sur-
prises, and he never revealed all he knew on any
subject. It wasn't a stretch to guess that whatever
was going on with Alicia, he probably knew or
guessed more than he was saying. If one of his people was going off the deep end, he'd find out—and
he'd be careful. He was a political animal, alert
enough, nimble enough, to jump out of the way before he got burned.

After he left, Quinn didn't feel any better for having told him about Alicia. She returned to her office
and stood at a leaded-glass window, staring down
at a center courtyard with a formal maze of shrubs,
flowering trees and stone benches. The pretty, se-
date scene made Quinn wish she'd had coffee with
Alicia there instead of down the street. The atmosphere might have calmed her and helped her to ar-
ticulate what was wrong.

Quinn checked her private office line, but she
had no messages.

If Alicia was okay, why not call and reassure her?

Dropping into her swivel chair, Quinn let her
gaze settle on the dark, ominous oil painting of her
great-great-grandfather that hung on the wall to
her right. His name, too, was Quinn Harlowe. His
portrait came with the office. Like her, he had black
hair, pale skin and hazel eyes, but his face had more

sharp angles than hers, and his expression was more dour than she could ever manage.

As a little kid, the painting had scared the daylights out of her. Her father would grin at it with pride. "What an incredible man he was. Nothing could stop him. He had guts *and* luck."

A scholar and adventurer, Quinn Harlowe had died at ninety-eight, having explored parts of all the continents. His son wasn't so lucky, dying in an avalanche in the Canadian Rockies at fifty. *His* son, Quinn's grandfather, Murtagh Harlowe, was a gentle soul, a Civil War expert who'd all but raised her while her parents were off on adventures of their own. Everyone who knew her father as a baby said they realized he was a throwback to that first Quinn Harlowe, a risk-taker, even before he could walk.

Quinn appreciated her family history, but she didn't worry about where she fit in. She liked her quiet cottage by the bay, her work as an analyst. She wasn't an adrenaline junky.

Right now she wanted to find Alicia. Whatever it took. She called several friends she and Alicia had in common, but no one had heard from her. Had she gone back to the cottage?

On a good day, with reasonable traffic, the drive to Yorkville took about three hours. Beltway traffic, however, was seldom reasonable.

"The osprey, the osprey."

An osprey pair had built a nest on a buoy just offshore in front of the cottage. The large birds of prey made Alicia nervous. They'd never held much romance for her.

5

Deputy Assistant Attorney General Gerard Lattimore had his driver drop him back at the Department of Justice. As he returned to his office, he could feel his pulse throbbing in his temple, as if Quinn's words were pounding themselves into his brain. Somehow or another, Alicia Miller's nervous breakdown—whatever was wrong with her—would come back to haunt him. He was her boss. He'd hired her. If she went off the deep end, it would reflect badly on him.

Depressed, drunk, drugged—did it matter what had caused her to make the scene earlier today at the coffee shop? She was a problem he should have addressed sooner.

Pushing back his concern, his anger at himself, he walked down the hall to the maze of cubicles where Alicia worked and wasn't surprised to find Steve Eisenhardt at his desk. Lattimore warned himself not to get worked up. He had borderline high blood pressure and feared that the next crisis would pop him over the line, and he'd have to go on medication. Provided, of course, he didn't drop dead of a stroke first.

A faint body odor wafted up from Eisenhardt. Odd, Gerard thought, because he was fastidious about his personal hygiene. He and Steve had similar backgrounds—family money, political connections—but the younger attorney didn't have the same drive to prove himself. The kid was brilliant—he didn't have to work hard to impress anyone. Alicia had tried to get him to be a little less arrogant, a little less obviously jaded, but she liked him. Most people did.

Gerard was the exception. From his first week on the job, Steve Eisenhardt bugged the hell out of him. It wasn't Eisenhardt's arrogance or his ambition, and certainly not his family money or connections—it was the little bastard's sense of entitlement. If only he'd been the one to go nuts, sobbing about ospreys, instead of Alicia. Gerard would love to have an excuse to get rid of him.

When Steve saw his boss, he made a move to get up. Lattimore held up a hand. "Sit, sit. I just spoke to Quinn Harlowe. She told me she's talked to you about Alicia."

"Oh, right. Yeah."

"You should have told me."

"Told you what? That Alicia Miller was upset about something?"

Fair enough, Gerard thought. Quinn had told

him that she hadn't given Steve all the details of her encounter with Alicia. "Have you heard from her?"

"Not since she left here Friday."

"Steve—Quinn downplayed Alicia's condition when she called you earlier. She's worried about her."

"To the point of calling the police?"

"No. At least not yet. You don't have any idea who might have picked her up?"

He leaned back in his chair and looked up at Lattimore. "I have no idea. I'm sorry. I wish there was more I could do. Did Quinn have someone check her cottage in case Alicia went back there?"

"She's on her way there now to see for herself."

Steve was silent a moment.

"What is it?" Lattimore prodded him. "Steve, this conversation's off the record. I have no more desire to see Alicia hurt than you or anyone else does."

"What if Quinn misread the situation? She and Alicia have had their problems. I don't want to get dragged into the middle of some squabble between friends." He shifted his attention back to his monitor and tapped a couple of keys, clearing the screen. "Why did Quinn tell you? When I talked to her, she didn't want to say anything."

He had no intention of letting this kid know that he'd gone to Quinn's office himself out of concern for her friend—*before* he knew about their encounter at the coffee shop. "She thought Alicia would turn up fine by now."

Steve shrugged, unconcerned. "She probably still will. Alicia told me she and Quinn would always be friends but not the kind of close friends they once were. Hey, it happens, right? People go in different directions. From what I gather, they haven't had much contact with each other since Quinn left here. Alicia could have new friends that Quinn wouldn't know to call—"

"Do you know any names?"

"We aren't that buddy-buddy."

Something in his eyes didn't feel right to Lattimore. He decided Steve was being disingenuous—he cared more about Alicia Miller than he wanted to let on. A romantic interest? Gerard would *never* put the two of them together.

"If you hear of anything, let me know."

Eisenhardt nodded. "Sure. Of course. Are *you* worried?"

Lattimore thought a moment. "Yes," he said. "Yes, I'm worried."

The younger attorney swore under his breath, but Gerard left, already late for a meeting that would drag on through dinner. Another night, he thought, that he wouldn't have time to stop at the house and see his kids—another night his ex-wife could use to prove her point: His work came first. Before her, before their children, before his own health.

And she was right. It had to be that way, at least while he was a deputy assistant attorney general. To pretend otherwise was dishonest, a disservice to himself and everyone he loved.

His ex-wife had wanted the goodies without the sacrifices.

No one, he thought, could have it all.

6

The osprey…

Cold rain pelted onto Alicia Miller's bare head and her red kayak, into the cockpit, drenching her to the skin. Lightning lit up the gray sky, followed by a roar of thunder. The waves had kicked up, frightening her.

Sobbing, shivering, she tried to slow her racing thoughts and control the rush of panic, the sudden spasms in her arms and legs. Especially her legs.

I'm going to die.

The osprey will kill me…

"Why?" she screamed, stabbing the paddle into a three-foot swell. "Why am I out here? What am I doing?"

Her words were lost in the wind, the rain, the pounding surf. She couldn't see. Everything was gray. Where was the land? Where was Quinn's cottage?

"Quinn! Help me, Quinn!"

Why should Quinn help me? I haven't been a good friend to her, to anyone.

Negative self-talk…Alicia remembered she was supposed to avoid it.

She felt the kayak bump against something firm. Land?

She looked up, into the rain.

Above her, suspended on a pole, was a sprawling, giant, frightening bird's nest, a mass of sticks and twigs and dead grass.

Her heart raced even faster. She couldn't suppress an overwhelming sense of doom.

I don't want to be here. The osprey…

She'd been paddling forever. She didn't know where she was. The cove? Was this Quinn's osprey nest?

The kayak bumped against the pole, turning sideways into the surf. The men in the car—she remembered them.

Travis.

One was called Travis, and he had encouraged her to take the kayak out. By himself. She didn't know what had happened to the other one. She remembered Steve getting out of the car back in Washington.

Travis's voice had been so soothing.

"Kayaking'll calm your nerves. Nothing like a good paddle."

But the ospreys—he knew she was afraid of them.

He hadn't mentioned the dark clouds moving in

from the west. She saw them and assumed they meant nothing.

She'd shoved her kayak into her car. He hadn't helped her. She drove out the loop road by herself and launched in a pretty spot, where there was a strip of sandy beach and she wouldn't have to deal with the slimy underwater grasses that were by the cottage.

No one was around on the loop. No one had seen her put in her kayak.

Steve—what had he been doing in the back of the car with her?

How long ago was that?

Everything was a jumble in her mind.

Why can't I think straight?

"Oh, God. What's wrong with me?"

The poison. Had she told Quinn about the poison?

No.

Alicia dropped her paddle across the kayak's cockpit and placed both hands on the sides of her head and squeezed, hard, as if that would help to quiet her mind.

She'd left Yorkville to go see Quinn in Washington that morning.

Yes.

Quinn, living the life she wanted now that she'd quit her job at Justice. That was good, wasn't it? Having coffee and a croissant on a beautiful spring afternoon.

The little boy—Alicia could see his frightened look.

Her chin on her chest, she sobbed quietly, embarrassed, exhausted, yet unable to sit still, unable to
quiet her body or mind.

A screech.

She jerked her head up, and the bird was there.
She could see its talons and black wings, its beady
eyes. It was the same one that had ripped apart the
duckling.

Terror gripped her.

"What do you want from me?"

She picked up her paddle and swiped it at the
bird.

"Ospreys are fascinating. I just love them."

Quinn's words, months ago, when their friendship was solid and they'd laughed and talked on
the cottage porch, drinking pinot noir, comfortable
with each other.

So much had changed.

Alicia sobbed, tears streaming down her face.

I don't have your courage, Quinn.

The osprey had disappeared.

Alicia spun around in the cockpit, looking for the
big bird. She was so cold. "I know you're out there!
I know you want me!"

Part of her knew she wasn't making any sense.
Yet she couldn't stop herself.

She dropped her paddle into the gray, churning
water.

A huge swell came at her. Lightning and thunder struck at the same time. She slumped deeper
into the cockpit, exhausted, her hands purple and
blue. She hadn't worn a life vest. She didn't have a

safety whistle to alert anyone on shore or in a nearby boat.

She saw her paddle floating on the oncoming swell. It looked so peaceful. No one, nothing, could do it harm.

Once more, her kayak banged against the pole where the ospreys had built their nest. She reached for the nest, but didn't know why, except that she needed to—she needed to stop the ospreys. She needed to save someone. Herself.

I can't think.

The swell hit. She was too far out of the open cockpit, and the wave knocked her kayak from under her. She tried to hook it with her feet, but her movements were impossible to control. Her entire body twitched, her teeth chattering as she grabbed hold of the pole.

She was cold. So cold.

She looked down at the water and saw only gray, churning water, her kayak, like her paddle, gone.

7

Huck cranked open the tall, narrow casement window in his dorm-style room at Breakwater and let in the cool, poststorm breeze off the bay. The unnaturally still gray-blue water lay past the immaculate lawn and over a barbed-wire fence. Supposedly, erosion had brought the Chesapeake Bay closer to the converted barn than when it was built in 1858. A plaque at the main gate gave a brief history of the house, barn and surrounding hundred acres.

The place felt like a summer camp.

Huck reminded himself he wasn't there for the accommodations. He was there to penetrate an elusive, violent criminal network and find out who they were and what they were up to. Had Oliver Crawford set up Breakwater Security to train vigilante recruits for future operations? Was he being used? *Are we all on a wild goose chase?*

Vern Glover appeared in the doorway. "The Riccardis want to see you."

"Now?"

"Yeah, now."

Huck knew he got under Vern's skin. "Where?"

"Outside."

"Vern, that leaves about a hundred acres—"

"You're an asshole, Boone, aren't you?"

Boone. Huck didn't flinch at the phony name. He'd gotten used to it during his months of deep-undercover work. "Who, me?"

"Be outside in three minutes."

He almost asked why three—why not two? Why not five? That kind of deliberate effort to get under a person's skin was more natural to him than he cared to admit, but he also knew it helped with his cover, the persona he'd established when he'd first gone undercover after his fugitive. Breakwater Security had done a thorough background check on him before letting him into their Yorkville compound. The U.S. Marshals Service and the FBI together made sure any paperwork and people needed to verify his new identity were in place, down to a retired deputy who posed as Huck's former first-grade teacher. *That little Boone boy. What a corker.*

Glover left Huck to what remained of the three minutes. He got a clean shirt from his built-in dresser. Because he was working for a private security firm, he got to carry his Glock 23 in his belt holster and a snub-nosed .38 revolver on his ankle. He had the proper paperwork as Huck Boone, bodyguard extraordinaire, so he couldn't arrest himself for gun-law violations. His Breakwater colleagues all were good with their paperwork—not that he would arrest them for low-level gun violations. There were rumors the vigilantes had shoulder-fired missiles, grenades, chemical sprays, illegal explosives—a long list.

Supposedly, they wanted to buy an armored helicopter.

The task force didn't want him blowing the whistle too soon.

Most of all, they wanted to know names and plans. Who were these guys, and what were they up to?

He sat on the edge of his bed. White no-iron sheets, cotton blanket, one pillow. He could feel the metal springs through the thin mattress. He was five-ten, one-eighty. On a good day, he had a face that scared children and small dogs.

An extra blanket was up on a closet shelf for cool nights. He had three Breakwater Security shirts, one sweatshirt and one windbreaker. A navy blue suit hung in his closet, and on the floor were running shoes, water shoes, lightweight combat boots and black dress shoes. If he needed anything else, he'd have to find a store.

When he ventured outside, the air smelled of wet earth and bay, but it was fresh and clean, the storm having blown out any remaining rain and humidity. The grounds of the Crawford compound were old-Virginia lush, with trim grass, flowering trees and shrubs, spring bulbs—certainly not the kind of landscape anyone would picture when imagining a start-up private security firm.

The sprawling main house, white clapboards with black shutters, overlooked the bay, a spot most people would be content to live. Not Oliver Crawford. He'd stirred up Yorkville when he announced that he was converting his picturesque country estate into Breakwater Security. Although people still had their doubts, outright protest was short-lived, at least partly because Crawford had only recently survived his harrowing kidnapping and his Yorkville neighbors understood his need to take action—except, perhaps, for Alicia Miller.

Huck stepped over a puddle left over from the storms. The late-afternoon sun angled through a stray gray cloud. It'd been a rough series of storms, rain and wind slapping the converted barn's windows, trees swaying outside, flashes of lightning, claps of thunder—the works. Diego had brought in his boat just in time.

The Riccardis, the couple who ran Breakwater Security, walked down the stone path to the converted barn. Joe had let his iron-gray hair grow out maybe a quarter-inch since he'd retired from the army. He was forty-two, six feet even and without any obvious excess fat. He had on a navy polo with the Breakwater Security logo embroidered in gold, pressed khaki pants and black running shoes. He wore his Glock on a shoulder holster. His wife, Sharon, was thirty-five and pretty, even delicate, with her dyed blond hair and blue eyes. She was unarmed and wore a skirted suit. Navy blue. She had worked as Oliver Crawford's executive assistant for fifteen years but now oversaw everything nonoperational for Breakwater Security.

Sharon spoke first. "How're you doing, Mr. Boone? Settling in?"

"Doing just fine, thanks."

Huck didn't have a solid read on the Riccardis, athough the task force had provided Huck with a brief workup on them. They were married last summer right there at Breakwater. Sharon's first marriage, Joe's second. He had two kids in college in Colorado. Nothing in their backgrounds shouted *vigilante*.

"Mr. Crawford is arriving from his Washington home in the morning," Sharon said. "He'll want to see what all we've accomplished in the week since his last visit. Joe will go over the details with you tonight at dinner."

Huck had yet to meet Crawford. He and Diego had read a write-up on him, too, but nothing in it indicated any wing nut vigilante propensities. Then again, who knew what a terrifying ordeal like a kidnapping could do to a man.

A towheaded kid of maybe twenty-two burst out of the barn. Sharon Riccardi gave an impatient sigh, but her husband greeted him pleasantly and shook his hand, welcoming him to Breakwater. The kid all but saluted. Joe couldn't stop a smile. "Relax, O'Dell. You're not in the army anymore. Boone, Glover— meet Cully O'Dell, our newest recruit. He's from the Neck. A local boy. He can tell you the best fishing spots, and you can show him around the property."

O'Dell shook hands with Vern, then Boone. The kid seemed to have a sunny disposition and was obviously excited about entering the high-stakes, high-possibilities world of private security. Vern didn't look thrilled at having to help show Cully O'Dell around Breakwater, but one thing Huck had discovered in his two days in Yorkville—he was never left to wander around the property on his own. Someone was always watching.

Being senior, Vern gave O'Dell the quick rundown of the various buildings and what was up and running and what was only in the planning stages.

No mention of private interrogation chambers and thumbscrews.

No mention of a plot to destroy the federal government, to assassinate judges or to snatch bad guys off the streets and toss them into their own private jail cells.

Vern talked about maintaining the highest standards of professionalism, ethics and training as they provided individual and corporate security ranging from routine background checks and threat assessment to investigations, protection, surveillance and crisis management. Those who started now, when the company was still more dream than reality, would have the opportunity to move up as Breakwater Security grew.

"Cool," the new recruit said under his breath.

Huck grimaced. If Cully O'Dell was a budding psycho vigilante, Huck would cut off his big toe. In the meantime, he'd try to make sure nothing happened to the kid.

They started up the stone path to a new, perfunctory structure that was out of keeping with the aesthetic of the estate. It housed classrooms and the gun vault. Huck figured if Breakwater had any shoulder-fired missiles, illegal explosives, illegal chemicals or vials of anthrax, they'd be in the vault. He wanted to get in there on his own, but it wouldn't be easy.

On the other hand, if he'd wanted easy, he would never have worked undercover at all.

They ran into the Riccardis again on their way down to the indoor firing range.

"I forgot to ask," Huck said. "Any word on the woman who was out here this morning? Miller—Alicia Miller, right?"

"She went back to Washington," Sharon said stiffly.

"That's what I heard. Did she drive herself?"

"I don't know if she did or didn't drive herself. She objects to Breakwater Security having its headquarters and training facility out here. This morning's histrionics were nothing but a rude, inappropriate protest."

"Was she drunk?"

"I have no idea." Sharon caught herself, softening. "I don't mean to sound cruel. Obviously Alicia Miller's a troubled woman."

Joe touched his wife's elbow. "We should get back to the house. Didn't you say Oliver was calling at seven?"

"Right. Yes, of course." She shifted her attention to Vern and O'Dell. "Mr. O'Dell? What do you think of Breakwater so far?"

The kid beamed. "Awesome."

* * *

Quinn buttoned her sweater and crossed her arms against the cold early-April wind as she stood at the water's edge across from her bayside cottage. Even in the small cove, the bay was choppy after the line of thunderstorms had blown across the Northern Neck and off to the northeast. The heavy rain had slowed her drive to Yorkville but left behind dry, fresh, much cooler air.

She'd arrived thirty minutes ago, parking her silver Saab practically in the branches of her huge holly, her hope of finding Alicia's ten-year-old BMW in the driveway or even the black sedan that had picked her up immediately dashed. The side door to the cottage was locked. Alicia had cleared out of the cottage—the only traces of her weekend stay were the hastily made bed in the guest room, towels in the bathroom hamper and an unopened nonfat, sugar-free strawberry yogurt in the refrigerator.

Quinn had walked next door to the only other cottage on the quiet, dead-end road, but the Scanlons, the couple who'd retired to Yorkville just before Quinn bought her place, were still not home.

A wasted trip, she thought, watching an osprey—a female—swoop up from the marsh into the clear sky above the bay. In spite of her concern for Alicia, Quinn felt some of her tension ease at the familiar sight of the huge bird. Once facing extinction, ospreys had become opportunistic in choosing their nesting sites, using channel markers, buoys, old dock posts and even the occasional bench on a quiet private dock. The nests could only be removed with a permit.

The two young ospreys that had constructed the oversize mess of a nest on a marker at the mouth of Quinn's cove had returned. The nest had survived several fierce winter storms. With luck, the ospreys, mates for life, would have baby ospreys in a matter of weeks.

But they were raptors—birds of prey. Although they dined primarily on fish, if Alicia had indeed walked out to the water early one morning and saw an osprey scoop up an unsuspecting duckling in front of her, she would have been horrified. Stressed out as she was from the pressures of her job, perhaps on the verge of a breakdown, she could have latched onto such a gruesome sight as she'd melted down, twisting it into a metaphor for all her fears and troubles.

Speculation, Quinn thought, turning away from the water.

Built in the 1940s, her cottage occupied a half-acre lot with lilacs and azaleas, not yet in bloom, and a vegetable garden out back that she meant to revive. Right now, it was mostly weeds. Alicia had promised to rent a tiller and dig up the garden, but Quinn had known it was just well-meaning talk. She loved Yorkville for its simplicity. A picnic, kayaking, walking on the beach, prowling mom-and-pop shops for books and antiques, sitting on her porch and reading. What Quinn enjoyed most about Yorkville, Alicia found lacking. Quinn grew up in the Washington suburbs, but Virginia's Northern Neck, with its wide, shallow rivers, its marshes and inlets, its beaches and rich history, spoke to her soul.

She walked across the road and up the stone walk to her cottage, the grass, which needed mowing, wet from the pounding rain. She stepped onto her porch, no railing to impede the view of the water from her wicker chairs. On one of her weekends on the bay, Alicia had put out a blue ceramic pot of yellow pansies as a gift for use of the cottage.

Quinn tucked her hands up into the sleeves of her sweater. Dusk was easing into night, the wind quieting, the air cold and fresh. Shivering, she went inside, her small living room dark enough now that she needed to switch on a lamp.

When she'd bought the cottage, it was a wreck. For two years, she'd poured herself, and coaxed various friends, into fixing it up. The scrubbing and painting and foraging for deals served as a welcome contrast to her days spent researching and analyzing criminal networks with tentacles that knew no borders, no boundaries, no ethics or morals but the lust for power, money and violence. She painted the simple wood floors and replaced the wainscoting, splurged on tile for the bathroom that she had put in herself.

Quinn remembered a sun-filled weekend in Yorkville, shortly after Alicia had moved to Washington. They'd gone on long walks together and had crab cakes at the marina restaurant, then drank wine and talked until midnight on the front porch, rekindling a friendship strained by busy lives and different interests and goals.

It was just before Alicia had introduced Quinn to Brian Castleton, the Washington, D.C., reporter for a Chicago newspaper, and they'd begun an on-again, off-again six months together that now, in retrospect, seemed doomed from the start. Brian found Yorkville too small, too boring, too unsophisticated, too, as he liked to say, 1947. He'd drag himself along with Quinn as she scavenged flea markets and yard sales for bargains—her mishmash of dishes, a Depression glass pitcher and tumblers, a copper pot for kindling, tables and chairs she'd refinished and painted.

The cottage, ultimately, had helped end their relationship. He wanted to buy a boat—he said he *might* stand the occasional weekend in Yorkville if he had a boat. They'd bought two kayaks together. Then he said a kayak wasn't the sort of boat he meant.

Before long, he was staying in the city on weekends, and she'd drive out to the bay by herself.

Yet, in spite of how easily and completely they'd drifted apart, Brian was the first to see that she needed to leave the Justice Department and strike out on her own. If she was content to spend a weekend stripping paint off an old chair, he reasoned, the day-to-day grind of her work was getting to her. She needed to take a risk and broaden her horizons. Dare to go out on her own.

"I'm too young," she'd argue. "I need more experience."

"You're from a family of daredevils. Go on, Quinn. Jump."

It was another month after they broke up for good before she finally turned in her resignation.

Her withering relationship with Brian had put an added strain on her friendship with Alicia, who couldn't hide her disappointment, even irritation, at Quinn's decisions. "First you dumped Brian, then you quit your job. What's next, Quinn? *Who's* next?"

She hadn't dumped Brian, and Alicia knew it. She'd exaggerated. What really got to her was how hard Lattimore had tried to get Quinn to stay at Justice—and then, once she'd made up her mind, how he continued to press her to come back. Last month, when he'd invited Quinn to an informal party at the Yorkville marina restaurant—his first social event without his wife—she had debated not going. The party was a good opportunity to network, but she also found herself wanting to go, hoping she could get Lattimore and Alicia to accept that she'd had to move on—it wasn't a slap in their faces.

Alicia was at the party. She and Quinn chatted outside on the dock, shivering in the cold as they'd danced around the recent tension between them. Whatever had bothered Alicia about Quinn's behavior over recent months seemed to have evaporated.

When she asked to use the cottage for a weekend getaway, Quinn hadn't questioned Alicia's motives. She'd simply handed her a key and told her to come and go at will.

Not once that night or in the next weeks did she sense that Alicia was seriously troubled or burned out.

8

When she took her tea out to the porch in the morning, Quinn told herself that Alicia must have shown up at her apartment last night and by now was on her way to work, yesterday's drama behind her. Quinn had tried calling, but her cell phone was balky. She'd walk down to the water after her tea and try again.

She sat on a wicker rocker and pulled her feet up under her, cupping her mug with both hands to feel the warmth of the steaming tea. She had on her oversize sweater, a flannel shirt, jeans and just her socks. She expected the cool air and the cry of seagulls in the distance, the sounds of the tide washing in and out, but not, she thought, the very buff man in running shorts and a ratty T-shirt jogging on the road in front of her cottage.

He didn't seem to notice her. When he reached the end of her road, just past her cottage, he did a

wide turn and paused briefly to stretch. His dark
hair was cut very short, not quite a crewcut, and he
had a thickset build, with a flat abdomen and muscular arms, shoulders and thighs. He was obviously
a physical man, not some guy dragging himself out
for an early-morning jog to lose a few pounds.

When he reached the end of her stone walk,
Quinn couldn't resist calling out to him. "Nice
morning for a run, isn't it?"

She didn't seem to have startled him. He
stopped, not even remotely out of breath as he
squinted at her on the porch. "That it is. I'm new
in town. You live here?"

"It's my weekend place."

"Today's Tuesday."

She set her mug on a small table to one side of
her rocker. "I was speaking in broad terms. My
name's Quinn—Quinn Harlowe."

"Huck Boone."

"Are you one of the new guys at Breakwater Security?"

Just a flicker of hesitation. "That's right." He
nodded toward the dead-end road and the barbed
wire. "I guess we're neighbors."

"No one but a seagull or an osprey would try to
get to Breakwater through the marsh. It's rough going. When did you get here?"

"Over the weekend."

"This your first time jogging out this way?"

"No, why?"

He was calm and very direct, but obviously wondering why she was asking such questions. But she

had dreamed about Alicia last night, not good dreams. "I got here late yesterday thinking a friend of mine who borrowed my cottage for the weekend might still be here. I guess I'm wondering if you've run into her."

"Was she supposed to be here?"

"I don't know where she's supposed to be. It's a long story."

"Hope you find her."

"Does that mean you haven't seen her?"

He paused a moment. "What's her name?"

"Alicia Miller. Her car's not here, and none of her stuff's here."

And no suicide note, Quinn thought. In a fit of paranoia, she'd searched the cottage before going to bed last night and found nothing that eased her mind about Alicia—nothing, either, that indicated she'd had a complete mental breakdown. The place was clean and tidied up, not even a dish left in the sink.

Huck Boone, she noticed, hadn't moved a muscle.

"I'm sure she's fine," she said quickly.

"You don't sound sure."

Quinn found herself wanting to tell him about Alicia's odd behavior yesterday, but she resisted. "I'm heading back to Washington this morning. If you do hear of anything—" She debated her options. "Can you hang on a second? I'll give you my cell-phone number."

Boone shrugged. "Okay."

She ran inside and grabbed a notepad and pen

off the coffee table, where she'd spread out files and papers and had tried to work last night. She quickly scrawled down her number, folding the small sheet in half as she returned to the porch.

She walked along the stone path in her stocking feet, Boone meeting her halfway. His eyes, she saw, were a dark green, at least in the cool morning light of early April. Quinn tried to smile, but knew she didn't quite manage. "Since you're in private security…" She let her shoulders lift and fall in an exaggerated manner. "Never mind. I'm just covering all the bases I can think of, in case something's happened to her."

"Why do you think anything's happened to her?"

"I don't—"

"Yes, you do."

She felt sudden tears in her eyes and hoped he would blame them on the cold air.

"Does she know Oliver Crawford?"

"Not well. They met briefly at a party last month." Quinn blinked back the tears. "He and I have met a few times, but I don't know him well, either."

Interest rose in Boone's expression. Little, she suspected, escaped this man's attention, a skill that had to be a plus in private security work.

But she brought her mind back to the subject at hand, adding, "Oliver Crawford and my former boss—Alicia's current boss—are friends. They went to college together."

"And your boss would be—"

"Gerard Lattimore." She didn't know how she'd ended up giving him this information about herself. "He's a deputy assistant attorney general at the Justice Department."

"What are you, a lawyer?"

"Historian."

Boone took a second to digest that information but had no visible reaction. "You don't work for this Lattimore anymore?"

"No. I left Justice in January."

"He knows your friend's missing?"

Quinn realized the tables had turned and now Huck Boone was interrogating her. He was a security type, she reminded herself, and such tactics probably came naturally to him. But she didn't feel particularly reassured. "Alicia's not missing. She's just—I just haven't accounted for her."

Boone didn't relent. "But Lattimore knows?"

"Yes."

"And Mr. Crawford?"

"I have no idea. I haven't talked with him."

"You don't socialize with him in Washington?"

"I told you, I don't know him that well. And these days, Mr. Boone, any socializing I do is work related."

He grinned unexpectedly and leaned toward her. "Then it's not socializing, is it?" He straightened, his eyes softer now, not as intense. "Since we're neighbors, you can just call me Huck."

She felt a twitch of a smile. "Huck Boone. That's quite a name, isn't it? Makes me think of Huckleberry Finn and Daniel Boone—"

"My folks have a strange sense of humor. I should get rolling. You okay? Anything I can do for you?"

His concern took her aback, and she wondered just how tight and preoccupied she appeared. She glanced out at the osprey nest at the mouth of the cove and almost told him about Alicia's pleas, but she'd told Boone, a man she didn't know at all, more than she'd meant to as it was. "I'm okay. Thanks for asking," she said. "Don't let me keep you from your run."

"Just getting loose. We're getting put through our paces today at Breakwater."

"Good luck."

He winked at her. "Thanks."

He jogged off toward the loop road at a moderate pace.

Quinn didn't immediately return to her hot tea. The bay glistened in the morning sun, the water quiet and very blue under the clear sky. She wondered how many of Oliver Crawford's guys would be jogging past her cottage now that he'd converted his estate into a private security outfit.

She started across the road, then remembered she was in her socks. But they were damp now, anyway, and she continued on her way, taking the narrow, sandy path through the tall marsh grass down to the water. The tide was out, leaving behind wet sand, slippery grass and swirling shallow pools. Using one hand to block the sun, she squinted out at the enormous osprey nest, but it was empty, the female, presumably, still out hunting.

As she turned to head back to the cottage for her cell phone, a fishing boat out in the water beyond her cove caught her eye. Something bright drew her gaze downward, out past her waterfront to the edge of the protected marsh.

Red.

What would be red on the shore?

"I have a red kayak," she said aloud.

Had Alicia left it in the marsh?

Why? Dropping her hand from her eyes, Quinn ran back up to the road and down to the marsh, pushing her way through thick marsh grass onto a narrow path. Her socks were soaked through now, covered with sand. Barely breaking stride, she lifted one foot and pulled off her wet sock, then lifted the other, leaving the socks on the path and pressing forward barefoot, the cold sand a shock.

She kept running toward the water, noticing gulls up ahead.

Gulls...

Why so many? Quinn counted five near the shore.

The path curved, and she saw the red kayak lying parallel to the beach, partly submerged in the receding tide. The gulls seemed to be picking at something in the tall marsh grass.

Quinn felt a crawling sensation at the top of her spine. Her mouth went dry. She tucked her hands up into the sleeves of her sweater and slowed her pace, ignoring her frozen feet.

More gulls arrived.

"Shoo!" She waved her arms at the birds, but they stayed with their find, whatever it was.

She looked up toward the road, hoping to see someone—anyone—she could call to walk with her down to the kayak and the gulls and see what was there. But there was no one.

With a nauseating sense of dread, she forced herself to veer off the path through the knee-high grass, still cold with the morning dew, slapping at her as her feet sank into the wet, shifting sand.

A dolphin? A small whale? Was it possible something had beached itself here on the edge of a Chesapeake Bay marsh? She was a historian, not a naturalist. She'd fancied that in her spare time, on long, lazy weekends, she could study bay life, learn the names of the birds and fish and wildflowers and grasses.

She came to the kayak and forced herself to look where the sea gulls were feasting.

A leg.

"Oh no."

Now Quinn could see blond hair.

She recognized the blue sweater and the jeans Alicia had worn yesterday morning.

"Alicia!"

Quinn's scream didn't faze the gulls. She turned around, facing the road, and yelled for help, her stomach knotting, bile rising in her throat. She didn't know if her screams were louder than the cries of the gulls or the tide, if anyone was nearby to hear her.

She made herself turn back toward Alicia and flapped her arms and yelled at the gulls, kicked sand at them, but only two flew off. When the rest refused to leave, Quinn took a closer look.

Alicia was sprawled facedown in the shallow water, strands of underwater grass tangled on her lower legs. Her feet were bare. Her sport sandals must have come off.

Quinn dropped onto her knees, shivering, her teeth chattering from cold and fear.

Please don't be dead.

But she quickly saw there was no point in checking for a pulse.

"Oh, Alicia," she whispered, sobbing. "You can't be dead. Oh, God, no."

"Quinn—"

Startled, she leaped up, spinning around right into Huck Boone. She took a step back, tripping on the kayak, but he grabbed her by the upper arm, steadying her.

He looked past her and tightened his grip on her.

"It's—it's my friend." Quinn's voice was hoarse. "Alicia. Alicia Miller. She's…" *I can't say it.*

"We need to call the police. Do you have a cell phone?"

"What?"

"A phone."

"Yes. It's at my cottage."

He released her arm and touched her shoulder. "Go. Call 911. I'll wait here." When she didn't respond, he squeezed her shoulder gently. "You've had a hell of a shock. There's nothing you can do for your friend now except to call the police and get her out of here."

Quinn knew he was right. He hadn't known Alicia—he wasn't facing the horror of seeing a friend dead. "The kayak…" Her entire body shaking now, teeth chattering, Quinn tried to point to the kayak. "I didn't realize it was missing."

"No reason for you to have noticed. Quinn—"

She tried to focus on anything but Alicia's body, disfigured by seawater and seagulls. "The storms— Alicia must have been out in the storms yesterday. Why would she do that?"

"I'll go make the call. Where's your cell phone?"

"Kitchen counter." But she grabbed his arm, her fingers digging into his hard muscle. "Wait. Did you see the kayak on your run?"

"I wasn't looking at the scenery."

Suspicion rippled through her. "You weren't out here to find her?"

Huck pried her fingers off his arm, holding on to them just for a second. "No, Quinn, I was out for a run. Come on. Let's go back to the cottage and call the police together—"

"I can't leave Alicia. I need to keep the gulls away."

His expression softened.

"I'll be okay," Quinn added. "The shock—" She cleared her throat, stiffened herself against the trembling and shivering. "I didn't expect to find her out here."

"Of course not. I'll be back in two minutes. Don't touch anything—"

"I know," she said quietly. "The police will need to investigate."

Huck gave a curt nod and, after a slight hesitation, as if he was reconsidering leaving her there alone, he headed back up the narrow path.

Quinn heard the sharp cry of a gull, and felt her stomach lurch. *An autopsy. They'll have to cut Alicia open.*

Her knees buckled and she tasted bile.

She knew Alicia was dead and yet wished she could shield her friend from what came next. Police, paramedics. Reporters. People who never knew her asking questions. Speculating. Judging.

They would want to know what had happened and why.

They'd ask Quinn about her encounter with Alicia yesterday in Washington.

Strangers would determine whether Alicia's death was an accident or suicide.

Would anyone even suspect murder?

"The osprey will kill me."

The crazy words of a disturbed woman.

No, Quinn thought. No one would suspect murder.

9

Nate Winter glanced at the picture on his desk of the small cape house he and his wife, Sarah, an historical archaeologist, had bought. It was a fixer-upper. Worst house, best location. They looked forward to doing a lot of the work themselves. Moving day was coming up. They'd enlisted the help of family and friends. Sarah was already loading up the freezer with southern-style casseroles to feed their helpers. Her friend John Wesley Poe had promised to show up. That he was the president of the United States was only one of the many complications of Nate's life.

The prospect of their new house only distracted him for a moment. He had wanted to give Juliet Longstreet the chance to digest the news he had just given her. Although she was a top-notch deputy U.S. marshal, even on a good day she didn't like coming into the USMS headquarters in Arlington.

Today was not a good day.

"Nice of you to wait until this Huck Boone–Huck McCabe character finds a body before you tell me about him." Juliet was known for her blunt manner. She was tall, in butt-kicking shape, but she was letting her fair hair grow out; it was curling past her chin now. "When did he arrive in Yorkville?"

"Saturday." Nate could feel his usual impatience working at him. "And he didn't find Alicia Miller. Her friend did."

"Quinn Harlowe," Juliet said.

Nate had already laid out for her what he knew about the tragic events in Yorkville. Juliet had made it clear she wanted to be in the field, tracking the vigilantes herself. She was directly responsible for disrupting one of their plots after a run-in with them last fall. Ethan Brooker, a former Special Forces officer, had helped. Now at the White House and romantically involved with Juliet, he was also on the task force. Both of them understood that this time, their unique expertise was best put to use at a distance. Let the guys from California do their thing.

"Ethan knows about McCabe?" Juliet asked.

Nate nodded, knowing his answer wouldn't go over well with her. "Ethan did a mission a few years ago with Diego Clemente, McCabe's backup." Hesitating a moment, Nate added, "I asked Ethan to keep the information to himself."

"Well, he did." Juliet scowled. "I hate being kept out of the loop."

"McCabe's in a precarious situation. He doesn't

know us. He came into this investigation through the back door. He's doing us a favor—"

"I get it, Nate. This guy feels safer with as few people as possible knowing he's an undercover federal agent. If we're right and these psycho vigilantes have infiltrated Breakwater Security, he's a dead man if his cover gets blown."

Leave it to Juliet not to mince words. Nate glanced again at the picture of his house. It had dove-gray shingles and white shutters, all of which needed replacing.

"Where's McCabe now?"

"Back at Breakwater."

"The local police are in the dark about who he is?"

"That's right." If they ever found out the truth, the locals wouldn't appreciate getting sidelined, but Nate thought that, given the stakes, they would understand. "We have several problems."

Juliet sighed. "Alicia Miller worked for the Justice Department. Is someone from the FBI looking into her death?"

That was one of the problems. "Special Agent T.J. Kowalski."

"I take it he doesn't know about McCabe, either."

"Correct. At the moment, there's no indication her death was anything but a terrible accident."

Nate looked out his window a moment and thought of his wife happily digging in the dirt at her newest archaeological site, an old family dump. A treasure trove to Sarah Dunnemore Winter. On a day like today, he would like nothing better than to join her in her search for artifacts.

He glanced back at Juliet. Huck McCabe had stumbled onto a lead that could be the thread they needed to pull to unravel a violent, paranoid criminal network. He was a topnotch federal agent, but Nate didn't know him. McCabe hadn't been handpicked picked for the job.

"Did McCabe talk to the police?" Juliet asked.

"He told them he was out for a run. Quinn Harlowe was drinking tea on her porch and said hello to him. He resumed his run, heard her scream and returned—"

"She'd found her friend's body."

"She spotted a kayak—hers, as it turns out—and went to investigate." Nate pictured the scene, although he'd never been to Yorkville. "McCabe says he didn't see the kayak or the body on his run."

"You believe him?"

Nate shrugged. "No reason not to."

"Quinn Harlowe. What do we know about her?"

"Not enough, obviously."

"Her friend—the dead woman. She said ospreys were out to kill her?"

"Something like that. That's what she told Harlowe."

Juliet sat back in her chair. "Ospreys. That's a new one. Harlowe didn't get a plate number of the Lincoln that picked up Alicia Miller?"

"No. She only caught a glimpse of the car. She did what she could to find her friend. Checked the woman's apartment and her office, made a few calls to friends and colleagues. Then she drove down to her cottage."

"McCabe give you all this?" Juliet asked skeptically.

"He managed to get to Diego Clemente. Then Diego called me."

She shifted in her chair, her concern plain on her face. "McCabe knows his safety is paramount, doesn't he? He's not to take unnecessary risks."

"Clemente says he reminded him."

"And?"

Nate let his gaze settle on Juliet for a moment. "McCabe told him all risks are unnecessary. Otherwise they wouldn't be risks." He grimaced. A dangerous, delicate undercover investigation depended on a man Nate didn't know. "I have a feeling that's a typical Huck McCabe answer."

"What about Gerard Lattimore?" Juliet asked. "Alicia Miller worked for him. Until January, so did Harlowe. He and Oliver Crawford are longtime friends—"

"I'll speak with Eliza Abrams," Nate interrupted, well aware of the facts, none of which he liked. Abrams was the U.S. attorney overseeing the vigilante investigation on behalf of the Department of Justice. "I expect she'll want to give this thing some time. If Alicia Miller was in the middle of a mental breakdown, it's possible her death had nothing to do with our investigation. We don't need to jump the gun."

"Meaning..."

"Meaning we continue to tell Gerard Lattimore nothing."

10

Joe Riccardi intercepted Huck outside the converted barn before he could get back to his room and change his shoes, not yet dry after he'd charged into the marsh. Quinn Harlowe's screams of horror had stopped him dead in his tracks on his run. Diego had said he'd heard her, too, out on his boat.

A hell of a shock, finding her friend's body.

One DOJ lawyer dead. A former DOJ analyst talking to the feds and the local police. Huck thought he could understand his new boss's tight look.

"Where have you been, Boone?"

"I was out for a run. There was a problem in town."

Riccardi's face didn't register any obvious emotion. "Alicia Miller. We heard the news about her death." He paused, his eyes unchanged. "Police suspect she drowned."

"I'd say so."

"What was your involvement?"

"I was on my run. I'd just gone past Quinn Harlowe's cottage when I heard her scream. I went to see what I could do."

"She could have screamed for a dozen different reasons—"

"Didn't matter."

Riccardi nodded. "You'll do well in this work, Boone." But his voice was toneless. "The body—"

"There was no hope for Miss Miller by the time I got there. She'd been dead for a number of hours." For some reason, Huck pictured Quinn barefoot, flapping at the gulls, her black hair whipping in her face as she'd tried to protect her dead friend. "Her body washed up in the marsh near a kayak—she must have been out during yesterday's storms."

"Why would anyone—" Joe shook his head. "It doesn't make any sense. Why would she go kayaking in severe weather? Did this Quinn Harlowe have any ideas? What's she doing in Yorkville?"

"She was worried about Alicia—Miss Miller. Apparently they had an encounter in Washington early yesterday afternoon. Sounds as if she was in even worse shape than when she showed up at the front gate here that morning at the crack of dawn. Harlowe tried to find her—checked her apartment, made a few calls. When she didn't have any luck, she came down here to see if Miller had returned to the cottage."

Joe inhaled sharply. "What a tragedy. Did you tell the police about our encounter with Miss Miller yesterday morning?"

"No. I didn't actually see her myself. I figured—" Huck regarded Joe Riccardi, clearly nothing about this day sitting well with Breakwater Security's chief of operations. "It wasn't anything I wanted to get into."

"Understood."

"Alicia Miller worked for the DOJ. The FBI's investigating. Her boss was Deputy Assistant Attorney General—"

"Gerard Lattimore. Yes, I know. He and Oliver Crawford are longtime friends. Law enforcement officials are welcome to ask questions of any of us." Riccardi's square chin came up slightly. "We have nothing to hide. Do we?"

"I sure as hell don't."

A flicker of impatience rose in Joe's hard face, but his wife joined them, shuddering in the cool wind as she stepped out of the converted barn. "What an awful thing suicide is." She crossed her arms on her chest, her windbreaker, with its prominent Breakwater Security logo, not warm enough for the cool temperature. "When I was in high school, one of my classmates killed himself. I'll never forget it. There was no reason, not that any of us saw."

"As far as I know, Alicia Miller didn't leave a suicide note," Huck said.

"Maybe there wasn't one. Maybe she wanted her death to look like an accident." Sharon shook her head, staring at the ground. "Maybe it *was* an accident, but she was reckless and didn't care what happened to her, didn't fight to save herself."

Joe Riccardi's jaw seemed to clamp down on itself. "We shouldn't speculate."

His wife didn't seem to hear him. "I wonder if Miss Miller had an underlying mental illness—would that make her death easier for her family and friends? If they could latch onto a reason, maybe—"

"There's never a reason to kill yourself," her husband snapped.

Her head jerked up, and she looked taken aback at his sharp tone. "No, of course not. That's not what I meant. A reason in her own mind—"

Joe broke in as if she hadn't spoken. "You'd think if Miller had obvious emotional problems the Justice Department would have taken some kind of action. Insist she take a leave of absence. They wouldn't just sit back and do nothing." He stopped himself. "Now *I'm* speculating. We don't know what happened."

"How well did you all know her?" Huck asked.

Sharon turned to him. "We met last month at a party Gerard Lattimore held at the marina restaurant here in Yorkville. Joe and I were there with Oliver."

"Quinn Harlowe?"

"She was there, too."

Joe straightened, even more rigid than usual. "Let's leave the investigating to the authorities. We have our own job to do. Boone? You all set? If the police have further questions to ask you—"

"I'll be in the shower."

His deliberately flip answer got a reaction out of

Lieutenant Colonel Riccardi. He made two fists. Huck thought he'd end up with at least one of them coming at his jaw, but his new boss restrained himself.

His wife touched his hand. "Joe."

Neither Riccardi said anything as Huck ducked into the converted barn. A straight hall ran down the middle, with rooms on either side, like horse stalls. There was a kitchen with cafeteria tables, an office, a men's room, a shower room. The bedrooms were at the far end—mostly singles, but a few doubles and one triple with its own private bath, apparently for any women who showed up. So far, Sharon Riccardi was the only female on the premises, but she stayed in the main house with her husband.

Huck ran into Vern Glover at the far end of the hall. "I heard about the dead woman, Boone. Damn. Couldn't you have picked a different route for your morning run and kept us out of this thing?"

"Sure. Next time I'll check my crystal ball to find out where the dead people are."

"You ran past the body and didn't see it?"

Vern had him there. Huck had noticed the red kayak in the tall grass out by the water, but hadn't thought much of it. If he'd investigated, he could have spared Quinn the trauma of discovering her friend's body.

"Hindsight's twenty-twenty," he said.

Travis Lubec emerged from the room across the hall from Huck's. Lubec had just moved into the converted barn. He had worked security for Oliver

Crawford for a couple of years and wasn't among those fired after his kidnapping—apparently, Crawford had ignored some piece of sage advice Lubec had given him before his trip to the Caribbean.

Nick Rochester, a kid maybe a hair older than Cully O'Dell, joined the men in the hall, coming in through the back door. He and Lubec were scrubbed, serious and ultrafit, wearing Breakwater Security polo shirts and khakis, their weapons in shoulder holsters.

Lubec's gaze fell on Huck. "You're bad luck, Boone."

Rochester nodded. "Hell, yeah. You're here, what, three days, and you've already managed to stumble on a body and end up under the hot lights, talking to the feds."

"Just one fed," Huck said. "The rest were local guys."

"You're a cheeky bastard, aren't you?" Travis took a step closer to him. "I'd watch that mouth if I were you."

"Cheeky. That's a PBS kind of word, isn't it?" Huck replied. "Shouldn't you say 'cheeky bastard' with an upper-crust British accent?" Huck yawned. "You know that Lubec and Rochester are both names of towns, right? Lubec, Maine. Rochester, New York."

Vern rolled his eyes at Huck's taunting the two meats. Lubec's fair cheeks turned red, but he didn't say anything. The kid told Huck to fuck off.

"Boone's had a rough morning," Vern said. "Don't kill him."

Lubec took a couple of breaths through his nose, then glared at Vern. "I'll excuse him this time. Next time, I'm not cutting him any slack."

After Lubec and Rochester left, Vern stuck a thick finger in Huck's face. "I'm not bailing you out again. If you want to mouth off, you can take the consequences."

"I was just stating a fact. Lubec and Rochester—"

"Shut up, Boone. I don't care if you did find a dead woman this morning. Just shut the hell up."

Huck thought he was displaying just the right amount of rule-breaking attitude for the vigilantes among Breakwater Security to take notice. On the other hand, he could just be pissing people off. He couldn't make himself care. He pictured poor dead Alicia Miller and her friend Quinn Harlowe, fighting tears and panic—and guilt. A lot of guilt.

Not that he had much hope for Harlowe heading back to Washington and minding her own business. Huck knew a few research analysts and he'd never met one who'd leave well enough alone.

11

FBI Special Agent T.J. Kowalski joined Quinn on her porch, the smells of low tide heavy in the air. She'd been sitting out there for more than an hour trying to grasp the reality that Alicia was dead.

Kowalski looked out at the water. "Nice spot." He was trim, lean and very good-looking in his dark gray suit and red tie, with his classic G-man square jaw and close-cropped dark hair. He also had a not-so-classic two-inch scar under his left eye. "You must like coming out here."

"I love it. But after today—"

"Don't think about that right now. Alicia cleared out of here yesterday morning and drove back to Washington. Then she came back here. Why?"

"I don't know."

"Where's her car?"

"I don't know that, either. Maybe it's still in Washington, and whoever picked her up there could have driven her to Yorkville and dropped her off here. She was very upset when she came to me at the coffee shop. I couldn't make sense out of half of what she said."

"Would she have taken her car to go kayaking?"

"It's possible. I generally put in right out front, but if I'm taking a different route, I'll launch somewhere else to save on time. Alicia didn't like launching here. It's fairly deep, and the underwater grasses—" Quinn stopped, staring at the porch floor but seeing the kayak, Alicia's body, the wet grass on her. "But she ended up back here in the cove."

The FBI agent's expression softened. "The local police are looking for her car. You don't need to worry about it."

"Alicia was fixated on ospreys. There's a nest out here in the cove—she could have wanted to avoid getting too close to it." Quinn shook her head, sinking deeper, if possible, into her wicker chair. "I just don't know."

"Did she have her own key to your cottage?"

"Yes. I gave her one in March."

"Is there a spare?"

"It's outside on the kitchen windowsill. I haven't checked to see if it's there."

Without a word, Kowalski headed down the stone walk and across the yard to the side entrance. Quinn didn't move, didn't think. The cove was quiet, nothing like it must have been yesterday at the height of the storms.

The FBI agent returned. "Key's still there. What about your kayak? Where do you keep it?"

"I have two. One red, one green. I keep them in the garden shed out back. The door's padlocked."

"Did Ms. Miller have that key?"

"Yes—it's here in the kitchen."

"And you didn't notice one of your kayaks was missing?"

"No, I didn't. I never looked. There'd been storms..."

Kowalski waited a moment for her to continue, and when she didn't, he rubbed the back of his neck and looked out at the glistening bay. "Was Alicia an experienced kayaker?"

"Not very, but she could handle quiet water—"

"Not big waves?"

"I'm not sure. We haven't gone kayaking together in a long time." Her stomach clenched at her automatic use of the present tense. Taking a quick breath, she continued. "She might have improved."

"You're a pretty good kayaker?"

Quinn nodded without looking at him.

"Would you have gone out yesterday?"

"No," she said almost inaudibly.

He turned, facing the water. "Wish I had a friend who owned a cottage on the bay. You and Ms. Miller were good friends?"

"We were."

"Were?" the FBI agent prodded her.

Unable to sit any longer, Quinn shot to her feet. "We haven't been as close in recent months, especially after I left the Justice Department."

"You didn't like your job?"

"I wanted something else."

Kowalski managed a quick grin. "A life?"

"Something like that."

"Do you have one?"

She gave him a sharp look, not deluded into thinking any of his questions were idle or friendly. "I work hard, Agent Kowalski, but what I do now is on my terms. I saved aggressively when I was at Justice and could afford—" Quinn broke off. "It doesn't matter. I have no regrets."

"Alicia was a spendthrift? Did she have a lot of debt?"

"I didn't say that. We spent our money on different things." There it was, she thought. The past tense. Her eyes filled with tears, but she didn't explain them to T.J. Kowalski. "Money was never a serious issue between us as friends, if that's what you're getting at."

"She have enough money to do what she wanted to?"

"Do any of us?"

He shifted his gaze from the water and settled it on Quinn. "You don't have to defend her, Ms. Harlowe."

"Please, just call me Quinn. And I'm not defending her. She was upset yesterday. Frightened, paranoid. She didn't say anything about wanting to kill herself. In fact, the opposite. She was afraid of being killed."

"By an osprey," Kowalski said.

Quinn didn't respond.

"The local police are in charge of the investigation into her death, but it's still too early to make a judgment about what exactly happened." The FBI agent sounded almost sympathetic. "Are you going back to Washington tonight?"

"No, I can't imagine making the drive." She glanced at the pot of cheerful yellow pansies that Alicia had left for her. "This place is supposed to be my refuge. I love it here."

"You have any friends around here who can stay with you?"

"No, I—" When she realized what he was implying, Quinn groaned. "Oh, come on, Agent Kowalski. I am *not* afraid to stay here by myself."

His eyebrows went up.

"I'm not!"

"I'd be scared if I found a friend of mine—"

"No, you wouldn't be. You'd be sad."

He didn't argue with her. "What about your neighbors?"

"We get along. Why? Are you going to talk to them?"

"After I finish up here." But she could tell that wasn't what he was getting at. "Are the Scanlons the kind of neighbors who will take you in if you get creeped out in the middle of the night?"

Quinn looked at him with what she hoped was a measure of resolve. "I'm not going to get creeped out. Alicia's drowning was almost certainly an accident. There's no evidence that she—of anything else, is there?" But when he raised his eyebrows again, as if she should know better than to ask such a question, she sighed. "Right, you wouldn't tell me if there were."

He reached into an inner pocket of his crisp dark gray jacket and withdrew a card, setting it on the small painted table next to her wicker chair. "Call me if anything else comes to you. Anything at all. About what you saw this morning, what your friend said yesterday. Don't dismiss anything as unimportant. Call me."

"All right, I will. What about the guy this morning—Huck Boone?"

"What about him?"

"Is there anything I should know about him?"

"He seems legit, but next time he runs past your cottage, I'd let him keep running." Kowalski pointed to his card. "If for some reason you decide you don't feel safe, you'll call me, right?"

"As opposed to Breakwater Security?"

He didn't smile. "As opposed to anyone."

Quinn tried not to let his serious tone affect her. If he had information she didn't, or if he had any suspicions, he wasn't sharing them with her. She had never met him before today, but FBI agent or not, T.J. Kowalski was obviously closemouthed by nature.

She glanced at his card. "It says T.J. there, too. What do the T and the J stand for?"

Now he smiled. "T.J."

After he left, Quinn sank against a porch post and gazed out at the water, watching a fishing boat make its way into shore just to the south of her cove. Seagulls hovered over it. In the bright late-afternoon sun, the osprey nest sprawled undisturbed on its buoy, no sign of the birds that had so preoccupied Alicia in her last hours.

When Quinn started to sob, she pulled herself from the peaceful scene and dashed inside, putting on a kettle for tea. As the water came to a boil and the kettle whistled and rattled, she almost missed the quiet knock on her side door. She saw her neighbors in its window and turned off the heat under the kettle, then let them in.

Maura Scanlon sniffled, tears in her eyes. She was in her early sixties, a sturdy, five-foot-tall retired nurse with more energy than most people half her age. "Oh, Quinn. We're so sorry."

Don, her husband, a retired accountant, nodded in agreement. "We know it's an awful day for you. Alicia was a good girl. We enjoyed seeing her."

Maura tried to smile. "She was so proud of those yellow pansies she put out on your porch."

"They're beautiful." Quinn could feel the steam from her tea kettle warming the small kitchen. "Alicia…"

"We'll miss her." Maura held up a steaming covered pot. "We brought you dinner. We couldn't think of what else to do." She walked straight to the stove and set the pot on a gas burner. "Crab stew. Nothing fancy. It'll stay hot for a while, but if you need to reheat it, just don't let it come to a boil."

"Thank you so much. I love crab stew."

"Well, you could hardly have a cottage on the Chesapeake and not love crab, could you?" But Maura's lightheartedness was forced, and she shook her head sadly, her amiable face drawn and pale. "What an awful day."

"Did the FBI talk to you?"

"Oh, yes. Special Agent Kowalski."

Don, a lanky man at least a foot taller than his wife, remained by the side door. "We weren't around much yesterday. We saw Alicia leave in the morning—"

"In her car?"

"That's right." He paused, glancing over at his wife as he scratched the back of his neck. "We knew she'd had an emotional weekend."

"We could hear her crying out on the front porch," Maura added. She shook her head again, as if she was still trying to absorb the reality of what had happened. "We thought she just needed a good cry. You know, sometimes people do."

Her husband sighed with a palpable sadness but said nothing. Quinn grabbed the old cookie tin where she kept tea bags. "I was just making tea. Would you like to join me?"

But they declined, and she understood. If they stayed, they would end up either rehashing everything or avoiding the topic altogether and staring awkwardly at each other, talking about anything but the events of the past two days.

Quinn followed the couple out the side door and down the driveway to the road, the air still, the tide going out again. "I met a man from Breakwater this morning," she said abruptly. "Huck Boone. He was out here jogging just before I found Alicia."

Don shook his head. "We didn't see anyone this morning. To be honest, Maura and I didn't realize anything had happened until we heard the police sirens."

His wife took his hand, her eyes shining with fresh tears. "I wish we'd been able to help."

"I don't know there was anything any of us could have done," Quinn said quietly.

Maura stood up straighter, dabbed her eyes. "The Breakwater Security people are out this way from time to time. Jogging, boating. It wouldn't be unusual to see one. They're generally polite."

"Do they happen to drive black Lincoln Town Cars with tinted back windows?"

"Black SUVs for the most part," Don replied. "Why?"

"Alicia came to see me in Washington yesterday. She was upset. Before she could tell me what was wrong, with any clarity, a black sedan picked her up and whisked her off. I have no idea who it was."

The Scanlons exchanged glances with each other. After more than forty years together, they were on each other's wavelength. Maura said, "I don't know whose car it was, Quinn, but I don't mind saying that we don't approve of Oliver Crawford turning his estate into the headquarters and training facility for this private security firm. Too much can happen. It's not his field of expertise. I know he went through a terrible ordeal, but how is having a bunch of guys with guns on his place out here going to help him feel safe?"

"It seems to us he's leaped without looking," Don said. "A lot of people in town feel that way, even if they're sympathetic to his situation."

Quinn could understand that sentiment. She had felt something similar ever since Alicia had blazed onto the coffee-shop patio in her semicoherent frenzy. "Did Alicia go out to the Crawford compound that you know of?"

"No," Maura said quickly. "Not that we know of."

Don dropped his wife's hand and slung an arm over her shoulder. "We should go. We're so sorry about Alicia, Quinn. If you need anything, let us know. Knock on the door or give us a call."

"Thank you." Quinn smiled at the couple. "And thank you for the crab stew."

After they left, she smelled the rich stew, grateful to have such decent people as neighbors, even if she had the feeling they had held back something, if only out of respect for her friendship with Alicia.

If they knew anything important—anything that would help people understand what had happened to Alicia—Quinn was positive that Maura and Don would tell the authorities.

She couldn't eat.

Quinn finally gave up trying and put the crab stew in the refrigerator and made herself a pot of chamomile tea, hoping it would help soothe her. She used a flowered teapot she'd found at a flea market and a mismatched, cheerful cup and saucer, sitting at her little kitchen table with its view of the bay. She opened a box of saltine crackers, eating a stack, like a little kid, with her tea.

And crying, silently at first, tears dripping into her tea until, finally, she was sobbing. She couldn't stop. She stood up, knocking over her chair, then gave it a good kick as if somehow that would make her feel better.

She cried until she couldn't stand up any longer.

Then she pulled a quilt, another flea-market find, off her bed, wrapped it around her shoulders and went for a walk.

Yesterday at dusk, after the storms, when she'd stood on the water's edge, Alicia was almost certainly already dead. Quinn kept picturing herself by the cove after she'd arrived in Yorkville, but she couldn't remember seeing anything out of the ordinary. Her red kayak. Gulls. Anything in the water.

She tightened her quilt around her, passing the Scanlon cottage, continuing along the waterfront on the loop road. There were more cottages, people working out in their yards on the cool but pretty spring evening. She smelled charcoal and barbecue sauce, and she heard children laughing.

She caught sight of an osprey high in the sky.

"The osprey will kill me."

Had Alicia had a premonition of her own death?

Or had her fears and delusions lured her out onto the bay at a dangerous time and become a self-fulfilling prophecy?

Quinn forced herself to pull her gaze from the osprey.

She could feel where the frigid, wet sand had rubbed her winter-tender feet raw, but at least they were warm now. After the police had arrived, Huck Boone had taken her back to her cottage and insisted she find dry socks.

She came to the small local motel that marked the

halfway point of her usual waterfront walk. Instead of continuing, she sat on a bench, listening to the steady rhythm of the tide. A lone gull perched on a post of the motel's rickety dock and turned to her, staring at her. Quinn shivered, wondering if it was one of the gulls from that morning, if it recognized her somehow.

It flew off, and its cry into the empty sky seemed to echo her mix of sadness and loneliness.

Alicia had come to her for help, and now she was dead.

A shadow fell over her, and a dark, drop-dead-handsome man handed her a tissue. "Thank you," she mumbled, wiping her eyes.

"Aren't you going to ask me how I happened to have a tissue?"

She managed a smile. "How?"

"My mother. She said a man should carry tissues in case a pretty woman needs one."

"That's very old-fashioned, isn't it?"

"It was her way of getting a fourteen-year-old to be prepared. If she said I should keep tissues in case I needed them for myself—" He shrugged. "I'd have told her that's what shirtsleeves are for."

Quinn laughed, sniffling. "I'm Quinn Harlowe, by the way."

"Diego Clemente. I'm staying here at the motel."

"I hear they serve good breakfast."

He made a face. "Two kinds of sugary cereal, stale Danish and bananas a monkey would throw back."

"How can you screw up a banana?"

"I don't know. Ask them." He nodded toward the hotel. "It's not a picky clientele. How're you doing? Feeling better?"

She nodded. "Thanks." When she rose, her knees wobbled under her, but Diego Clemente had the grace to give her a moment to steady herself. "Have the police been by here?"

"The police?"

"A woman—there was—" Not normally at a loss for words, Quinn couldn't seem to focus. "A woman drowned. She was probably out on a kayak yesterday. A red kayak. I was wondering if the police asked anyone out here if they saw her."

Diego had narrowed his dark eyes on her. "I didn't see anything."

"I wasn't suggesting—" She pulled up her quilt, which had drooped to the ground. "I don't know what I'm saying."

"The woman was your friend?"

"Yes."

"Stinks, losing a friend that way." He tugged on an edge of her quilt. "What, you don't own a coat?"

"I just grabbed the quilt…"

He frowned at her. "Your cottage is on that dead-end road out by the cove? You're not going to make it that far."

"The walk will do me good. Thanks for the tissue."

"Sure."

Quinn took a few steps back down the road, but stopped and turned back to him. "By the way, have you seen an abandoned dark blue BMW around here anywhere? Alicia—my friend who died this morning. Her car's missing."

His gaze held hers. "I'll keep an eye out for it."

"Thanks."

Twenty yards from the motel, Quinn tripped over her quilt and almost went flying, but rearranged it quickly, glancing back toward the dock in case Diego Clemente wanted to say he'd told her so. But he'd disappeared, and she wondered if he'd already forgotten their conversation.

She made it the rest of her way back to her cottage without tripping or crying. The walk and the chilly air had helped her appetite, and she got the crab stew out of the refrigerator and set it on the stove. While it heated, she checked her cell phone for messages. Gerard Lattimore and Steve Eisenhardt had called. Lattimore asked her to call him back. Steve left it up to her. He seemed to understand that they didn't know each other well enough for her to want to talk to him after such a day.

When she tried Lattimore's number, she got his assistant. He was in a meeting.

Thank God, Quinn thought, dipping up a bowl of the steaming crab stew and taking it into the living room with her. She wrapped back up in her quilt and sat on the sofa, a yard-sale find that she'd covered in a sea-green plaid herself.

The Scanlons were good cooks, and the stew was wonderful.

But Quinn took two bites and set the bowl down on a side table, assaulted by images of Alicia paddling in the storm, trying to keep her kayak from overturning in the swells and failing, capsizing, drowning.

And no life vest, no emergency whistle in case she got into trouble.

Either might have saved her life.

Quinn sank back against the soft couch and could almost feel Huck Boone's arm around her as he'd walked with her back to the cottage.

Heck of a name, Huck Boone. Was it real? How many guys working private security changed their names?

Probably a lot.

She thought of Diego Clemente and his tissue, and his neutral expression when she'd mentioned Alicia's car. Maybe too neutral? Had he seen something yesterday and didn't want to get involved?

You're exhausted.

A sudden gust of wind rattled the windows, so startling her that she almost fell off the couch.

She got up and ran through the cottage, making sure all the windows were locked, checking the porch door and the side door. If she felt unsafe, she could call Kowalski. But what would he do? And he'd meant truly unsafe, as in killers were on her doorstep, not the wind rattling the windows and unnerving her.

Again, Quinn thought of Huck Boone's thick arm around her.

Not good.

She collapsed back on the couch, rolling up in her quilt and listening to another gust of wind come at the cottage, concentrating on it, trying to push back more images.

But there she was at the University of Virginia, on a warm spring day among the dogwood, she and Alicia falling onto their backs in the soft grass and laughing hysterically over something that had just happened. Quinn couldn't remember what, but the laughter was clear in her mind and all she wanted was to reach back in time and warn Alicia not ever to move to Washington, tell her that a job at the Justice Department wasn't worth the cost—wasn't worth her life. Even if her work—her friendship with Quinn—hadn't caused her death, if Alicia had taken a different route and stayed in Chicago, maybe she'd still be alive.

12

Despite her many years as a nurse, Maura Scanlon couldn't stop thinking about what pretty Alicia Miller must have looked like when Quinn had found her dead, drowned, on the beach.

Thank heavens I didn't have to see her.

Maura rubbed lotion into her hands, rough from her work in the garden. Unable to eat supper, she'd gone into the backyard and divided daylilies, not wearing gloves, relishing the feel of the dirt—letting it remind her of life, not death. She'd had to use a brush to get the dirt out from under her nails. She hadn't gotten all of it.

"Quinn Harlowe hasn't gone back to Washington yet," Don said, joining his wife in the kitchen. "I thought she might head back tonight, but her car's still in the driveway."

"She'll probably rest tonight and leave in the

morning. She should go back to her work, her friends. There's nothing for her here."

Maura sat at the round oak table that had belonged to her mother. Alexandria, where she and Don had lived their entire lives, suddenly seemed so far away. She rubbed a long-existing crack in the table as if it were some kind of genie lamp. *Three wishes. If only I'd be granted three wishes. Right here, right now, I'd bring that poor girl back to life.*

"Can I get you anything?" Don asked.

"No, thanks."

They had cleaned up the supper dishes. Don had eaten very little, his appetite, too, curtailed by the trauma of the day. Maura looked out the window by the table, but it was dark now and she only saw her reflection. She and her husband enjoyed the simplicity of their lives in Yorkville. They didn't care about riches or a jam-packed social life. Taking their coffee onto the porch on a warm morning and watching the bay was enough to satisfy them.

"Do you suppose it'll ever be the same here?" Maura asked, hearing the haunted tone in her voice.

"Of course it will."

"The FBI—Don, we were interrogated by the FBI."

He tried to smile. "'Interrogated' is a bit strong, don't you think? It'll get better with time, Maura. The shock of what happened today will ease."

"If only we'd been here—"

"There still might have been nothing we could have done. The water's cold. Even if we'd seen Alicia out on the bay in the storm, once she fell in, she wouldn't have lasted long. As a nurse, you know that."

"No one's suggested she died of hypothermia—she drowned." Although, as Maura well knew, hypothermia could have contributed to her drowning.

"We weren't there. We couldn't have saved her." Don pulled out a chair and sat down heavily, his gentle eyes troubled. "And if she was intent upon killing herself…"

"You don't believe her death was an accident?"

"I don't know what to believe."

Maura pumped out more of the pink lotion she'd bought on sale in a bottle big enough to last through summer. "Should we have told the authorities about her and Oliver Crawford?"

"Special Agent Kowalski never asked—"

"He asked us if there was anything we could think of that might help them understand what happened. So did the local police."

Don shook his head. "I see no reasonable purpose served by spreading gossip. We don't know for a fact that Oliver Crawford and Alicia Miller were having an affair."

"We know he visited her at the cottage."

"We don't know if he ever stayed the night."

Maura squirted another dab of lotion into her palm and rubbed it in, then pushed the bottle into the center of the table. "Neither of us likes spying on the neighbors."

"Oh, Maura, we weren't spying—"

"It feels like spying when we know such things. If Oliver Crawford had wanted people to know he was visiting Alicia, he wouldn't have been so sneaky about it."

"Perhaps he saw it as being discreet, not sneaky." As always, her husband kept his tone even. "He's friends with Gerard Lattimore, and he's—he was Alicia's boss. They could have been discussing something about him. A surprise birthday party, maybe."

"A surprise birthday party?" Maura laughed. "That's rich, Don. I don't like Crawford or Lattimore. I saw their type often enough at the hospital. Their hunger for power and ambition goes right to their pores. Neither holds any interest for me, even less so as I get older."

Don smiled, taking her hand. "A good thing, because I've never been powerful or particularly ambitious. Maura—"

She set her jaw. "I still think Oliver Crawford and Alicia were having an affair, but I agree we shouldn't be spreading rumors and gossip. If her death were a homicide, that would be one thing."

"Even if you're right about the affair, if Alicia committed suicide, it wasn't Crawford's fault. It wasn't anyone's fault."

Including mine, Maura thought. But she'd seen the signs of depression in Alicia, worsening in the weeks since she'd starting coming to Yorkville—and over the weekend, the increased agitation.

"I knew something was wrong," she whispered. "I should have taken her to the hospital myself and insist she get checked out. Accident or not, she wouldn't have taken such a risk in those conditions if she'd had her head screwed on straight."

"We'll take a long walk tomorrow. It'll help."

Maura knew he was right. Self-recriminations and speculation would get them nowhere, and they had their own lives to lead.

13

Just after dark, Special Agent Kowalski knocked on Quinn's porch door. She'd spotted his car pull up in front of her cottage, but still her heart pounded when she saw him through the door's window. She had difficulty unlocking the door, her fingers stiff from the cold air and her long, difficult day. When she let him in, a breeze stung her face, her skin raw from crying. Another time, she might not have wanted an FBI agent—anyone—to see her in such a state, but tonight she didn't care.

"Are you spending the night in Yorkville?" she asked him as he walked past her into the small living room. "It's getting late."

"I live in Spotsylvania. It's not too far from here." His expression suggested he hadn't come for chitchat. "We found Alicia Miller's car."

"How—where?"

"We received an anonymous tip. It was out by an

old boathouse on the waterfront, about two miles up the loop road from here. It's closer by water. Apparently it's a favorite spot for kayakers to launch."

"I know it well. It's an easy paddle over to the wildlife refuge from there. But Alicia must have headed back this way, since she ended up in the marsh." Quinn's voice caught. Had Kowalski hoped to catch her off guard? She noticed her quilt on the couch, her running shoes under the coffee table, her bowl of cold crab stew, but stayed focused on what he'd just told her. "When did you get this anonymous tip?"

"I didn't. The local police did, maybe an hour ago."

An hour. Had Diego Clemente recognized her description of Alicia's car and phoned in the information anonymously, not wanting to use his name and have to answer questions?

"Quinn?"

"If Alicia had her head together enough to drive out to the boathouse to launch, don't you think she'd have checked the weather? At least worn a life vest?"

"Happens all the time. People don't pay attention."

"But she must have just arrived back from Washington—"

"If she'd been agitated, then stuck in a car for three or four hours, she could have cut corners in her rush to get out on the water," Kowalski reasoned.

Quinn sat on a 1950s wooden-armed chair, its cushions covered in a flowered fabric that went with the plaid on the couch. Alicia had helped her pick it out. "Alicia always wore a life vest. I insist anyone using one of my kayaks wear one. I keep several sizes in the shed. It's not like her to go without."

Kowalski didn't respond right away. "Have you had anything to eat?"

His question took her by surprise. "Crab stew—"

"Uh-uh." He pointed to her bowl, still on the side table. "You've had, what, three bites?"

Not even that much. She didn't answer him. "Does Huck Boone know you found Alicia's car? He was with me this morning—"

"I know. I can't discuss the details of an ongoing investigation with you."

"The black sedan that picked Alicia up in Washington—it hasn't turned up?"

Kowalski sighed at Quinn. "You are tenacious, aren't you? Why didn't you sign up for the FBI? What are you now—thirty?"

"Thirty-two."

"You still could. You've got four years. Then you can run an investigation and ask people questions."

"If I weren't a former Justice Department employee—"

"I treat everyone the same."

She snorted. "Ha."

"I know a couple guys planning to sit in on your workshop at the academy."

"If you tell me things you're not supposed to, I'll give them A's."

That got him to crack a smile. "Good to see you

have your sense of humor. It'll help you in the coming days."

But she sensed he was trying to tell her something more. "And?"

"And leave the investigation into your friend's death to law enforcement. Don't meddle."

"What makes you think I've meddled?"

"Good night, Miss Harlowe."

"A minute ago it was Quinn."

He leaned toward her. "Eat. Get some sleep. Go back to Washington in the morning and make up a hard test for my friends." But he sighed, shaking his head. "I know it's been a rough day for you. I'm truly sorry about your loss."

"Thank you."

After Kowalski left, Quinn took her crab stew to the kitchen and popped the bowl in her ancient microwave. If she had something to eat, she thought, she might be able to figure out how T.J. Kowalski had discovered that his anonymous tipster was Diego Clemente and she'd asked him about Alicia's car, because obviously he had. Otherwise why read her the riot act about minding her own business?

Kowalski must have gone to the waterfront motel himself and asked people hanging around if they saw anything. Ordinary legwork. He'd talked to Clemente and figured out he'd provided the tip about Alicia's car. Had Clemente actually told him that Quinn had been asking questions?

The microwave dinged. The stew was bubbling hot, but she didn't think it had come to a boil. She opened another sleeve of saltines and sat at the table, and after three spoonfuls of the rich, flavorful stew, she knew what she was doing and why Kowalski had warned her off. She was grasping at straws and looking for distractions—meddling in a law enforcement investigation—in order to alleviate her own guilt, to take her mind off her shock and grief and, even for a few moments, the image of Alicia in the marsh.

However she'd died, she was gone, and Quinn didn't want to accept that reality.

T.J. Kowalski hadn't made the effort to come to her cottage and tell her in person about the discovery out of any sympathy for her, or because he'd needed to ask her more questions.

He'd wanted to tell her to butt out.

Message delivered, message received.

Quinn stared at her crab stew. It had turned gloppy, and she had lost any urge to eat. She forced herself to take a few more bites, but couldn't really taste anything. Finally, she gave up and, as she washed out her bowl, she wondered what T.J. Kowalski knew that he wasn't telling her. Or was she just grasping at more straws?

She thought of Huck Boone. He worked for Breakwater Security—he could have his own read on the investigation.

Maybe she'd look him up tomorrow and ask him what he thought.

Feeling better, Quinn fell back onto the couch and wrapped up in her quilt, listening to the wind and the tide and trying not to think.

14

Steve Eisenhardt bought a tall coffee-to-go at a Starbucks between his apartment and the Department of Justice and hoped the caffeine jolt would help clear his head.

Alicia was dead. He might as well have killed her himself.

After he'd heard the news, he tried to rationalize his behavior and absolve himself of any guilt. But he knew what he'd done.

The devil's come for you…

Rain-soaked fallen cherry blossoms rotted on the sidewalk. He drank his coffee through the plastic lid and noticed his hands were trembling, a mix of fear and self-loathing, he thought, eating away at him. He would never be the same. There was no going back now. All he could do was hope these scumbags who had him by the short hairs had finished with him.

But as if he'd conjured them up himself, the two Nazis from Monday eased in next to him, the older one on his left, the younger one on his right. The three of them walked down the street together, like tourists who'd met by accident.

"Quinn Harlowe," the older goon asked. "Tell us about her."

"Quinn?" Steve snorted. "She's a pain in the ass. If you stupid assholes left a bread-crumb trail, she'll find it and follow it right back to your hidey-hole."

The goon didn't react at all. "What's her relationship with Lattimore?"

"He worships her. Thinks she's brilliant. Thinks she can help him shine. He'd do damn near anything to get her back at Justice."

"Any romantic interest?"

"Have you had a good look at her? Who wouldn't have a romantic interest in her?"

The kid to Steve's right sneered. "Not everyone wants to screw every woman he sees, Eisenhardt. You're a piece of work, aren't you?"

A squeaky-clean type. Steve ignored him. He looked up at the superfit goon on his left. "Quinn doesn't like to sit on the sidelines."

"That doesn't surprise me. Keep an eye on her. If she meets with Gerard Lattimore, we want to know." The SS guard took another few steps. He spoke mildly, never raising his voice or giving his words any emphasis. Just stating the conditions under which Steve got to live. "We don't want the Justice Department to use Alicia Miller's death as an excuse to start nosing around in our affairs."

Steve felt sweat breaking out on his brow, the back of his neck, his lower back. "I don't know her that well. What if I can't find out what she's up to?"

"You're a well-connected, intelligent, successful attorney. You'll find out."

They walked a few more steps in what would look to anyone on the street like companionable silence. Finally, Steve licked his lips. "This wasn't part of the deal."

"There was no deal."

"We had a verbal agreement—"

"Lawyer talk," the kid said.

The older guy—the SS guard—seemed to like that one. "One more thing. We want you to find out if anyone at Justice is investigating what they would call a vigilante network."

"What?"

"Names. We want names."

"What vigilante network?"

The SS guard didn't react. "Last fall. You remember. Deputy U.S. Marshal Juliet Longstreet and Special Forces Army Major Ethan Brooker uncovered a vigilante plot to expose traitors. One of the vigilantes was killed. Another—a low-level thug, really—was taken into custody."

Steve remembered. They'd nearly killed a White House advisor and Juliet Longstreet's family in Vermont. "You guys?"

Cold, steel-blue eyes leveled on him.

Steve felt his stomach drop to his knees. He had a sudden urge to go to the bathroom. He tugged at his shirt collar, his fingers coming away wet with sweat. "If you're involved with those kooks from last fall, you can bet your ass they're investigating you. I wouldn't have access to that kind of information."

The older goon reached into his pants pocket and withdrew a pack of gum, tapping out a piece as if they were discussing the spring weather forecast. "Get access."

Sipping more of his coffee, as if somehow it made him feel normal, Steve decided these guys needed to know he wasn't afraid of them, that his life depended on it—never mind that his intestines were telling him in no uncertain terms that he was scared shitless. "So, is Oliver Crawford in on your new world order, or are you all just using him for his money and connections? He *is* who you work for, isn't he? Makes sense, given what happened to Alicia down in Yorkville."

Steve wasn't into their crazy thinking. Justice, breaking the law to save freedom. Throwing out two hundred years of jurisprudence and starting from scratch, rewriting the law their way. If they were involved with those screwballs from last fall, they were into vigilante violence and their own idea of the new world order.

Thumbscrews. These bastards are into torturing people.

The steel-eyed Nazi responded to his remark in the same mild tone. "We want the names of anyone involved in the investigation into last fall's events. The lawyers, the FBI, the ATF, the marshals. Any White House liaisons."

"Liaison. That's a big word for you, isn't it?" Instead of shooting him, the Nazi offered Steve a piece of gum. He shook his head. "No, thanks." For some reason, the gesture made him sweat even more. "Doesn't anything get to you?"

A quirk of a smile. "Justice Department lawyers entrusted with the people's business having kinky sex with underage girls."

Steve forced himself not to react. The bastards had pictures. They'd sent him a link to a Web site with an entire photo album of him and the congressman's daughter. They didn't just have a couple of grainy pictures he could explain away. With a few clicks of the keyboard, they could post their little montage to the world.

"No one was hurt."

"Tell that to her father," the Nazi Youth said. "She was *fifteen*."

"If Daddy sees a picture of his daughter with your dick in her mouth, you won't just not work in Washington again." The SS guard chewed his gum, obviously relishing this part of his job. "You won't work anywhere."

"The daughter was rebelling against her parents. That's not my fault."

True enough, but the ropes and the rough sex were his idea. She'd gone along at first, just itching to get back at her father for ignoring her, at her mother for putting image above anything else—at both of them for not understanding her. Steve had used her disenchantment with her life to his advantage.

He'd done it all before, and she hadn't; his speed, his expertise, his excitement at her moans had frightened her. He'd gotten off on the risk of what he was doing and couldn't make himself stop.

Several of the pictures showed her trying to get away from him.

She didn't want anyone to know what she'd done. If nothing else, Steve figured he'd taught her a lesson about not getting ahead of herself in doing payback. She wanted to punish her parents by misbehaving, but the gain needed to be in balance with the pain.

He'd also promised himself he'd stay away from the troubled teenage daughters of powerful Washington types.

Two weeks ago, just when he thought he'd dodged this latest speeding bullet he'd fired at himself and his fun with the congressman's daughter would stay their dirty little secret, the goons turned up. The pictures would embarrass the girl, too—not to mention her family—but they didn't care. Steve didn't know how they had managed to get the pictures. They must have followed him. Did he look like a pervert? Had one of his previous consensual partners talked?

Since seeing himself on a computer screen, he'd been celibate.

No wonder he couldn't stand still, couldn't think straight. Sex, especially kinky sex, relieved his stress.

They came to Pennsylvania Avenue, busy on the warm spring morning. Normal people, Steve thought, going to normal jobs.

The two Nazis flagged a cab and climbed in, ignoring Steve. The cab pulled away. He melted into a crowd crossing the street, his hand shaking wildly, his bowels clamping down. He didn't know if he'd make it to the DOJ in time.

What would the atmosphere be like, with Alicia's death? Word of the discovery of her body hadn't reached the office until late in the day.

I didn't mean for any of this to happen.

But it had, hadn't it? And it was never going to end. Never, unless he did something, walked into Lattimore's office and told him everything, or called this Brooker or Longstreet. At least maybe they could stop these guys from hurting anyone else.

Steve could hear his jail-cell door locking shut even now. If he talked, he faced a prison sentence as well as public humiliation.

He wasn't going to do anything except what the two Nazis had asked him to. It was his only chance to save his own neck.

15

Quinn noticed curious looks from a few people as she settled into her booth at Shippey's, a diner in a former hardware store on Yorkville's wide main street. With its red vinyl booths and Formica counter, its draw was its comfort-food menu and pleasant staff, not its decor.

The village did, however, have its quaint places. Some of the tourist-oriented seasonal shops weren't open yet, but most of the mainstays—bookstore, pharmacy, antiques shops, galleries, sporting goods store—had out their welcome signs. Quinn had no intention of going shopping. She just wanted breakfast. She'd spent the night on her couch, sleeping in fits and starts, and woke up starving, with nothing to eat but Alicia's abandoned yogurt.

After two years in Yorkville, with her scores of trips to yard sales and flea markets, she knew many of the locals and second-home people. Shippey's was a gathering place, quieter on a weekday morning in early spring, but, still, half the stools at the counter and most of the booths were occupied. On a weekend morning in the summer, there'd be a line. Several people recognized her and told her how sorry they were about Alicia's death, and Quinn quickly decided that coming to the diner, being among people, had been a good move.

Donna, the redheaded thirty-year-old daughter of Shippey's owners, set a mug of coffee in front of her and took Quinn's order of French toast and bacon. Food, she knew, would help steady her.

"You just missed your FBI agent," Donna said. "He had the French toast, too."

Shippey's French toast, golden-brown and sprinkled with cinnamon sugar, was famous. "Special Agent Kowalski? He's not *my* FBI agent—"

"I don't know. He's kind of cute." Donna grinned, pointing her coffeepot at Quinn. "There. I knew that'd put some color back in your cheeks."

"Did he say where he was headed?"

"No—I figure he's gone to Breakwater. He was talking to some people in here, and he didn't realize the woman who drowned—Miss Miller—" Donna suddenly grew awkward. "I'm so sorry about what happened. I know she was your friend."

"Thank you." Quinn left it at that. "What didn't Agent Kowalski realize?"

"Oh. That your friend was acting weird all weekend. I don't mean to speak ill—"

"It's okay, Donna. Had anyone seen her?"

"A couple people saw her on Sunday and said she was real jittery. Then on Monday morning, I was up early as usual to get here for five-thirty, and I saw her out at the Crawford compound's front gate. I go by there on my way to work. She looked pretty upset."

"She was at the Crawford compound at five-thirty in the morning?"

"That's right." Donna blushed. "I'm not saying anything out of turn, am I?"

"No, no, of course not. I just hadn't realized she was there, either."

"I'm sure it doesn't mean anything, her being out there. She'd walked from the cottage, I guess. It's a couple miles, but she kept in good shape—we used to see her jogging around town all the time on the weekends she was down here. I didn't think too much of it, except she was so upset."

"Did anyone at Breakwater know she was there? They've tightened up security—"

"Oh, yeah. They knew she was there. You *know* they did. They've gone downright crazy with security, if you ask me. They've got snipers on the roof. I live three miles up the road, and half the time I don't remember to lock my doors. And they're just getting started. There's way more to come."

Quinn doubted Breakwater had snipers, much less any posted on the roof. Donna's exaggeration, however, wasn't unexpected. Obsessive about his privacy even before his kidnapping, Oliver Crawford was a popular subject of gossip, and his new private security venture only added to his aura of wealth and eccentricity. He had the money, freedom and connections to indulge any whim.

"Could you hear what Alicia was saying?" Quinn asked.

Donna shook her head. "I couldn't make out any words. I was going to stop and help, but some of Crawford's security guys came out the front gate. Bet they drove her back to your cottage."

"Did you see which guys—"

She gestured with her coffeepot out the window. "Not those two. They're new." But she collected herself. "I'm talking too much. I should put your order in."

As she sipped her coffee, Quinn turned to see who Donna had pointed to and watched Huck Boone and another man, just as buff, shut the doors to a black SUV that had pulled up in front of the diner. She was so startled, she dropped her mug, coffee spilling over her table. She jumped aside before it could hit her and pulled napkins from a dispenser, and began to sop up the coffee.

In an instant Huck was there, scooping up the wet napkins as she grabbed for more. "Got butterfingers this morning, huh?"

"Looks that way." Using a fresh napkin, she took the wet napkins from him and tried to smile. "I didn't expect to see you here."

"A granola bar at 5:00 a.m. doesn't go far. We were up early for training." Instead of running clothes, this morning he wore neat khaki pants and a black lightweight jacket with Breakwater Security over his heart, in discreet gold lettering. He gestured to the man next to him, also in khakis and a black Breakwater Security jacket. "This is Vern, by they way—Vernon Glover. He's another Breakwater flunky. Vern, meet Quinn Harlowe."

"My pleasure," Vern said, but he didn't offer a hand, nor had he helped clean up the spilled coffee. He turned to Huck. "I've got a few things to do in town. I'll be back for you in thirty minutes."

He left abruptly. Huck smiled at Quinn. "Looks as if Vern's not having breakfast with me."

Quinn started to invite him to join her, but Donna arrived with a damp towel and he took a stool at the counter. Donna mopped the table, nervously glancing at Boone. She leaned close to Quinn and whispered, "Him and the one that just left—they're armed to the teeth."

"I'm sure they have permits for any weapons—"

"Shh."

Quinn started to say something else, but Donna scooted off dramatically, giving Huck a dazzling smile as she disappeared into the kitchen.

With her table wet, Quinn moved to the counter, deliberately sitting next to Huck. He glanced sideways at her. "How are you this morning? Besides jumpy."

"I'm doing okay. Thanks for asking. I thought getting out would do me good." She smiled. "Plus, I had no food. Alicia left a yogurt…"

"You need a real breakfast. You look pale."

Donna returned with two mugs of coffee and set them on the counter. "Your breakfast will be right up," she told Quinn, then took Huck's order of eggs, home fries and wheat toast.

As she peeled open a thimble of half-and-half, Quinn was aware of him so close to her. "What exactly do you do at Breakwater?" she asked.

"Whatever I'm told."

"You don't give the orders?"

"No, ma'am," he said with an undertone of amusement. "I take orders. I'm just a low-level bodyguard."

"Whose body do you guard?"

His eyes settled on hers, then drifted lower, taking her in with a frankness she wasn't used to. He shifted back to his coffee, drinking it black. Without looking at her, he said, "Makes no difference to me."

"How does one get to be a bodyguard?"

"I fell into it."

Quinn persisted. "How?"

"Harvard didn't want me."

"You're using sarcasm to avoid answering my question. Is that your custom?"

His dark green eyes narrowed on her. "You're asking questions to avoid thinking about your friend."

She felt heat rise in her face. "I wouldn't know if that kind of avoidance is typical for me because I've never had a friend drown."

"I'm sorry," he said abruptly. "That wasn't very nice of me."

"Are you a nice man?"

He gave her a quick, unreadable smile. "You ask a lot of questions for someone who hasn't had breakfast. Aren't you hungry?"

Donna returned with a plate of French toast and a glass shaker of cinnamon sugar, but this time she kept any comments she had to herself.

Quinn picked up a knife and spread butter across the golden toast. "Whatever training you did this morning must not have been too rigorous. You were a lot sweatier yesterday. And you don't look as if you just got out of the shower."

Sudden humor sparked in his eyes. "How would I look just out of the shower?"

Oh, hell. She set the knife down quickly, before she ended up dropping it. "More avoiding of the subject. My point is," she went on, "that I don't believe your story. I think you and your friend Vern saw Special Agent Kowalski coming in the front door and you went out the back door. So to speak. I don't even know if the Crawford compound *has* a back door."

Huck drank his coffee without responding.

As she sprinkled cinnamon sugar onto the melting butter, Quinn tried to regain her appetite. The smell of food combined with the tension of interrogating this man—who probably *was* armed, if not to the extent Donna assumed—had turned her stomach. "Why didn't you tell me Alicia was at the Crawford compound early Monday morning? Never mind me—did you tell Special Agent Kowalski?"

"I didn't see her."

"Did Vern?"

"No."

Donna brought his breakfast and refilled the two

mugs, her knuckles white on the handle of the coffeepot. Quinn wondered how much she'd overheard.

After Donna retreated nervously, Huck picked up a slice of bacon. "What are you now, Kowalski's helper? Think the FBI can't investigate, and they need your help?"

"I was just making conversation."

"No, you weren't."

She cut into her French toast. She needed a sugar boost. Something to help get her back to normal. "The police found Alicia's car last night up on the loop road."

"So I heard."

"She must have taken the kayak up there—"

Huck turned to face her. "Quinn, just stop. Don't do this to yourself. Go back home, resume your life and mourn your friend. Let the authorities figure out what happened to her."

"She drowned."

Quinn jumped off the stool, ready to bolt.

He touched her elbow. "I'm sorry. Sit down. Finish your breakfast. I'll leave you alone."

"I can't eat. It's not you…" Her throat caught. "Good luck with your job. I'm sorry we had to meet under such difficult circumstances. If you stay at Breakwater—" She didn't know what she was saying. "Well, who knows."

"You're heading back to Washington?"

"Yes, as soon as I pull myself together. I have work today, and there's nothing—I guess there's nothing for me to do here."

She left money on the counter for her breakfast and a generous tip. As she headed for the door, Huck didn't stop her. Once she was outside, she let herself sob, brushing back tears as she started down the main street. She'd walked into the village, which meant she had to walk back. The gorgeous morning made her want to stay on the bay for a few days. Hide there, she thought. Pretend she was on vacation and Alicia was at work in Washington, not on a slab in some medical examiner's office.

Pushing the image out of her mind before it could take hold, Quinn focused on the pretty scenery, walking along the loop road past the motel where she'd met Diego Clemente last night. She stood on the dock, pretending to look for birds, but she didn't see him or his boat. She recognized Buddy Jones, the motel's owner and a Yorkville fixture, a wiry, leather-skinned man in his late sixties, a cigarette hanging off his lower lip as he tied a boat with a thick, worn rope.

"Excuse me," Quinn said. "Have you seen Diego Clemente?"

"Who?"

She repeated the name. "He was out here last night. I think he's a guest at your motel—"

"Oh, right. Yeah. The Yankees fan." Buddy paused, removing the cigarette from his lip. "I hate the Yankees. Diego's a nice guy, though. He went out early this morning. He does most mornings."

"In his boat?"

"Yeah, in his boat."

"He's here alone?"

Buddy regarded her with curiosity more than suspicion. "Why do you want to know?"

"I don't, really. I was just asking."

"He's a good-looking fella."

"That's not why—"

"He and his wife split up. He's taking some time to get his head screwed on straight. Nothing like fishing for that." He flicked ashes into the water. "You fish?"

"No—I kayak."

"Kayaking." He grimaced with disdain. "I hope you know what you're doing. Half the kayakers I see out here are a menace. A wonder more of them don't get killed. That girl yesterday—you hear about her?"

Quinn felt the blood run out of her head, but she nodded. "What a tragedy."

He sighed. "An unnecessary tragedy, if you want my opinion. Now she's gone, and her family and friends have to live with what she did. Sorry. I don't mean to speak ill of the dead. You want me to tell Diego you were asking for him?"

"Oh, no, that's not necessary. How long has he been in Yorkville?"

"Couple weeks." The old man stabbed a callused finger at her. "You take my advice and stay away from him, okay, missy? He's on the rebound from a bad marriage. Nothing but heartache in it for a pretty girl like you."

"Thanks. I'll remember that." In spite of his old-fashioned attitudes, Quinn couldn't help but like the man. "He doesn't have anything to do with Breakwater Security, does he?"

The old man grunted. "Those psychopaths? No, not that I know of."

"The security guys—do they sometimes do training runs out this way?"

"A few do—"

"A rough-looking guy with short dark hair? He was out for a run yesterday morning—"

"I think I know the one you mean. He found that woman's body yesterday—he and her friend from D.C. I heard his name's Boone. I can't remember if it's his first name or his last name. He just got here. I saw him running Monday, before the storms hit."

Quinn took a breath. "What time, do you remember?"

"Before five." He grinned, stained teeth showing. "I wasn't drinking a beer, and I don't drink beer until after five."

"A sensible rule."

"He stopped to stretch. Diego was out here having a cigarette—they talked for a minute or two. That's it. Why?"

"I'm just curious." It was the truth, but she remembered Kowalski's warning about interfering. "To be honest, I'm not sure how I feel about having the Crawford compound turned into a private security facility."

Buddy waved a hand in dismissal. "A day late and a dollar short on that one, if you don't mind my saying so. It's a done deal."

Quinn couldn't argue. Thanking him for his time, she continued her waterfront walk back to her cottage. Finding Alicia yesterday was horrible. She'd been in shock most of the day and wasn't doing that great now, but if she didn't pull herself together soon, people like T.J. Kowalski would either think she was on the verge of a breakdown herself or hiding something.

A sound overhead—close—drew her out of her thoughts.

A helicopter. Private. Flying low over the cove.

Oliver Crawford.

Quinn pictured Huck in his neat khakis and Breakwater jacket, rushing out to meet his boss, and found something about the image was off, simply didn't work.

She didn't know the man at all, but she'd learned to be a quick judge—to trust her instincts. And he hadn't struck her as bodyguard material. Not that she knew anything about bodyguards.

Huck Boone is not your problem, she told herself.

She'd take a shower and head back to Washington.

There was no reason to stay in Yorkville another minute.

16

Huck followed a mixed barbed-wire and white rail fence down to the water, where the rail fence gave way to just the barbed wire. As deterrents went, it was nothing elaborate, barely enough to warn off trespassers. Getting to Breakwater along the water would be difficult enough, given the surrounding marshes and the absence of a dock.

Joe Riccardi was smoking a cigar and staring out at the water. Without looking at Huck, he said, "I understand you met Quinn Harlowe in town just now."

"I didn't meet her. I ran into her."

"She was in the diner when you arrived?"

"That's right."

"You didn't go there because of her?"

"No, I went there for breakfast."

Riccardi nodded, his gaze still on the quiet bay. "Mr. Crawford is here. We don't want any problems. He's met Quinn Harlowe several times, because of his friendship with Gerard Lattimore."

"Did he know Alicia Miller?"

"Not really. They'd met." Riccardi shifted his gaze to Huck, but his expression was difficult to read. "The FBI agent looking into her death was here. T.J. Kowalski. He'd heard Miss Miller was out here on Monday morning. I hate to see that story come to law enforcement's attention. The scrutiny—" He looked back out at the water. "I don't know what's to be gained by that kind of scrutiny."

Find out if she was murdered. During the night, Huck had brainstormed all the different ways Alicia Miller could have ended up in the marsh, drowned, with her kayak, that didn't involve an accident or suicide. The thunderstorms could have provided a killer with cover, a reason for the authorities *not* to think murder.

But if he had a list of possibilities, speculative though they were, so did T.J. Kowalski and the local cops and probably half the village of Yorkville.

"Do you ever wonder how you got into this kind of work in the first place?" Riccardi asked quietly.

"Sometimes."

"If I'd stayed home in Michigan, I don't know." He puffed on his cigar. "There was no work in town. I wasn't that excited about college. I went, anyway, and got a useless degree. Then I joined the army."

"How long did you stay in?"

"Twenty."

"Miss it?"

Riccardi shook his head. "Not anymore. I lost a wife because of the demands. She just wasn't suited to having a husband at war. Then I met Sharon. We've been married less than a year. I thought Breakwater would be a path to a more normal life. I'd have a chance to get ahead." He stubbed out his cigar on a fence post and tucked it into his jacket pocket. "It's beautiful out here. We sure as hell could do worse."

"I guess so."

"Alicia Miller's death is a tragedy. Monday morning, when she came out here, Lubec and Rochester did what they could for her. She was ranting. They took her back to the cottage. They tried to get her to go to the emergency room or call a friend, but she sent them away. What more could they have done?" Riccardi didn't wait for an answer. "She went back to Washington, then came back here. For whatever reason."

"Tough break to get mixed up in her problems."

"What about Harlowe? Is she going to stir the pot?"

She already has. Huck shrugged. "Once she gets back to Washington and resumes her normal routine, she should be fine."

"She doesn't want to believe her friend killed herself yesterday or died in a tragic accident, does she?"

"She's operating under a lot of guilt."

Joe Riccardi's dark gaze fell on Huck. "Be careful of her."

It wasn't a statement that required a response.

Riccardi changed the subject. "Oliver Crawford is meeting with Sharon right now. I'm joining them in a few minutes. We're updating him on where we are with the company. He wants to see you, Vern Glover and Cully O'Dell at the house in an hour."

"Any reason?"

"He takes a personal interest in all of his employees."

Huck couldn't tell if Joe Riccardi was dead-on serious or indulging in a little sarcasm about his employer. He left, and Huck stayed by the barbed-wire fence, looking out across the marsh. He hoped Quinn had packed up her Saab and was on her way back to Washington. From what he'd seen of Special Agent Kowalski, he wouldn't take to having her sticking her nose in his investigation, even one into a likely death-by-accidental-drowning. She'd already given Diego fits. Huck had managed to check in with him by phone before breakfast, and Clemente was spitting fire about her bumping into him last night.

Huck had made the mistake of reminding him that because of Quinn, they'd found Alicia Miller's car. Diego had growled. "I'd have figured out it was Miller's car without Harlowe's help."

Unable to resist, Huck had prodded his partner. "When?"

"You're a prick, Huck. If you weren't a prick, you couldn't do what you do."

Diego was just giving as good as he got, but Huck thought his partner and backup—his friend— had a point. The past months of deep undercover work had changed him. When Huck looked in the mirror in the morning, he didn't know who he was.

A jackass.

If he had to be a jackass to get the job done, fine. If being nice would do it—he'd be nice. But he had no clear idea of how to win the trust of the vigilantes among his new colleagues at Breakwater enough to get them to let him in on their plans. What did the Riccardis know? What did Oliver Crawford know? Who were the key players? Or had Vern Glover landed in Yorkville just because he needed a job, and Huck was barking up the wrong damn tree?

Alicia Miller's death had set everyone on edge.

Somehow, as unfeeling as it sounded, Huck knew he had to turn all the free-floating tension around him because of the tragedy into an advantage. Something that would help him get answers.

A soft breeze blew across the marsh, bringing with it tangy, earthy smells of salt and wet dirt. He was from northern California. As a deputy U.S. marshal, he could be assigned anywhere. But he wasn't a part of the vigilante task force and didn't like coming in through the back door.

He saw Diego Clemente's wreck of a fishing boat out toward the horizon. *Tough life.* Diego didn't know a damn thing about Alicia Miller's death, either. That black-haired, hazel-eyed Quinn Harlowe, reportedly a very fine analyst and an expert on transnational crime, had managed to find the one other federal undercover agent in town last night didn't sit well with Huck at all.

Diego's decision to use his own name hadn't seemed to be a big risk. There was no reason for anyone to run a background check on him. Now—he'd sparked Quinn's interest. If she threatened their undercover status, Nate Winter and his team would yank Huck and Diego out of Yorkville, and the psycho vigilantes they were hunting would crawl back under their rocks.

Huck turned back to the house. He knew Diego would see him on shore. His primitive all-clear for his backup. Things were okay at the Crawford compound. He wasn't scheduled for a beating or an execution. With all the technology they had at their disposal, they were working with smoke signals.

Back at the converted barn, he found Cully O'Dell preening in front of a mirror in the bathroom. He'd spent the morning in the classroom, taking written tests. "I look okay for Crawford?"

"Yeah, you look fine. What's that smell?"

O'Dell sniffed. "Aftershave. Too strong?"

"Well, this place has chemical-attack sensors. Don't want anyone thinking you're trying to kill Crawford."

The kid blushed. "Should I wash it off?"

"No, you're fine." Huck grinned. "Hell, Cully, you're going to be a great bodyguard, especially for women. The bad guys will underestimate you, which will be their mistake, and the women will think you're their little brother and undress in front of you. Either way, you're good."

If possible, Cully reddened even more. "I see myself as a professional, Mr. Boone."

"Huck, okay?"

He nodded. "Yes, sir."

No way, Huck thought, was Cully O'Dell a half-crazy vigilante mercenary willing to break the law and torture, even murder. He was just a kid from Virginia who wanted to make a respectable living. If the shit hit the fan, O'Dell wouldn't be backup or an enemy—he'd be someone Huck needed to protect.

Unless all his instincts were wrong and the kid was plotting to kill him in his sleep.

This was no time to start questioning his instincts, Huck thought, then washed up and put on a fresh shirt for the big meeting.

17

Quinn decided she couldn't go back to Washington without making herself get out on the water. She didn't want Alicia's death to keep her from kayaking. She *had* to get back out there. She dragged her second kayak, a dark green, down to the cove and shoved off smoothly. The water was colder than she'd anticipated, but the sky was bright and clear and the light chop just enough to be exhilarating.

With the osprey pair circling overhead, she gave their sprawling nest wide berth and headed north along the marsh, up toward the Crawford compound. As she dipped her paddle into the soft water, she quieted her mind and listened to the gentle breeze in the marsh grasses and trees and the light lap of bay against kayak. A two-hundred-mile estuary, where saltwater met fresh water, Chesapeake Bay played host to more than three thousand species of plants and animals and, with its inlets and islands, had more than eleven thousand miles of shoreline. Sixteen million people lived within the bay region. Pollution, erosion, competition for resources and space were fierce, the delicate ecological balance constantly threatened and yet—always there was hope for a better future.

Feeling more positive, Quinn continued along to the southern edge of the Crawford compound, her muscles tight after the tension of the past two days. Cold bay water splashed into her boat. She was wet up to her thighs. She'd put on water shoes and a bright yellow life vest, with a whistle secured to a zippered pocket, but she was wearing jeans. Although she should have worn a wetsuit, she didn't expect to be out long. She'd be back at her cottage before she got really cold.

Peering past the barbed-wire fence, she saw the graceful old house that was now headquarters for Breakwater Security and noticed a new building—classrooms, she recalled from local gossip. The tactical facilities—shooting ranges, simulation environments and defensive-driving courses—were farther inland, not right where Oliver Crawford could see them from his front porch.

A large swell seemed to serve as a challenge—a dare. Quinn turned her kayak into the wave and let it take her to shore, onto the grass and sand in front of the barbed wire. She climbed out, splashing into the cold water.

Unfastening and unzipping her vest, she laid her paddle across the kayak and caught her breath, hands on hips, as she surveyed the narrow strip of sand and wild grasses. The wash of waves behind her soothed her taut nerves.

Why had Alicia come to Breakwater at dawn? As out of her head as she'd been, she still had reasons for what she'd done. She'd come to the coffee shop for Quinn's help. Why here?

Huck Boone and Vern Glover appeared on the other side of the fence. Neither man looked pleased to see her. Quinn shrugged off her life vest, dumping it into the cockpit of her kayak as she squinted at them. "You both look quite spruced up. Having lunch with the boss?" She pointed at the sky. "I saw his helicopter arrive."

"Lunch is over," Glover said.

Huck pushed down the barbed wire and stepped over it onto her side of the beach. "I thought you were going back to Washington."

"I am. Just not yet." She nodded to the fence. "Worried about lost kayakers and wanderlust bird-watchers?"

He just narrowed his eyes on her, as if he could see through her bravado to all her messy motives and emotions and knew exactly why she was there.

She kept on. "Not much protection, is it?"

Glover grunted. "There's what you see and what you don't see."

"You mean, like land mines?"

Not liking her answer, he took a step forward, but Huck grinned, glancing back at his colleague. "She's got her sense of humor back, anyway."

"It's a sick sense of humor," Glover said, his eyes darkening. "I know people who've lost limbs to land mines. They're a serious business."

Quinn started to say something back to him, but Huck held up a hand and gave her a sharp, warning look, silencing her. "What do you want?" he asked.

She realized she had no idea. She'd acted impulsively, getting out her second kayak, dragging it down to the water, paddling up the bay. A wonder she hadn't ended up in Maryland. She squared her shoulders, feeling the cold bay water dripping down her legs inside her jeans. "Oliver Crawford's here, right?" She didn't wait for an answer. "I'd like to see him."

Without waiting for any by-your-leave from the two men, Quinn pushed down the barbed wire with one foot, then climbed over to Glover's side of the fence. The ends of her hair had gotten wet from paddling up to the compound. She shivered, suddenly feeling cold.

Vern snorted in disgust. "You handle this, Boone," he said, about-facing and stalking up across the yard.

Quinn frowned at the departing bodyguard. "Mr. Warm and Fuzzy must make nervous clients feel safe and secure."

"You want a Mr. Rogers protecting you or a Vern Glover?"

"I don't want anyone protecting me."

"Why doesn't that surprise me?" Huck stepped back over the fence. "Your lips are purple."

"It was colder on the water than I expected." She shifted just enough to get out of his shadow. As she stood in the sunlight, his eyes seemed to have darkened. "If you take me to see Ollie, I can warm up at the house."

"Ollie, huh?"

"That's what my former boss calls him. To each other, they're Gerry and Ollie. To the rest of us, they're Gerard and Oliver." She tried to smile, but it felt strained. "In case you're wondering, I'm never Quinny."

Huck settled back on his heels, studying her a moment. "Quinn, go home. I can take you back to your cottage—"

"Okay, I'll find Ollie on my own." Feeling light-headed, a little out of control, she pointed toward the white house with its black shutters and gracious landscaping. "He's up there, right? All you have to do is let your guys know I'm friendly, so no one shoots me."

"No one's going to shoot you."

"What about you? Are you armed?"

He didn't answer her.

Taking a few steps in the soft, cool grass, she could feel her heart racing and knew the shock of Alicia's death was having an effect on her. She hadn't slept or eaten enough in the last two days. She was half-frozen. Normally, she was self-disciplined, thinking before acting. "My great-grandfather died in an avalanche because he was impulsive."

"What?"

She paid no attention to him, barely paused for a breath. "But my great-great-grandfather lived to almost a hundred, and he took more risks than any of us. When is a risk calculated and when is a risk reckless?" She glanced back at her companion, then answered her own question. "Depends on whether you live or die."

"Sometimes, there's no choice—"

"Not with my family. They all could stay home and read books, but they don't. My parents—" She stepped onto a brick walk that curved around dogwoods, lilacs and azaleas that soon would be in bloom. "I used to worry myself sick about them when I was a kid. They're marine archaeologists. It sounds like a safe profession, doesn't it? But they've had so many close calls, diving into sunken ships, exploring remote places. They'd leave me with my grandfather."

Huck eased in next to her. "He's not a risk-taker?"

"He's a historian, too. His area of study is the Civil War. These days he's a volunteer guide at Fredericksburg and Chancellorsville."

"Old guy?"

"Eighty-two." Feeling the sun warm on the back of her neck, Quinn took a breath, some of her tension letting up. "My point is, Alicia could have done everything right the other day, and still could have drowned."

"Quinn." Huck's tone had lost some of its edge. "You did what you could. It sounds as if she had problems—"

"She didn't kill herself."

"Maybe not on purpose."

Quinn swung around at him. "Where are you in the Breakwater hierarchy?"

"I'm the new guy. I'm at rock bottom."

"That's not good. I was hoping you could pull strings for me. I guess I'll manage on my own, especially since no one's going to shoot me—"

"I could just throw you over my shoulder and dump your butt back in your kayak."

"Then you could kiss your new job goodbye, couldn't you?"

He didn't answer, but she thought he gritted his teeth.

The brick walk led to the front of the house. If she was going in the wrong direction to find Oliver Crawford, Huck wasn't going to tell her. He didn't want her there at all. She could hardly blame him.

"Why was Alicia here on Monday?"

"I have no idea—"

"She and Gerard Lattimore, her boss, my former boss, get along well. He thought she was burned out at work and needed some time off, understood the appeal of Yorkville in springtime." Quinn cast Huck a look. "He wasn't here, was he?"

"No."

"Oliver Crawford—"

"Him, either."

The Riccardis intercepted them in front of the porch steps. She'd met them, briefly, at Lattimore's party in March. In retrospect, she suspected the party was his way of showing his approval of his friend Oliver's private security firm—of legitimizing it without having to go on record.

Sharon Riccardi, in a Breakwater sweatshirt a size too big for her, stepped forward, ahead of her husband. "Miss Harlowe?" There was a decided sharpness to her tone. "Is there something we can do for you?"

Before she could respond, Huck answered. "She

was out kayaking and stopped just outside the fence—"

"I'd like to say hi to Oliver," Quinn interrupted. "I saw his helicopter arrive."

Joe Riccardi gave Huck an irritated glance, then turned to her, smiling pleasantly. "Miss Harlowe, Mr. Crawford's on a very tight schedule."

"You look half-frozen," Sharon said. "My God, you're shivering."

"I underestimated how cold the water is this time of year."

Joe straightened. "Huck can drive you and your kayak back to your cottage. We're very sorry for your loss yesterday. We'd met Alicia…" He hesitated, as if he didn't know what more to say. "We're sorry."

"She was lovely," his wife interjected. "Absolutely lovely."

Quinn decided to push harder, although she wasn't sure why. "Can you tell Oliver that I'm here and—"

"Quinn!" Crawford himself trotted down the porch steps. He had gray-flecked dark hair and was about six feet tall, paunchy, dressed in baggy jeans and a navy cotton sweater with the elbows blown out. He took both Quinn's hands into his. "It's good to see you, although I wish the circumstances were better. I heard about Alicia, of course. I've already called Gerry to express my condolences."

"Thank you."

"What can I do for you?" He squeezed her hands. "You're freezing."

Now that she was here, seeing how distraught

everyone was over Alicia's death, Quinn didn't know what to say, and she was so cold, she just wanted to crawl back into her quilt at her cottage and stay there. "Nothing, really. I just wanted to say hello."

"You've never been out here, have you?" When she shook her head, he let her hands go and gestured broadly, taking in his entire hundred-acre estate. "We're transforming the place into a state-of-the-art security company. We want to keep it small, elite."

"Looks as if you have your own mini-Quantico here." She thought of Donna at the diner, the talk in town surrounding Breakwater. "There's a rumor going around town that you've got snipers on the roof and everything."

Huck didn't react at all, but the Riccardis seemed appalled at such a suggestion, Sharon in particular, wincing, taking a sharp breath. Oliver Crawford, more accustomed to controversy, chuckled. "Well, not quite."

"Corporate security isn't what it used to be, is it?" Quinn could feel her teeth starting to chatter and knew it was the cold. But she couldn't seem to stop herself. "Gone are the days when you just needed a couple of scary-looking guys in black suits."

Sharon stepped forward. "Miss Harlowe—"

"Quinn's fine."

Crawford held up a hand, apparently guessing that his Breakwater CEO was losing patience. He smiled. "Scary-looking guys never hurt."

Quinn refused to look at Huck, who was tight-jawed, not moving from his spot. She kept her attention on the boss, the owner of the hundred-acre compound. "You heard that Alicia came out here to Breakwater early Monday morning, didn't you?"

Crawford's smile faded, and he sighed heavily, his eyes shining with regret and sympathy. "I heard, yes. Quinn—Gerry told me your friend had been on the verge of a breakdown for several weeks."

"A couple of your guys took her back to my cottage—"

"Travis Lubec and Nick Rochester, Oliver," Sharon said, her voice steady but laced with impatience. "They were trying to help."

"Did they follow her to make sure she got back to Washington?" Quinn asked, noticing that purple splotches had appeared on her hand—she needed to get on dry clothes. But she didn't stop. "A black Lincoln Town Car with tinted back windows picked her up at a coffee shop down the street from my office."

Huck quietly fell in next to her. "I can take Miss Harlowe back to her cottage now. If you'll all excuse us—"

"No, wait," Crawford said. "Boone, right? Thank you, but I want to know what she's getting at. Quinn, if you're suggesting my men had anything to do with your friend's death, that they have anything to hide, then you're quite mistaken."

"I have no idea who was in the car that picked Alicia up in Washington."

He softened. "Perhaps this mysterious black car belonged to another of Alicia's Washington friends, someone who also tried to help her. With a sudden death—especially of a vibrant young woman—we all want to find answers where sometimes there simply are none."

Quinn suddenly felt tears hot in her eyes, high on her cheeks. She looked away.

Crawford draped an arm over her shoulders. "It's okay, it's okay," he whispered. "Cry all you want. It's a terrible loss. Please, if there's anything I can do, personally—anything at all—you'll call, won't you?"

"Thank you. I should get back. It's a long drive to Washington." Stepping out of his embrace, Quinn managed a quick, fake smile. "And I don't have a helicopter."

He seemed to relax at her attempt at humor.

Joe Riccardi, who'd maintained a tight-lipped silence, glanced at Huck. "Boone?"

"I'll see her out of here."

18

As he led Quinn back across the lawn, Huck was relieved no one joined them. He was thinking that one more word out of her and she'd have everyone pissed off, and someone would start shooting. Then he'd have to blow his cover and say he was a deputy U.S. marshal and get her safely away.

He didn't need a shivering kayaker poking around in his investigation.

Not that she was just some black-haired, slim and sexy yahoo out for the afternoon. He wasn't that lucky. Nope. His kayaker had to be Quinn Harlowe, an expert in transnational crime who had recently worked for the Justice Department and the best friend of Breakwater Security's owner.

For all Huck knew, she was more familiar with his psycho vigilantes and how they operated than he was.

Whose side was she on?

If a vigilante mercenary ring was using Breakwater Security as a front for smuggling weapons and training a private army—helping murderers escape custody—Gerard Lattimore would look bad, even if he wasn't involved. He and Oliver Crawford were friends. It wouldn't matter what either man knew. Appearances were everything in Washington.

Quinn, too, could get burned.

Not your problem.

"You're in no shape to kayak back to your cottage," Huck told her. "We can grab your boat and throw it in the back of my Rover."

He could see her stiffen, her eyes, red-rimmed and puffy from fatigue and grief, focused on something in front of her, determinedly *not* focused on him. "That's not necessary. It's just cold. There's no fog or thunder and lightning. No rain. Not like Monday. I'll be fine."

She shot ahead of him, jumping over the barbed-wire fence. She picked up her kayak by a short line tied to the bow and started dragging it toward the water, her soaked shoes sinking into the sand.

Huck remained on the other side of the fence. "You're already a candidate for hypothermia."

She dropped the kayak and put her hands on her hips, then, heaving a sigh, let them drop to her sides. "All right. You win. If I get into trouble out there, I don't know if I'd have the energy to blow my whistle. And Buddy Jones would tack my picture up on the bulletin board behind his front desk as a warning to others. He thinks most of us kayakers are idiots."

"Buddy Jones is—"

"The owner of the shabby little motel on the loop road." She raised her eyes. "I'm sure you've seen him on your runs."

Diego's motel. Huck didn't react. "I've only been in town a few days."

"You stopped there on Monday before the bad storms hit. You chatted for a couple of minutes with a fisherman named Diego Clemente. He was having a cigarette."

For two cents, Huck thought, he'd shove Quinn Harlowe's butt into the back of his Land Rover and drive her to Nate Winter and have him put her in protective custody. Or some kind of custody.

Better yet, he'd leave her with Diego and let him deal with her.

Since he didn't know what role, if any, she had with Breakwater—since he didn't know if she'd been on the straight and narrow about her friend's death and had nothing to hide—Huck put one foot on the barbed wire and pressed it down. "Coming?"

"I'm almost certain this Clemente character is the one who phoned in the anonymous tip about Alicia's car."

Sweet pea, Huck thought, *you're lucky I'm not wired, because if Diego were listening in, he'd be on his way.*

He kept his foot steady on the barbed wire. "I'm not surprised. These fishermen can see things from their boats that other people might miss." *Especially with high-powered binoculars and night-vision equip-*

ment. "Why don't you leave your kayak. I'll bring it by your cottage later."

"I think our Special Agent Kowalski should talk to this Clemente character, don't you?"

"I don't tell the feds what to do."

She shrugged. "They don't intimidate me."

Huck wished to hell they did. But he found himself almost smiling. Traumatized and half-frozen, Quinn still was paying attention to details, processing, analyzing, thinking. The woman had guts.

She glanced down at her kayak, then let her shoulders slump as she muttered something under her breath. Leaving her boat behind, she walked back to the fence. "If you all can hold on to my kayak, I'll stop by and get it when I come back down here."

"Don't want to give me the key to your shed?"

"No, I really don't." She smiled. "No offense."

As far as Huck was concerned, her reluctance to give him the key demonstrated that some of the shock of her friend's death was easing and she was thinking more clearly.

It was a big step for Quinn to get over the barbed-wire fence, but instead of putting a hand on his shoulder to balance herself, she reached to her right and held on to a fence post that was about eight inches too far away.

Huck could see she was tilted too far to the right but said nothing.

She got her left leg over the barbed-wire fine, then lost it with her right leg and plunged directly into him. He caught her around the waist, breaking her fall, and set her on the wet grass. She didn't weigh anything, but she was fit.

He grinned at her. "Your stubbornness just cost you, didn't it? If you'd just hung on to my shoulder—"

"I wasn't being stubborn. I'm tired. That's all."

"Uh-huh."

She changed the subject. "What did you do before you became a bodyguard? Were you in the military? Law enforcement?"

"I played a lot of video games."

With a skeptical look, she started back across the lawn. She didn't seem quite as distracted. He got a step ahead of her, leading her to the gravel parking area near the converted barn. When he pointed at his Rover, she opened the passenger door and took a step backward, as if she'd been bit.

Looking over her shoulder, Huck noted his locked gun box in back, his bulletproof vest, various holsters and other gear a well-equipped law enforcement officer or private security expert would need.

Blue-lipped and pale, Quinn gestured at the stuff. "Your personal equipment?"

"Yes, ma'am." He reached past her and grabbed a fleece pullover, handing it to her. "Put it on before you freeze."

She nodded and mumbled a thank-you. The fleece made her look even smaller, but Huck reminded himself not to underestimate this woman. He walked around to the driver's side, wondering what he'd do if he were Quinn Harlowe. Get in the Rover or make a break for it?

She got in. "The fleece'll help," she said. "I'll be fine."

"You really are in the early stages of hypothermia, you know."

"I'll warm up fast." She seemed to shrink into the fleece. "I apologize if I've seemed curt or ungrateful. You've been very decent."

"Decent, huh?" He gave her a mock shudder. "I'll have to work on that."

She smiled a little. "You have a sense of humor. It must help in your work."

Huck pulled the Rover onto the paved driveway, waving at Travis Lubec, looking as mean as ever in front of an azalea not quite in bloom.

When they reached the narrow road that led back to the village, Quinn wasn't looking as frozen. She had her hands up inside the fleece's sleeves. Its dark sage green seem to bring out the mix of colors in her pretty, hazel eyes.

But she wasn't ready to stand down. "Did you have anything to do with Oliver Crawford's rescue last year?"

"No."

"Have you done anything like that yourself? Rescued people?"

He remembered what was on his Breakwater résumé. "Vern and I did a few things in Venezuela."

"Really? When?"

"Over the winter."

"I was at Justice until January. I know a bit about Latin American kidnappings."

That would figure, Huck thought. "Sweet pea,

the people Vern and I rescued didn't want the U.S. Department of Justice knowing what had gone down. It's over. The way I live, last winter's ancient history."

"What have you been doing since?"

"Looking for work."

"So," she said, "basically you're a mercenary."

Suddenly, Huck didn't want to lie to her. He'd been lying to everyone for months, for good reason, but the constant deception took its toll.

Yet, he couldn't tell her the truth.

"Yeah. Basically I am."

He parked behind her Saab. The temperature had dropped farther, with just a few rays of sunlight breaking through the gray clouds pushing in from the west. Quinn started to take off the fleece, but Huck touched her upper arm. "Keep it. You can return it another time."

"Thank you for your help."

"Anytime."

He got out of the Rover and followed her to her side door. Yesterday, he'd paid very little attention to the cottage. She'd obviously worked hard on it, kept it fun—nothing about the place was uptight, especially for a woman whose job it was to assess and analyze international criminal networks and the threats they presented.

"How long have you owned your cottage?" he asked her.

"About two years. I love it." She turned into the wind, looking out at the cove, the water gray now under the clouds. "Even after yesterday."

"That's good."

"Breakwater—it's the most beautiful spot, isn't it? And yet now…" She kept her gaze on the water, not looking at him directly. "It was strange seeing all you bodyguard types among the lilacs and azaleas."

"Wait'll they're in bloom. We'll look even more out of place."

She lifted her eyes to him. "Yesterday couldn't have been easy for you, either. I hope you get a chance to catch your breath."

"Rescuing women with borderline hypothermia is kind of relaxing."

"I wasn't even close—"

"You were close."

She held her ground. "And you didn't rescue me."

No, he probably hadn't rescued her. Huck wondered if she knew just how much of a risk she'd taken in coming to Breakwater—and never mind the hypothermia.

"Not that I'm not grateful for the ride," she added quickly.

When she pushed her door open, he saw that she'd left it unlocked. "Quinn—"

She turned to him. "It's okay. I forgot. I'll lock up when I leave." She smiled, a hint of real amusement in her eyes. "You can relax, Mr. Bodyguard. I'm used to being on my own."

Her smile, bright against her pale skin, and that spark of humor rocked Huck right to his toes. He'd have to steel himself next time he saw a smile coming his way. "Listen…" He paused, getting his feet back under him. "Oliver Crawford is a charismatic guy and richer than most, but he's been through his own hell. I don't know what kind of people he's bringing into Breakwater Security."

"Then why are you there?"

"I can handle myself and get out if I need to."

"If you're suggesting Crawford is overcorrecting, in a way, after what happened to him, and hiring thugs instead of professionals—okay, point well taken. I'll be careful." She smiled again. "I come from a family of reckless people. I'm always careful."

"Why do I have a feeling your idea of 'careful' is different from most people's?"

"Because I'm standing in my open kitchen door with you right here?"

He tucked a finger under her chin, her skin soft and not quite warm. When she didn't tell him to go to hell, he let his fingers drift up to her mouth. Her lips were still cold. "Be sure to warm up before you go back to Washington."

"I will." Her voice seemed to catch. "Huck—you be careful, too." She smiled again. "I have a feeling caution isn't one of your top traits, either."

"Quinn…"

McCabe—what the devil are you doing?

The woman didn't even know his real name. But she didn't move from the threshold of her cute little cottage, and he didn't resist anymore. He kissed her softly, and his mouth must have felt burning hot against hers. She held on to his upper arm, and when he forced himself to pull away, he saw that some color had returned to her face. He touched his thumb to the pink in her cheek. "I'll have to remember how best to warm you up. Never mind the ratty old fleece."

She dropped her hand, clearing her throat, more color rising to her cheeks. "I guess it's been a weird couple of days for both of us."

"You can trust me. Remember that, okay?"

She just stared at him.

Before he went any further, Huck returned to his Rover and got back on the road, hoping Quinn would heed all sensible advice and resume her normal activities back in Washington. He had a job to do, and she was one hell of a distraction.

19

Alicia Miller's death had cast a dark shadow over her unit at the Department of Justice. Gerard Lattimore could feel the despair of her grieving colleagues. For weeks, they'd watched her struggle emotionally, casting about for balance, pushing herself to be positive. For a brief window a couple of weeks ago, she'd seemed to pull herself together and was almost happy. By late last week, she was clearly falling apart.

And I did nothing, Gerard thought.

He stood at Steve Eisenhardt's cubicle. Steve was among those having the most difficulty coping with Alicia's death. "How're you holding up?" Gerard asked.

"I'm managing."

"I don't know what to say—"

"There's nothing to say." Eisenhardt, who hadn't even glanced at his boss, tapped on his keyboard.

"It was a terrible accident. Alicia—she deserved better."

"Her family's handling arrangements. They want to keep everything quiet, private. There's been talk of holding a small memorial service here—"

"I'll say goodbye in my own way."

Prickly. Gerard nodded. "We all will."

Eisenhardt swiveled his chair around, looking up now, his eyes sunken, as if he hadn't slept since he'd heard the news about his colleague—and friend. Perhaps, in his own mind, at least, Gerard thought, more than a friend.

"Steve—get some rest. Go home early if you need to."

"Thanks, but I can do my job. It helps. You know—Alicia never was right for this place."

Gerard didn't argue with him.

"She was beautiful and well connected, but she didn't belong." He swiveled back to his monitor, his tone accusatory as he continued. "Maybe I noticed because I'm new."

"She wasn't one to confide in anyone—"

"I saw what was happening. I didn't say anything." His look turned into an accusatory glare. "Doesn't Justice have protocols for handling someone who's obviously falling apart? If we'd all done something—said something—Alicia might still be alive."

"We all did the best we could, Steve. We'll probably never know for certain what was going on in her mind. You're talking as if she committed suicide. We don't know—"

"Kayaking in a thunderstorm is suicide, period."

"I understand how you feel. If there's anything I can do—if you want to talk—"

"What about Quinn?" His tone had lost some of its edge. "Do you know where she is?"

"On her way back to Washington, I imagine."

"She'll push for answers, won't she? I don't know her all that well, but she strikes me as the type not to be satisfied with surface answers."

Gerard sighed, regretting his gesture of sympathy. Steve Eisenhardt had his own way of thinking—he didn't make life easy for himself. "I don't know what Quinn will do."

"Your friend Oliver Crawford—he can't like having a body wash up onshore practically on his doorstep down there. Alicia said she'd met him. You don't think Quinn will blame him for anything, do you?"

"Blame him for what, Steve? He and Alicia only met each other a month ago. Oliver's a busy man—"

Steve was barely listening. "Think Quinn knows anything about his kidnapping over the winter?"

Gerard frowned. "What?"

"Nothing. I'm sorry." He smiled feebly, looking awkward. "I can't focus right now."

"I understand." Gerard had no intention of pursuing Steve's crazy line of thinking regarding any connection, even a professional one, between Quinn and Oliver's kidnapping. Eisenhardt was in no shape to make coherent judgments. "At least give yourself today before you try to work on anything important. We all need some time."

When he returned to his office, Gerard was surprised to have Oliver Crawford on the line. They'd
already exchanged condolences over Alicia's death.
The last thing he wanted to do was to dwell on the
tragedy, keep being reminded of it. If he could just
dive into his work, he could pretend that he'd never
heard the terrible news, at least for a little while.

But he shut his door and sat at his desk, then
picked up the phone. "Ollie. What's up?"

"I saw your Quinn Harlowe today."

Gerard squirmed. "I wouldn't say she's 'my'
Quinn Harlowe—"

Crawford laughed softly. "No, of course not. I
can see why you didn't want to let her go. She's an
attractive, intelligent, determined woman."

"There's nothing romantic between us. I admire
her though—"

"Bullshit. You can't fool me, Gerry. She kayaked
out here. She gave my security people fits. She's a
wreck because of her friend's death, but still she's
asking questions, trying to make sense of such a
tragedy."

Gerard took a breath, picturing Quinn in her
kayak, twenty-four hours after finding her friend
drowned. He hadn't lied—there was nothing romantic between them. He would keep at her to
come back to work for him, provided he thought he
had a chance of persuading her. He'd half hoped
she'd crash and burn on her own and have to turn
to him for help, but he'd just heard that she was being asked to sit on an independent, privately
funded council tasked to assess and prioritize key

emerging international crime threats. A coup for anyone, but for someone as young as Quinn, newly out of the Justice Department, it was impressive. As a historian, she would bring a different perspective from the politicians, the lawyers, the law enforcement people.

Although his interest in her was primarily professional, Gerard did think of her paddling on the Chesapeake.

"We're all still reeling here because of Alicia," he said, sounding lame even to himself.

"You must be. My staff tells me she was out here early Monday morning. I was in Washington in meetings all day—I had no idea. I gather she was very upset and not making a lot of sense. Hysterical, really. It's so sad."

Gerard didn't want to get into any details about Alicia's mental state, even with a friend. "It's a tough one, that's for sure."

"The FBI was here earlier. They know all we know." Another awkward, halfhearted chuckle. "I want to stay on law enforcement's good side, especially with this new security services company just getting up and running."

"You know I can't intervene—"

"Of course not. We'll see you out here soon?"

"I plan to get my boat out on the water again in a week or two. I haven't—I don't know if Yorkville will be the same now."

"Make it the same," his longtime friend said with an intensity—an urgency—that was palpable. "Make it *better*."

20

On her way back to Washington, Quinn stopped in Fredericksburg, parking at the brown-and-white marker for Lee's Headquarters. She'd put on dry clothes and a fleece vest before heading out from Yorkville, but now they felt slightly warm to her. She climbed up the steep hill, the only hiker on the old, well-traveled path. The trees weren't fully leafed out yet, but they would have been bare when the Battle of Fredericksburg was fought in mid-December 1862, the last Virginia battle of that difficult, bloody year.

She found her grandfather at one of the cannons atop the hill, where he said he'd meet her when she'd called from her car. The breeze lifted his thinning white hair, and the clear April air seemed to make his eyes, the same hazel color as hers, look even brighter and more alert. A slight man of eighty-two, Murtagh Harlowe had never had the restless soul of his father and grandfather.

As she walked along the cold hill, Quinn imagined Robert E. Lee directing his commanders. The Confederates had won the battle, but at enormous cost to both sides—nearly eighteen thousand injured and dead.

"Hey, Granddad," she said. "Aren't you freezing?"

He shrugged. "It's a fine day for a walk. I'm just glad I can still make it up that hill."

Her grandfather had met Alicia back when she and Quinn were at the University of Virginia together. Alicia's interest in the Civil War was minimal, but she'd loved listening to Murtagh Harlowe tell stories. Quinn had dragged her along on a battlefield tour, explaining how Lee had entrenched his army on the hills above town and fought off Union assaults—too much detail, too much history, for Alicia, the budding, ambitious lawyer. She liked the views of the Rappahannock River and their lunch after the tour in a quaint restaurant in Fredericksburg's historic downtown.

Quinn tried to pull herself out of her pensive mood. "What was it Robert E. Lee said up here? About war—"

"At the height of the battle, Lee was reported to have said, 'It is well that war is so terrible, lest we grow too fond of it.'" Her grandfather looked out from the summit toward the surrounding hills and valley, once witness to so much carnage. "Quinn, are you going to be all right? I'm sorry about your friend's death."

On her way to Fredericksburg, Quinn had turned

on the radio and realized Alicia's death had made the news, although no mass of reporters had descended on little Yorkville—not for the drowning of a kayaker. "I've been acting like a crazy woman since I found Alicia."

"You've never experienced anything like that before."

"And I never want to again. It was horrible." She thought of the gulls but wouldn't paint that particularly awful picture for her grandfather. "There's so much I can't get out of my head."

"Give yourself time," he said quietly.

"I have about a thousand questions, it seems like. So much doesn't add up, at least not in the way people want it to."

"What people?" But he didn't wait for her response. "It's how things add up for you that matters right now. Is there anything you need to do?"

Quinn fixed her gaze on the old cannon. During the battle, Lee's Hill—Telegraph Hill, as it was known in 1862—served as an artillery position as well as Confederate command headquarters, firing on Union positions and being fired on. Lee himself was almost killed. But his death those bleak days wasn't meant to be. He would live through the deaths and maiming of thousands more on both sides over the next two and a half years, until the Confederate final surrender at Appomattox.

The Union army, so badly defeated at Fredericksburg, would go on to win the war.

"I keep thinking there's something I'm supposed to do," Quinn whispered.

"You're a catalyst, Quinn. You always have been. You push for answers. You make things happen. You don't settle." Her grandfather put a bony hand on her shoulder. "That's why you wanted to go out on your own. It'll be why you succeed."

"It's only been three months. The jury's still out—"

"Not for me. If your questions about Alicia's death need answers, you'll get them."

"I don't want to get arrested."

He smiled gently. "I'd like you not to get arrested, too. I'm not suggesting you break the law. Short of that, do what you have to do."

She sighed. "You make it sound so simple."

"A lot of difficult things ultimately are simple." He studied her a moment. "Is there a new man involved?"

She thought of Huck Boone, his thick arm around her, his compelling, uneasy mix of self-control and unbridled energy. He hadn't told her everything, Quinn thought. He hadn't even come close. "Just another wrong man."

"Ah."

A longtime widower, her grandfather nonetheless understood the ups and downs of romance. He'd had relationships but had never remarried after his wife died when Quinn was two. She had no memory of her grandmother, but understood her to have been a gentle soul, too, although both her grandparents had encouraged their only son to be true to his nature as an adventurer and risk-taker.

Her grandfather walked back down the hill with

Quinn, and she gave him a ride out to his car at the end of the road, passing intact trenches from the legendary long-ago battle. Somehow, the peacefulness of the landscape seemed to make her feel even more the horror of the death and destruction that had taken place there.

"Trust your instincts," her grandfather said when she hugged him goodbye.

Traffic back to Washington didn't bog down. Quinn arrived at her apartment before dark. She had a studio on the third floor of an unremarkable ivy-covered building a few blocks from her office, sacrificing the space she would have had in a cheaper area for location.

Collapsing onto her sofa, she listened to messages from her parents, a string of friends she and Alicia had in common, Gerard Lattimore again and—to her surprise—Brian Castleton, her ex-boyfriend's voice cracking as he said how much he'd miss Alicia. But Quinn couldn't help thinking that Brian must have been relieved she hadn't been around for his call and got her voice mail instead.

She didn't call anyone back. When the messages finished, she deleted them and stared up at the ceiling, trying to empty her mind. Her apartment, with its soothing, neutral colors, was so different from the eclectic cheerfulness of her bayside cottage. Normally, she could relax in both places, but not now, with guilt and questions swarming, with fatigue sinking her deep into the sofa.

She couldn't even remember what her plans for the week had been. Work. Dinner with friends one night. Laundry. Grocery shopping. An aide to an Arizona congressman she'd dated three times—two movies, one truncated dinner—had disappeared. She'd known they were doomed when Lattimore had spotted her at the dinner and made a special point of saying hello, and her date had leaned over the table and whispered, "I hate that son of a bitch."

That was in February. Quinn had decided to take a break from dating. If a guy whose company she enjoyed fell from the sky, okay. If not—she had things to do.

Just as she'd started to take her relationship with Brian for granted—started to think about the prospect of marriage, children—everything fell apart between them, and *poof*, off he went. And not just because of their different interests or Gerard Lattimore.

"Quinn, you're just too independent. You don't need me."

Now that she had some distance, she realized that he meant she didn't adore him enough. Love was one thing and all very nice, but adoration was something else altogether, and he needed it. He'd wanted to be stroked and admired and adored and for her not to work such long hours, have the responsibilities she had. He needed to be the center of attention—the total focus of her life.

For weeks, Quinn had believed he'd basically told her she was selfish and boring. Now she realized he hadn't been looking for the kind of equal, adult relationship she wanted. As much as he pretended he wasn't self-absorbed and liked a woman with her own career, he nonetheless, at his core, wanted a woman to acquiesce to his every whim— to *anticipate* his whims. Scoot off to the south of France at the drop of a hat. Blow the budget on a bottle of champagne.

Give up knitting. She remembered how irritated he would get when she was content to spend an evening knitting, sitting next to him while they watched TV or listened to music. Brian had felt as if they'd turned into his grandparents.

The last Quinn had heard, he was seeing *another* intern. He wasn't bored, anyway.

Why am I thinking about him?

Because of Alicia, who'd liked Brian. Because she didn't want to think about all her unanswered questions.

Restless, assaulted by memories, Quinn jumped up and headed outside, the streets crowded with commuters heading home from work, off to cocktail parties and early dinners, running errands. The normalcy helped soothe her taut nerves but made her feel even more isolated and alone.

All was quiet at the American Society for the Study of Plants and Animals. Thelma had gone home, but the executive director, no relation to any of the founders, was up in his office. A former anthropology professor, he and Quinn's parents got along well. She liked him, but didn't want to see him or anyone else right now.

Ducking into her office, she thought about the scut work she owed the Society. A few hours of prowling through closets and attic cubbies sounded more attractive than dinner with sympathetic friends or going back to her apartment and heating up a frozen dinner. But as she picked up a manila folder, its contents all junk from 1939, Quinn wished she'd remained in Yorkville, no matter whose feathers she ruffled.

21

Oliver Crawford stayed in Yorkville through the week, his presence ramping up the already intense atmosphere at Breakwater Security. When he left by helicopter late Friday afternoon, taking Travis Lubec and Nick Rochester with him, Huck noticed an immediate reduction in tension among those who remained behind. With a dozen trainees arriving in less than a month, there was still a lot of work to do. Courses were designed and the facilities almost finished, but Joe Riccardi had yet to hire all his instructors. According to Vern Glover, tapped as an instructor himself, Sharon had veto power over any of her husband's picks. She was the one with Crawford's total trust.

Vern didn't approve, grumbling as he helped Huck carry a wooden crate to the walk-in gun vault at the back of the classroom building. "Either the guy can be trusted to do his job or he can't."

"I thought they were equals with separate responsibilities, and they each reported to Crawford."

"In theory, not in practice. In practice, Joe reports to her."

Sometimes, Vern was smarter and more observant than he let on. Huck had decided not to underestimate him.

They set the crate in front of the locked, alarmed metal door.

"That's it," Vern said. "I'll take it from here."

"I can help you—"

"Don't need your help. You're not authorized for access." Vern was breathing hard from the exertion of hauling the crate from the parking area, where he and Huck had offloaded it from a van to the vault. "We're on a need-to-know basis around here. You don't need to know."

"Locked doors always kick my curiosity into high gear."

"Tough."

Huck shrugged. "An open environment can build trust. You shut too much up tight, people will start filling in the blanks, and not necessarily in a way you'd want."

"What kind of bullshit is that, Boone?"

McCabe, he thought. *My name is McCabe.* Reminding himself periodically helped him stay focused on who he was, what he had to do. "Maybe you have shoulder-fired missiles in there."

Vern didn't smile. "Think you're funny, don't you?"

"I wasn't making a joke, Vern. Shoulder-fired missiles could come in handy in our work."

He didn't bite. "We're a legitimate operation. You want to do well around here, you'll learn to take orders and keep your mouth shut."

"I was never good at clicking my heels together and saluting smartly."

Joe Riccardi had come down the hall behind them. "We need independent thinkers." He spoke in an even, measured tone. "I believe those were your words, weren't they, Vern?"

Vern gave a small hiss through his teeth. "I just want to finish this job and get out of here. I have a date tonight."

"In Yorkville?" Joe smiled. "Not much nightlife around here."

"I make my own nightlife," Vern said, grinning now.

Joe shifted his attention to Huck. "You can go. Why not get out of here, take yourself out to dinner? The crab cakes at the marina restaurant are the best in town. We've all had a hard week. A lot of work, a lot of emotion. Let's take the weekend to regroup." With a brief pause, he took a breath. "Alicia Miller drowned. That's now official. Her death was almost certainly an accident. Despite her odd behavior over the weekend and on Monday, she didn't leave a suicide note or specifically tell anyone she planned to kill herself, and, of course, there's no evidence of foul play."

"Toxicology results?" Huck asked.

"They screened for alcohol and drugs of abuse. She was clean."

"What about medications—"

"She wasn't on any medications."

Huck nodded, somehow not satisfied. "I guess that ends it, then."

"Yes." Riccardi's tone didn't change. He gave Huck a flicker of a smile. "Crab cakes, Boone. Take the night off."

Dismissed.

Huck returned to his room at the barn. Cully O'Dell had gone home to Fredericksburg for the weekend. Although he was just a kid, he was a whiz at all the techie stuff, working with Crawford's tech gurus in Washington to set up systems at Breakwater. But what he wanted to do was bodyguard work. *"I don't want to be the loser in the van with the headphones."*

Nothing about O'Dell was hard-cover vigilante.

Lubec and Rochester were another matter.

Huck showered and put on clean jeans and a clean shirt, fancy enough for crab cakes in Yorkville, Virginia.

Since he was alone in the converted barn, he slipped up the hall to Lubec's room—no complicated locks on the door. A credit card did the trick, and Huck was in, the room identical in setup to all the others and obsessively tidy, not so much as a wrinkle in the bunk. Moving quickly, Huck did a reasonably thorough search.

No photographs of the wife and kids or a girlfriend. No checkbook or credit cards in drawers, closet, pants pockets, on top of the dresser.

No rocket launchers under the bed.

No computer.

Lubec had ten one-hundred-dollar bills in a clip out in the open on his dresser. A cash-and-carry kind of guy.

Huck returned to his room. The search was a waste of his breaking-and-entering talents.

He took his Rover into town, driving past Quinn's cottage. Her Saab wasn't in the short driveway. Just as well she didn't come down to Yorkville for the weekend. He parked at the dead end and got out, a cold wind gusting off the water. The tide was coming in, the sun low in the west, leaving behind a dull, almost eerie light on the bay. He could see Quinn's osprey swooping toward its nest.

What are we missing?

What the hell are we all missing?

Getting into the gun vault and finding something incriminating in Travis Lubec's room would be progress where there was none, but Huck was more interested in the big picture. So was the task force. Who were the key players in this vigilante network? What were their plans?

If Quinn's neighbors, the retired couple, had drowned in the bay, that would be one thing. A tragedy, but it wouldn't have raised the questions that Alicia Miller's death did. She had been a DOJ attorney under Gerard Lattimore, who was friends with Oliver Crawford—an accomplished, self-controlled woman who'd sobbed to her friend about ospreys trying to kill her.

Doesn't add up.

If the events of the past few days didn't add up for him, they didn't add up for Quinn Harlowe, either. What had she been up to this week? But Huck stopped himself from going any further. His curiosity wasn't just professional—it was personal. If she'd been at her cottage, he'd have whisked her off for crab cakes, and he didn't need to be doing that. He'd been nearby when she yelled for help after finding the body of her friend. Otherwise, they'd have no reason even to know each other.

Not that Quinn *did* know him. As far as she was concerned, his name was Boone and he worked for a startup private security company and a man she didn't really like.

He took the loop road past Clemente's dump of a motel and saw him out on the dock having a cigarette with the crotchety owner.

Huck bit back his impatience. Diego Clemente and Huck McCabe, two of the U.S. Marshals Service's finest, and here they were, smoking cigarettes and off to eat crab cakes.

Sharon Riccardi, sitting on the porch steps of the main house at the Crawford compound, called to Huck as he headed up the brick walk after his dinner out, the night black under an overcast sky. Several lights were on in the house, but as he approached Sharon, he saw that she was drinking wine in the dark, wearing a long black, filmy sleeveless dress with a shawl and no jewelry. She tilted her head back and raised her glass at him. "I'll bet the mosquitoes don't dare to bite you."

"I don't know about that, Mrs. Riccardi."

"You're very fit, aren't you?" She rose, somewhat unsteady on her feet; she wasn't wearing shoes, although the night temperature was cold to go barefoot. "I like fit men."

"Mrs. Riccardi—"

"Sharon." She sipped her wine, her black shawl falling into the crooks of her elbows. Her gaze drifted over him. "All that hard muscle. You'll be an inspiration to the new men when they arrive."

"Where's your husband?"

"Inside, asleep." She gestured toward a second-story window. "We get to live here in luxury. Don't you think we're lucky?"

"It's a nice house."

"Joe doesn't even seem to notice. I think he'd be happiest living in a foxhole. All I'd need to do is drop in once in a while." Her eyes raised to his. "Conjugal visits."

Huck wondered how many glasses of wine she'd had and decided to keep asking questions. "He ever see combat?"

"I have no idea. I don't know him that well." She laughed at her own comment. "An odd thing to say, isn't it? He's a very private man. He was wounded by his first wife. Now he's more careful about what he reveals."

"You two seem to have a good thing going here with Breakwater."

She gave a dismissive shrug. "Oliver always has something new for me to do. He's had a rough time since he was kidnapped." This time, she took a bigger drink of wine. "I remember those terrible days."

"Did you ever lose hope?"

"No, I didn't. He says he didn't, but I don't know. The kidnapping still haunts him. I believe it will until the day he dies. All he can hope for now is to see justice done."

"The kidnappers—"

"Strange how fate works. We heard just this week that two of them were found recently in a remote camp in the Colombian Andes. They'd been tortured and executed."

"Who found them?"

"A couple of emerald miners." She tossed back her head, letting her hair curl down her back. "It looks as if the two thugs had enemies of their own."

"Why were they tortured?"

"For information, I assume. Perhaps for the fun of it. Revenge. I don't know."

"You think they deserve what they got?" Huck said.

She raised her chin to him. "Yes, I do. Don't you?"

"Absolutely." Huck could feel his crab cakes, fries and coleslaw heavy in his stomach, but he'd stayed away from alcohol. "I'm not saying you torture and execute people for no reason. If these guys had useful information, why screw around? If they're guilty of kidnapping, murder, drug dealing—hell. I'd pull the trigger myself."

"Who would have to give the order?"

"I'm not a lapdog. I think for myself. I base my decisions on the situation and the existing options."

Sharon Riccardi gave him a cool look. "What if the kidnappers had committed their crimes here, on U.S. soil?"

From his briefings, Huck knew what to say. "Doesn't make any difference."

"It's not our job as private contractors to conduct interrogations and executions."

He fixed his gaze on hers. If she wasn't one of the vigilantes, she would have good reason not to put her trust in him. If she was—he needed to find out. "Law enforcement doesn't have the necessary latitude to do what has to be done. They have to answer to politicians and protocols that don't necessarily make any sense. We don't."

"We can't break laws, of course," she said, her tone difficult to read. As she adjusted her shawl, the V neck of her dress skewed to one side, exposing the soft curve of her breast. She smiled, touching the stem of her wineglass to her breast. "Oliver left us imported chocolate truffles. Care to indulge?"

Huck debated how to react. What if Sharon Riccardi didn't give a rat's ass what he thought about anything and just wanted to flirt? Or more, he thought.

But her husband walked out onto the porch. He was fully dressed and didn't look at all as if he'd been sleeping. "Sharon? What's going on here?"

She didn't so much as glance back at him. "We'll

have truffles another time, Mr. Boone. Enjoy the rest of your evening."

"Thanks. I will." Huck addressed Joe Riccardi. "We were just chatting. I'll see you both tomorrow."

When Huck got back to his room, he considered washing his mouth out with soap after all the nonsense he'd just spoken. His head pounded, and he dropped onto his back on his bunk, picturing ospreys and Quinn Harlowe's quaint cottage and her pretty, hazel eyes, wondering what she was up to and why he didn't think he and Diego had heard the last of her.

22

On a bright, warm Thursday ten days after Alicia had found her on the coffee-shop patio, Quinn took her espresso and almond biscotti out to the same table where she'd been sitting that beautiful afternoon. Returning was her way of signaling to herself that she was beginning to accept the reality of what had happened.

Alicia was dead, drowned, the autopsy on her body completed.

Her funeral had been two days ago in Chicago, a small, private affair. Alicia's mother had all but asked Quinn not to attend, not out of any sense of animosity, she knew, but because they all would be tempted to rehash the last confused, troubled days.

"We want to celebrate Alicia's life and remember her as she was."

Nor, Quinn thought as she sank back in her chair in the warm sun, did anyone need to pretend that

she and Alicia had remained all that close, the best
of friends. The thaw that had started in March at
Lattimore's party had never had a chance to take
hold. Now that the initial shock of Alicia's death
had eased, Quinn wondered how much borrowing
the cottage had to do with her friend's own ends
and not with any conscious attempt to repair the
strains in their friendship.

Yet, when she was frightened and melting down,
Alicia had come to her, counting on the bond between them to see her through the crisis.

And I failed her.

As far as she was concerned, there were still unanswered questions—questions that she knew but
couldn't accept might never get answers.

Ivan, the coffee-shop owner, had told her that
the mother and little boy hadn't returned for their
alphabet book. He said he'd heard about Alicia's
death and was sorry.

Quinn sipped her espresso but couldn't work up
any appetite for her biscotti.

The cherry blossoms had vanished, and the trees
were leafed out, the shade welcome especially now
as the temperatures climbed. With the afternoon
temperature in the upper seventies, Quinn had
worn sandals and a sundress—turquoise, another
way to tell herself that she was better.

Someone pulled out the chair across from her,
and she looked up, startled, as Steve Eisenhardt
plopped down with an iced coffee. He gave her a
disapproving sigh. "I go inside, I stand in line, I get
my drink, I pay up—it's a good thing you're not a

spy, Quinn. You never even saw me." He grinned at her, his eyes crinkling in the bright sun. "I ducked out of work hoping I'd find you here. How're you doing?"

"Preoccupied."

"No kidding."

"I've been spinning my wheels ever since I got back from Yorkville last week." She drank some of her espresso. "I don't know what I'm doing."

"I heard you've been invited to present a paper at an international crime symposium in Vienna."

"That was easy. All I had to do was say yes, I'll do it. It's not until October."

He leaned forward and said in a fake conspiratorial whisper designed to make her laugh, "I also heard you met Oliver Crawford."

Crawford must have told Lattimore, who told Steve. Quinn smiled at Steve's natural irreverence. "I've met him before."

"But not at his estate. What did you do, just drive up and knock on the front door?"

"I kayaked and climbed over his barbed-wire fence."

Steve grinned. "Only you, Quinn. Lucky someone didn't shoot a hole in your boat."

"I had a greeting party." She thought of Huck's dark eyes as he'd tried to talk sense into her, and Vern Glover, impatient, scary. "Breakwater Security seems like a legitimate enterprise. It's still so new. The compound itself is gorgeous—I hate to see it get turned into a security training facility."

"You'd rather see it turned into a country inn?"

"Definitely."

"I hear Crawford hasn't slept soundly since he got snatched last year. If this helps him, who knows." Steve shrugged. "Maybe once he gets a few weeks of REM sleep, he'll close down Breakwater Security and open up Breakwater Spa."

"A spa." Quinn moaned. "I could use a week at a spa."

His expression turned serious, at least for him. "What about your cottage? Going back anytime soon?"

"I've been thinking about this weekend."

"Quinn—"

"It's not too soon. I *need* to go back. If I don't—" She looked down at her espresso. "If I don't, I'm afraid I never will."

"You will, Quinn. You put your heart and soul into that place." He sighed, pushing back his chair slightly. He hadn't touched his drink. "Alicia was a very special person. She was smart, and she was beautiful, and she was looking in all the wrong places for happiness. If she committed suicide, directly or indirectly, I wish she'd turned to her friends for help first."

"She did turn to me. I just couldn't get through to her. She ran off, and by the time I found her..." Quinn took a heavy breath. "Damn."

"If it was suicide, they say people just want to stop the pain. They believe that the people they love—who love them—will be better off with them dead."

"There's nothing to suggest it *was* suicide. She

was so upset she had no business being out on the water, storm or no storm. She could easily have turned over the kayak by accident, then got so disoriented that she couldn't get herself back into the boat."

"No life vest, no emergency whistle, a storm brewing. It sounds deliberate, Quinn."

"In her mental state, I'm not sure she was capable of planning her own suicide. She was a mess, Steve, and she drowned. It just happened."

"Yeah. Sucks, doesn't it?"

Quinn could feel the jolt of the espresso, and she looked out at the quiet street, could see Alicia running past the flowerpots, jumping into the Lincoln. "I've been doing a little research, more for my own peace of mind than anything else."

"What kind of research?"

"Just checking out what's on the public record about Oliver Crawford. He started Breakwater Security after his kidnapping. I've been looking into it. How it happened, when, why, where. Basic stuff."

Steve picked up his drink, giving her a dubious look as she took a sip. "You checked *only* public records?"

"Well, I did talk to a few sources—"

"And?"

"Just in the past week, two of his kidnappers turned up tortured and executed."

"Ouch. Where?"

"Colombia."

"I thought he'd been snatched in the Caribbean—"

"These guys weren't Colombian," Quinn said. "One was Puerto Rican and one was Dominican. Back in February, another of the kidnappers was also found tortured and executed. He was Mexican."

"An international group of thugs, huh?"

"They're all professionals. Low-level mercenaries. That's all on the record, by the way. There just haven't been any press releases—"

"Meaning the media haven't gotten hold of it."

If they did—if she put them on the trail—she wondered what they would uncover, and just how uncomfortable Oliver Crawford and his people would be. "I don't see how these thugs could have planned the kidnapping, and I sure as hell don't see what they could have known that would have prompted anyone to risk torturing them. Killing them—they were in a volatile area. But torture takes time. From that standpoint, it's riskier."

Steve grinned nervously. "I don't like the idea of either one, thank you very much."

"My sources haven't run across these guys before."

"Ah, a mystery."

"Oliver Crawford's an American citizen, even if his kidnappers weren't. The FBI is investigating. He was rescued by his own people—they received a tip."

"Wasn't there a huge reward for credible information leading to his safe rescue?"

"There was indeed. Sharon Riccardi, who's now running Breakwater Security, put out the word. His guys found him in the Dominican. They chose not to inform U.S. or Dominican authorities. They say they weren't convinced the tip would pan out."

Steve rolled his eyes. "And these are the goofs running Breakwater Security now?"

"I don't know how involved they are with Breakwater." Quinn picked up her biscotti, although she was no longer in the mood for it. "I haven't gotten that far in my research."

"You're digging around in some dangerous files, Quinn."

"As I said, most of it's on public record. I haven't done any more digging than your basic *Post* reporter would do."

"But you have a mind for this shit," Steve said.

She made herself smile. "Not these days. I'm just finding distractions. What about you? How's work, how's my erstwhile boss?"

"Oh, work's just a barrel of laughs with you gone and Alicia drowned."

"I'm sorry—"

"No." He held up a hand. "No, *I'm* sorry. That was insensitive. Work's fine. We're all bearing up. Lattimore's the same. He's got steel balls, you know? Nothing rattles him. Me—I'm a coward." But there was no self-pity in his tone. He winked at Quinn. "Not you, though. You've got brass tits, Harlowe. Especially for a page-flipping historian."

"Easy for me to talk tough. I'm not on the frontlines."

"You were last week," he said softly.

When Steve finally headed back to work, taking

the rest of his iced coffee with him, Quinn watched
him pick up his pace as he rushed down the sidewalk. Not for a single five-second stretch had he relaxed. She realized now why Alicia had said she
found him difficult to be around for any length of
time. The poor guy had been half in love with her
for so long, and yet he'd never stood a chance with
her—he drove her nuts.

But his distress over Alicia's death seemed genuine, and for Quinn, that was enough.

Steve was on Pennsylvania Avenue, on his way
back to work, when his cell phone rang. He recognized the tight, controlled voice of the older of the
two goons. "What, are you assholes spying on
me?" Bravado—he was sweating like the pig he
was. "I just had iced coffee with Quinn Harlowe.
Or do you know already? Are you following her—
or me?"

"Did she ask you to meet her?"

"No. I knew you'd be breathing down my neck
and just showed up. She's working up a dossier on
you bastards."

Silence.

"I'm serious. Your boss is Oliver Crawford,
right? Are you the ones torturing and executing the
guys that kidnapped him? I hope the feds are onto
you. I hope they're fucking *all over* you. I hope—"

"Calm down."

"I *am* calm."

But he wasn't. He could feel the blood pounding
in his arteries. His chest was tight. If he wasn't so

young, he'd be worried about a stroke or a heart attack. As it was, he thought he'd crack. Just collapse on the sidewalk and start blubbering. Was that what they'd done to Alicia? Scared the living shit out of her to the point she was drooling on herself?

"Where are you on the names we want?"

Steve wasn't fooled by the mildness of the question. He was running out of rope with these bastards. "I'm working on it."

"Work faster. What about Harlowe? Is she part of the task force investigating the vigilantes?"

"What?"

A hiss of impatience, like he was stupid. "Harlowe. What's her role in any vigilante investigation?"

Hell. Steve wiped sweat off his brow. *These* guys were vigilantes. Had to be. "She doesn't have one. No. She's just nosy."

Another couple seconds of silence.

"We're not the bad guys here," the goon said quietly, a hint of humor—and sarcasm—in his tone.

Steve glanced around him, but no one was eavesdropping. Still, he lowered his voice. "You're never going to leave me alone, are you? You've got me by the balls, and you're going to twist until I shrivel up and die."

"We're seizing an opportunity that you yourself presented to us. We're careful people. We have a great responsibility. There's much at stake." He sounded so persuasive, so reasonable. "I don't ask you to understand, just to do as you're told."

"What about Quinn? I'm guessing not everyone

thinks you're the good guys you say you are. She'll find out. She's like that. I've heard how she works. She throws out one little question in a meeting and turns it around, upside down and inside out. That's why she's in demand. Don't underestimate her."

Because if they did underestimate her, she'd be onto him as well.

"We'll do our job. You do yours. Keep us informed."

Steve clicked off and lifted his arms, trying to let some air in between his wet shirt and his skin, with little success.

He had no doubts now. He knew where he'd made his bed.

For better or worse, he was in the sack with fascist sociopaths.

23

Seeing his wife cry never failed to make Nate Winter think of his two younger sisters. He, Antonia and Carine were orphaned as children when their parents died in the White Mountains of New Hampshire, and he remembered his helplessness when he'd hear them sobbing into their pillows at night. He'd never admitted to his own tears.

Sarah wasn't crying so much as trying to keep herself from crying. She'd worked all day on a dig in back of the historic northern Virginia house where they lived and then had started packing for their move that weekend.

Honey-haired and blue-eyed, she was the most beautiful woman Nate had ever known, but right now, her cheeks had red splotches, and her eyes were bloodshot. She grabbed a tissue and blew her nose. "I don't know what's the matter with me."

"You've been working nonstop. Take the night off—"

"I need to finish packing these books." With a desperate gesture, she took in the floor-to-ceiling shelves she was unloading. "I've hardly even started."

"My family's coming tomorrow. They'll help. I can help—"

"No, no. You have a meeting tonight." She smiled. "I'm fine. Really."

"You've never been one to pace yourself."

This time, her smile reached her eyes. "You're one to talk. Go on. You don't want to be late. If I applied the right kind of pressure, would you tell me what your meeting's about?"

He laughed, kissing her, tasting her tears. "It's boring. Save your pressure tactics for something more worthwhile."

"I will," she whispered, exaggerating her southern accent.

When he got to his car, Nate couldn't dispel a nagging uneasiness. It'd been eating at him for days, ever since Alicia Miller's death in Yorkville. He looked back at the idyllic house and thought of his wife packing for their upcoming move while he was in a meeting about high-level killers. Sarah was a fighter, a survivor—one of the smartest people he knew. But she was also married to a senior federal agent in the middle of a troubling investigation.

Nate dialed his brother-in-law in New Hampshire. He and Tyler North, an air force pararescueman, had been friends since childhood, a relationship that became somewhat more complicated when Ty married the younger of Nate's two sisters.

Ty and Carine had a four-month-old baby boy, Harry, named after his paternal grandfather.

Ty was at home in New Hampshire on leave, planning to help Nate and Sarah move. He picked up on the second ring.

"Can you get down here sooner than tomorrow night?" Nate asked.

There wasn't even a flicker of hesitation on Ty's part. "I can leave for Manchester airport in an hour."

Nate didn't bother to hide his relief. "Thanks."

"It's Sarah?"

"I'd just feel better with someone else here with her."

"Should I leave Carine and the little guy up here?"

Nate thought a moment. His sister was a nature photographer and an independent soul—she and Ty had known each other since they were tots. "No. Bring them. I'm just on edge. There's nothing to worry about."

"You were born on edge," North said. "I'll see you later on tonight."

After he hung up, Nate continued to Washington and FBI headquarters, where the vigilante task force was meeting. He had virtually nothing to report from Huck McCabe or Diego Clemente. After two weeks in Yorkville, McCabe was no closer to finding out what was going on there than when he'd unpacked his bags. He had to be frustrated. Even if he was building trust day by day, establishing his credentials as a no-holds-barred vigilante, he didn't strike Nate as someone who would be satisfied with the status quo for too long. He'd seize his opportunity, and he'd make things happen.

Nate just hoped they all were ready when McCabe hit the switch.

24

On the warmest morning since he'd arrived on the East Coast two weeks ago with Vern Glover, Huck was in the back seat of a black SUV one block up from the American Society for the Study of Plants and Animals. Vern was in back with him. Nick Rochester was up front in the passenger seat. Humorless Travis Lubec was driving.

They all wore regular clothes, not a Breakwater Security logo to be seen.

"Quinn Harlowe's office is on the second floor." Lubec looked back at Huck and gave a half smile that didn't reach his flat eyes. "Octagon Room."

"What do you want me to do?"

"Take her for a walk. Talk to her."

"About what?"

"Ask her how she's doing since her friend drowned. What she's been up to." Travis paused and added, indifferent, "Tell her we're all worried about her after what happened to her friend last week."

Nick Rochester also turned around. "The receptionist is Thelma Worthington. Older than dirt, but a nice lady."

"What are you doing while I'm talking to Harlowe?"

Travis, obviously not liking the question, turned and faced front. "We're taking Vern to the White House. You've never seen the White House, have you, Vern?"

"No, just on TV."

For all Huck knew, they were taking Vern to see the White House. Lubec had presented them with their orders first thing that morning. *"Hop in the helicopter. We're going for a ride."*

Huck didn't have a chance to let Diego know what was going on. He had no backup. His butt was in the breeze.

Vern didn't like helicopters. Five minutes after they were in the air, he went green and threw up, just missing Huck's shoes. Travis and Nick both had a good laugh.

The helicopter landed on a private airstrip at Oliver Crawford's main estate in suburban Washington. The SUV was waiting for them. Without any explanation of what they would be doing, Travis got behind the wheel and drove them straight into the city.

Huck had the feeling he was being tested. If he didn't go along now, he'd never get any deeper into Breakwater Security and its layers.

He opened his door but didn't move. "Is Harlowe sticking her nose where it doesn't belong?"

Travis looked up into his rearview mirror. "Find out."

"See you in an hour, then. TGIF, huh?"

"Just do your job."

Huck got out and walked down the shaded sidewalk to Quinn's building. He had to shout his name into the intercom system and explain why he was there before the starchy receptionist would buzz him in. Even then, she didn't seem thrilled by his presence. Rising from her desk, she kept her hand near the telephone, which probably had 911 on speed dial. "Quinn's not expecting you, is she?"

"No, ma'am. It's a spur-of-the-moment visit."

"You're the bodyguard from Yorkville, aren't you?"

Huck gave her his most charming smile. "That's me. Mind if I go on up to see her?"

"Yes. As a matter of fact, I do." Thelma reached for her phone, then glanced back at him, a slight catch in her voice. "How do you know her office is upstairs?"

"I figure it wouldn't be down here with you and the stuffed birds."

"Ha-ha," she said, rallying as she lifted the old-fashioned phone, pressing two buttons. "Quinn? Huck Boone is here to see you. Shall I send him up?" She frowned into the receiver. "Quinn?"

"Just shocked the hell out of her, I'll bet," Huck said.

Cradling the phone, Thelma turned her frown on him. "Quinn will be right with you."

"Mind if I look around?" He showed her the bottom of his shoes. "I haven't stepped in dog poop or anything."

"Just take a seat, Mr. Boone."

She pointed at an ornate wooden chair against the wall across from her desk. "I feel like I need a crown to sit in that thing. Mind if I use your phone to make a call? It's local."

"Please, make yourself welcome." Her gracious words didn't match her frosty tone. "Dial 9 for an outside line."

Huck ignored her hostility and stepped over to the front of her desk, turning the heavy old phone to him. At least it was Touch-Tone. He dialed 9, then one of a handful of Washington numbers he'd committed to memory. He didn't want any of them showing up on his cell phone, in case Vern and the guys got hold of it.

Nate Winter answered. Huck quickly interrupted. "I'm in D.C. at the American Society for Plants and Animals. I can't talk right now. Something's up. Everything okay there?"

"Everything's fine." Winter sounded tight and impatient, but he always did.

"Here, too. I'll talk to you soon."

When Huck hung up and turned around, Quinn Harlowe was there, apparently having slipped down the thickly carpeted stairs without him noticing. In her slim skirt and stretchy top, she looked smart and professional and even prettier than she had in Yorkville. Her black hair was pulled back, so that all the angles of her face stood out, and her eyes shone brighter, more intense.

"It's the American Society for the Study of Plants and Animals," Quinn said, cool, obviously suspicious.

"Isn't that what I said?"

"You left off 'the study of.'"

"Oh."

"It changes the meaning entirely. Who were you talking to?"

"Dry cleaners."

Thelma returned to her oak swivel chair behind her desk. "I can hit redial and find out."

Nate would know what to do. Huck shrugged. "Go ahead."

"It's okay, Thelma," Quinn said, giving the older woman an affectionate smile. "Thank you. I'll take Huck upstairs—"

He remembered his orders from Lubec. *Take her for a walk.* He could think of worse tasks. "It's Friday. It's beautiful outside. Let's get out of here for a little while." To drive home his point, he touched a fingertip to her pale cheek. "You've been sitting up in your garret all morning, haven't you?"

"I naturally don't have a lot of color in my face. But you're right, it is a beautiful day, and I'd love to take a walk. Thelma, I have my cell phone if you need to reach me."

This was another way of telling Thelma to stick close to *her* phone, in case Quinn needed her. Considering how they'd met and the dubious circumstances under which he was in Washington, Huck thought she was being smart.

She'd have been even smarter, though, to have shown him the door.

Thelma clearly didn't like the idea of Quinn going off with him, but she kept quiet. Huck decided not to worry about her. They weren't leaving Thelma alone—the building was full of Society staff. As he headed for the front door, however, he couldn't dispel his sense of uneasiness. He would have preferred knowing where Travis and Company had gone.

Quinn trotted down the steps ahead of him. "Where do you want to go?"

"We could have coffee somewhere."

"Sure. I can show you where I was when Alicia found me. That's why you want to go for coffee, isn't it?" Without waiting for him to answer, she breezed down the shaded sidewalk. She looked back at him. "Coming?"

Something about her was off, Huck thought. Or not off so much as ramped up. As if, on some level, she'd been expecting him and had her own agenda for when he showed up on her doorstep.

He fell in beside her. "We don't have to do coffee. We can take a walk."

"Coffee's fine." She glanced over at him, her eyes still cool. "Who sent you here?"

"Ah. I can see you distrust my motives."

"I don't know what your motives are. I can speculate, but I'm not sure that would do any good. In my work, I try to avoid speculation."

"There's a difference between speculation and analysis?"

"Big difference."

"Travis Lubec sent me. He's a senior security—"

"He's Oliver Crawford's chief bodyguard. He might have a fancier title, but that's what he is. Yes, I know his name." She picked up her pace. "He was a key player in the rescue of his boss."

"You've been doing your homework."

"It was in the papers."

"Not Lubec's name," Huck said.

"No?" She didn't act as if he'd caught her in a deception. "Someone must háve told me."

"When?"

"Recently."

Now she was being openly deceptive, making him wonder what all she'd been up to in the days since she'd found her friend and her red kayak in the marsh. Lubec could have had good reason to send Huck in to talk to her. He kept up with her quick pace. "Ever think Crawford and his people are a little jumpy these days and might not want someone asking questions about them?"

"You mean me, because of Alicia, because she wasn't herself and she showed up at their front gate early one morning when they all were in bed." Quinn shifted to him, still moving at a fast clip, her eyes bright, shining with energy, a touch of indignation. "What, do they think Alicia and I conspired to make Oliver Crawford and his people uncomfortable?"

"Quinn—"

"*The Kayak Caper.*"

Huck sighed. "Having fun?"

"Not really. If I worried every time I asked a question someone didn't want me to ask, I couldn't do my job. I have to put that kind of resistance aside and focus on what I'm supposed to do. I try to keep an open mind and not let outside forces influence my conclusions."

"That's why you're good, but it's not your job to investigate what happened to your friend last week—"

"How would you know I'm good? Have you been researching me? Why is that okay but it's not okay for me to research you all?" She was on a roll now. "Maybe I should be taking you for a walk and picking your brain."

Huck decided to keep silent.

"That's what you're doing, isn't it? Picking my brain—finding out what I've been up to since I left Yorkville?"

"It was a good excuse to get to see you."

She obviously didn't believe him.

"Quinn—"

"I've only reached a few conclusions about Oliver Crawford and you Breakwater Security guys." She eased her pace slightly and gave him a sideways glance, the coolness suddenly back. "For instance, I don't believe Huck Boone is your real name."

"No, huh?"

"I told Special Agent Kowalski. And this Venezuela rescue of yours—" She shook her head. "I did a little investigating. Something doesn't pass the smell test there, either."

Huck was thinking about shoving her into a cab, taking her to Nate Winter and having him put Quinn Harlowe under lock and key. "Vern and I did a good deed. We worked under the radar, and the U.S. government might not approve—"

"I checked with a law enforcement source I have in Venezuela. Very reliable. She says that the kidnap victim you rescued wasn't a particularly good guy. He was involved in Colombian emerald smuggling. He disappeared after you freed him."

Because, Huck thought, unbeknownst to Vern, he'd managed to tip off fellow U.S. federal agents who subsequently took his rescued emerald smuggler into custody. Turned out he was an American citizen wanted for a long list of wrongdoing.

"Wouldn't you disappear if you were a smuggler?" he asked Quinn mildly.

"I don't think rescuing a smuggler is such a good deed." Quinn stopped in front of a small coffee shop with flowerpots and four round tables out front. "If you want, you can get us a table and I'll buy coffee—"

"That's okay." In her mood, she could be out the back door in a flash, and he'd have to explain why he went for coffee by himself. "I want to see what's on the menu."

"Every kind of coffee you can think of."

"I'm hungry."

"Biscotti, croissants, muffins, cookies…"

He smiled at her. "I want to see what looks good. Let's go."

He followed her into the coffee shop, and she said a cheerful hello to a big guy she called Ivan, who looked at Huck as if he were a criminal. Huck tried to take Ivan's suspicion as a positive signal that his deception was working. In any event, he figured it was good that Quinn had people looking out for her. She ordered an espresso. He ordered coffee, black, and a chocolate croissant.

"Make that two chocolate croissants," Quinn said, giving him a quick smile. "I can't resist."

She put everything on a tray and carried it outside, all four tables vacant. She set the tray on the middle one and unloaded it. "I'm right—Boone isn't your real name, is it?"

He wanted to tell her. *McCabe. It's Huck McCabe.* He wanted to tell her about his family in San Francisco and how his parents had adopted him, then four more kids, all of them of different racial and ethnic backgrounds. How they ran a boutique hotel and had never understood his interest in law enforcement but always supported him, wished him well, worried about him, believed in him.

How they thought he was training police officers in Eastern Europe.

So much deception, and here he was, supposed to figure out what lies Quinn was telling.

"It's all right," she said quickly. "You don't have to tell me."

He picked up his coffee. "I suppose you have

various scenarios to explain why I'm not using my real name. Assuming I'm not."

"Six scenarios, at least for starters. One, you're an ex-con. Two, you're dramatic and just like the idea of using an alias. Three, you're protecting your family, for whatever reason. Four, you're wanted by authorities under your real name. Five, you're making a clean break from a troubled past. Six, you're a cop."

"You met Joe Riccardi, right? Well, does he look like someone who'd hire a guy like me without having done a thorough background check?"

"Then either he knows you're using an alias," she said, picking up her tiny espresso cup, "or you've covered your tracks very, very well. Which these days would take money and help."

Why couldn't Alicia Miller have been best friends with a dental assistant? Nope. An expert in transnational criminal networks. "Going to take my coffee cup back to your fed friends and have them run my prints?"

"That's an idea."

"Of the six scenarios, do you have a favorite?"

She lifted her espresso to her lips. "Undercover cop. Federal. FBI, ATF, DEA, U.S. Marshals. Vern Glover associated with a California fugitive..." Her hazel eyes leveled on him. "Didn't you say you were from California?"

"San Francisco." He leaned over the table. "How long have you known?"

Color rushed to her face. She had to set her cup down. *"Damn."*

"Yeah. Damn."

"Your real name—"

"McCabe. Huck McCabe. I have a brother named Boone. He's a painter in northern California, as in canvasses, not houses."

"You're…what kind of—"

"I'm a deputy U.S. marshal working undercover." He smiled at her. "And you, Quinn Harlowe, are suddenly a very big pain in my ass."

"Not that suddenly," she said, rallying. "I got suspicious when you told me to trust you. You wanted me to know who you were. If you hadn't, you'd have handled the situation differently."

"I'm not that deep. You'd had a shock. You were scared. I wanted to make you feel better."

"That was decent of you."

"There you go calling me decent again," he said dryly. "Look what it gets me, a former DOJ analyst poking her nose into my investigation."

She didn't seem remotely guilt-ridden or even that concerned. "When I started digging into Breakwater Security and Oliver Crawford's kidnapping—certain things didn't add up right from the start. I doubt the Breakwater guys would draw the same conclusions I have. I have access to sources and materials they don't."

Not if Lubec has his way. Huck got rid of any hint of a smile. "Quinn, this isn't some intellectual exercise. You're not ten steps removed from an operation. You're right in the thick of it."

"Yes, I know."

But she couldn't sustain that cool demeanor, and Huck watched her break off a piece of her chocolate croissant, realizing that she hadn't fully expected she was right about him. She was more shaken than she wanted to admit, which probably should have pleased him more than it did. He found himself wanting to reassure her—and yet he warned himself that he didn't need that kind of distraction, that kind of emotional involvement. If she was a problem, he'd stick her with Nate Winter.

"I suppose you're not going to tell me what you're investigating at Breakwater?"

"Nope." He smiled slightly. "I'm not sure I know."

She eyed him. "Want me to take a guess?"

"That might not be a good idea."

"Maybe not. I have a high-level security clearance. I keep secrets well." She ate her small bite of croissant. "You don't have to stuff me in a trunk for the duration of your investigation."

"You have a lot of guts, Quinn, and you're curious by nature—your profession requires it. But you're not removed from the action. You knew Alicia Miller. You know Oliver Crawford. Gerard Lattimore has a soft spot for you, maybe a romantic interest in you."

"No romantic interest."

Huck didn't let up on her. "You have to stop asking questions, calling up sources. Do your job—"

"You're telling me to mind my own business."

"I'm suggesting that you're in over your head and you need to swim away to safer waters."

"What about Alicia?"

"There's just no indication her death wasn't an accident—"

"Or suicide. That's what you all believe, isn't it? That she killed herself, if just by not caring if she lived or died—just by being reckless and agitated."

"'You all' would be—"

"Your superiors, the local police, the FBI, the Breakwater Security guys. Everyone." Quinn didn't wait for a response. Tears, which she hadn't seemed to expect, shone in her eyes. "What about the black sedan?"

"Quinn, I'm not going there. I'm not speculating with you—"

She pointed at the street. "The Town Car met her at that intersection. Right there."

"You said she got in on her own. She wasn't pulled in. No one forced her."

"Were you in the car? The fisherman, Diego Clemente—Buddy Jones said he saw him have a cigarette with you that afternoon. Before five. It wouldn't give you much time to get back to Yorkville and into your running shorts, but it's possible."

Huck said nothing. What had she done, diagrammed time lines?

Quinn shot to her feet. "Oh. Damn." She almost knocked over her espresso. "Clemente—he's with *you*. That's why the anonymous tip about Alicia's car."

Hell.

She put a hand on one hip and blew out a lungful of air. "I didn't get that one until just this second.

Don't worry, it's not like anyone else in Yorkville will figure it out. Your guys at Breakwater—whoever you're after—none of them will necessarily put two and two together. I just happened to be in the right place at the right time with Clemente and asked the right questions."

"Don't screw around with Diego, Quinn. He *will* stuff you in a trunk."

She nodded, taking his comment seriously. "I've put together a basic dossier on Oliver Crawford and Breakwater Security. And on you, although nothing speculative—nothing that would blow your mercenary bona fides."

"Anything in writing?"

"Just notes. Everything's on my laptop."

Huck stood. "Let's go back to your office and take a look."

"I can't have dug up anything on Crawford and Breakwater that you all don't have already, but you're welcome to take whatever files you want."

"Quinn, Oliver Crawford's guys know you've been poking around. How?"

"I have no idea—"

"Who have you talked to?"

"No one who'd know *them*."

"Did you tell anyone you were looking into Crawford and Breakwater?"

She hesitated.

"Lattimore?" Huck prodded.

"No—I haven't seen him. We've talked once since last week, but just about Alicia and how much we miss her." When Huck started to say something else, she held up a hand. "Steve Eisenhardt. I told him a little about the research I was doing. We met here yesterday. He started working for Gerard after I left Justice."

"You're friends?"

"Sort of. I don't know him that well. He was half in love with Alicia—" She broke off, frowning. "He wasn't at Lattimore's party in March, when Alicia met Oliver Crawford. She asked to use my cottage right after the party. I suppose Steve could have wondered what was going on and hooked up with Crawford's guys somehow."

"He ever mention Crawford?"

She shook her head. "I'll talk to him—"

"Hell, no, you're not talking to him."

"I meant as a friend."

"If he's ratting you out to Travis Lubec, he's no damn friend. Let's go."

25

Sweating, heart thumping, Steve hit some keys to wake up Quinn's laptop on her desk.

Password protected.

He'd expected as much and didn't waste time moaning and groaning. He grabbed the spiral note-pad next to the laptop and flipped it open.

He'd never been in Quinn's office before. Very Sherlock Holmes, he thought, glancing up at the oil portrait of a man identified as Quinn Harlowe in raised lettering at the bottom of the frame. Steve couldn't help thinking the hazel eyes were boring right through him, seeing that he was a soulless piece of dung.

And why not? That is what I am.

He'd sold his soul to the Nazi devils who were waiting for him.

He had to produce.

Getting out of there with the laptop was out of

the question. Stuffing the notepad in his pants was only a marginally more credible option, but the old bat downstairs would never let him out the door. For all he knew, Quinn could have used the notepad to scribble down a speech to the Rotary Club.

If he didn't bring something to his goons, they'd be pressing buttons on their computer by tonight, sending pictures of him and the congressman's underage daughter, and he'd be Washington's next jaw-dropping scandal.

All the Nazis needed was confirmation that Quinn was, indeed, digging into their business and an idea of how far she'd gotten.

Do the dumb shits think she's some kind of undercover federal agent?

He glanced at her hen-scratching on the top page of the notepad.

Venezuela. Emerald smuggling. Oliver Crawford, Dominican Republic.

Tortures. Executions.

Steve shuddered. Who the hell were these guys? He wondered what would happen if they decided Quinn knew too much.

Not my problem.

He quickly tore off the top three sheets in the notepad, making sure he didn't leave behind any threads of paper from the spiral holes, and folded the sheets, tucking them into his suit-coat inner pocket. With a little luck, Quinn wouldn't notice anything was missing until it was way too late.

"Mr. Eisenhardt?" It was the receptionist, calling him sternly from the staircase. "Mr. Eisenhardt, I'd like for you to wait for Ms. Harlowe downstairs."

A man came out of another second-floor office down the hall and spoke to her, but Steve couldn't make out what the guy was saying. He returned the notebook to its spot on Quinn's cluttered desk. He hadn't broken into her office—he'd walked in. The Nazis had assured him they'd distract Quinn and give him a window of time in which to operate.

The old-bat receptionist would tell Quinn that he'd been there. If either of them suspected he'd been up to anything underhanded, they'd be on the phone with the cops in a heartbeat. Alicia's death had put everyone he knew in Washington on edge.

He went to Quinn's door. "Is that you, Miss Worthington?"

He could see her marching down the hall toward him. She inhaled deeply through her nose. "Mr. Eisenhardt, didn't you hear me?"

"No, I didn't. I mean, I heard you, but I couldn't make out what you were saying. What's up? Quinn back?"

She glared at him, not nearly as winded as he would have expected for a woman her age. "Quinn isn't back yet, no. I asked you to wait downstairs."

"You did? Sorry. I'm not used to the routine around here." He could see that charm wasn't going to work on her. "I was one of her friend Alicia's colleagues at Justice—we were in and out of each others offices all the time. Cubicles, actually." He gestured at the elegant Octagon Room behind him. "This is much nicer. Really swank."

"She needs to get used to locking her door."

He'd gambled that Quinn's office wouldn't be locked. A risk, but he was right. He didn't want to think about what would have happened if he'd been wrong—what he'd have had to force himself to do. Somehow, some way, he had to bring the Nazis what they wanted.

"Hey, I don't want to get you into any trouble," Steve said. "I can't wait around here, anyway. I was hoping to catch her. What's she doing, taking a walk in the park?" The Nazis had told him they had a guy distracting her, but Steve didn't know any details. He didn't want to know. "We've all had a rough time since Alicia's death."

Thelma toned down the sourpuss expression. "I imagine so. Miss Miller was your friend, too?"

He felt a prick of real sadness. "I didn't know her as well as Quinn did. I've only been at Justice a couple months. But, yes, I considered her a friend."

"I'm sorry for your loss, Mr. Eisenhardt." But, refocusing on why she was there, Thelma stood to one side of the door and motioned him toward the stairs. "I'll follow you downstairs."

Don't do me any favors. As he started past her, he noticed her give Quinn's office a suspicious scan. Steve wondered if he looked shifty, or if she just didn't trust lawyers. Stealing stuff off a purported friend's desk wasn't the kind of risk he preferred to take. Sexual indiscretions were one thing, but he didn't like breaking the law. If he'd known the congressman's daughter was underage, he'd never have touched her.

But he'd suspected. He just hadn't asked her or bothered to find out on his own, which he could have done just by going to her father's Web site. He'd wanted what he got from her, and he didn't let anything stand in the way of his obsession.

When he reached the first floor, he smiled at the receptionist. "You'll tell Quinn I stopped by?"

"I certainly will."

Steve thanked her and pushed through the heavy front door, then trotted down the steps, fresh waves of heat and perspiration breaking out from his brow to his feet. He cut up the street to an intersection, turning right, walking fast until he came to the black SUV.

The Nazi Youth stepped out, and Steve handed him the sheets from the notepad. "This should satisfy you. She's on your asses."

No reaction. "Mr. Lubec wants to speak with you."

"Asshole—no names. Okay? I don't want to know who you are."

The kid smirked. "You know we work for Oliver Crawford. You could give our description to the police, and in a matter of hours, they'd have our names and our pictures posted all over the media."

Steve felt his stomach drop. On the one hand, he didn't know anything. On the other hand, he knew too much—and that was what the kid was telling him. "I'm not going to do that."

"We know you're not." The kid stepped backward, motioning for Steve to get into the car. "Have a seat."

Not a chance. He stuck his head in the open door, Lubec—the SS guard—behind the wheel. "The Nazi Youth here says you want to talk to me. Talk. I'm not getting in here with you. If you try to shove my ass in, I'll scream bloody murder. Plus, I left a message on my cell phone. If I'm not back at my desk in forty-five minutes, the feds will know to come looking for me."

Lubec cast him a stone-cold look. He didn't like the feds. Steve had already figured that one out. In the same dead tone as always, Lubec said, "On Monday at 5:00 p.m., we will send the link to the pictures to the attorney general and the director of the FBI." He let his gaze bore into Steve for a couple seconds. "You have until then to get us the names we want. No more stalling."

"I can't…" But Steve knew he wouldn't get anywhere by trying to appeal to their common sense about his limitations. "I'm serious, okay? I don't have that kind of access. *Lattimore* doesn't have that kind of access—"

"We also want the names of any undercover agents trying to penetrate our network."

Our network. No more fooling around with semantics. Steve wasn't reassured—they weren't making him an ally. They didn't trust him. They didn't believe he was one of them. They had him by the balls, pure and simple.

"Come on." He tried to keep his desperation out of his tone. "Nobody's going to give me that kind of information."

"We want to know if Alicia Miller and Quinn

Harlowe were using the Yorkville cottage as a cover to infiltrate us on behalf of the federal government."

Steve held his hands to his ears. "I don't want to know details. *La-la-la.* I can't hear you."

Lubec rolled his eyes. "Monday at five."

The kid tapped Steve on the shoulder. "Move away from the car."

He complied, dropping his hands from his ears. The Nazi Youth got into the SUV. As it pulled away, Steve sank against a light pole, his bowels loosening. His only smart move of the day was telling everyone at work he was going home early. Now, he didn't have to go back to the office and instead could go home and be sick in peace.

Home?

If Quinn figured out he had swiped her notes, she'd be all over him. And the Nazis—they'd never be satisfied. They wanted what he couldn't give. He'd done too much for them as it was. He knew too much about them.

Lubec.

Steve shuddered. He had a *name* now, not just a description. Obviously, they'd helped out with that Tatro escape last fall.

They weren't going to leave him to his own devices. They'd have his office and apartment watched. For all he knew, someone was on his ass right now.

He couldn't go home.

Just go back to Quinn's office and tell her everything.

If anyone could put the pieces together of what these goons were up to, Steve knew it was Quinn

Harlowe. She'd help him sort through his options. Telling her everything had to be better than throwing his lot in with Lubec and the rest of his Nazis.

The pictures...

He thought of his mother, no prize herself, home in New Jersey, so proud of her son the Justice Department lawyer.

Narrowly stopping himself from puking on the sidewalk, Steve clasped a hand to his lower abdomen and started to run.

"Are you sure you know who your friends are?"

Seated in the back of a government car, Gerard Lattimore couldn't read Oliver's tone over his cell phone. He was on his way to a meeting at FBI headquarters and almost hadn't answered the call. "Do any of us?"

His old friend chuckled softly. "Good answer. I don't mean to make you paranoid. You have an important position in the government. Of course, I'm not privy to the details of anything you're responsible for, but I imagine none of it's trivial. I don't envy you, I must say."

"You've never envied anyone, Ollie. You wouldn't waste your time."

"Time *is* valuable."

"Speaking of which—I have a meeting in ten minutes."

"I'll be brief. It's been brought to my attention that your Quinn Harlowe has been asking questions about you. She's very bright, isn't she? And suspicious, if not by nature, after working for you for three years. Her friend's death can't have helped."

"What kind of questions is she asking? Of whom? You, Ollie?"

"I don't have the details. I'm working on getting them. Are you by any chance under investigation?"

Gerard kept himself from shooting up out of his seat. "Of course not."

"Would you know if you were?"

"Ollie, I don't play those games. I'm as straightforward as they come. If people want to maneuver and plot behind my back, fine. I'll just keep doing my job."

"Spoken like a true patriot," his friend said.

"Are you suggesting Quinn is part of some kind of conspiracy to undermine me?"

"Oh, no. I'm suggesting no such thing. I'm not trying to make you paranoid. Just watch your back." Oliver paused, taking a sharp, audible breath. "I didn't, and I almost lost my life. I don't want the same to happen to you."

So that was it. A touch of post-trauma paranoia. "Ollie—I'm sorry. I wish I had more time to talk."

"You're coming out to Yorkville this weekend, aren't you? My people tell me your boat's been cleaned and is ready to go. I'm in Washington at the moment, but I expect to be back at Breakwater tonight. I'm having an open house there tomorrow afternoon."

"Tomorrow? At Breakwater?" Gerard didn't hide his surprise.

"Yes. It's Sharon's idea, but I think it's a good

one. We're still meeting resistance here in Yorkville, which we need to confront, especially with a dozen trainees arriving in the next couple of weeks."

"I understand, but it's so soon after Alicia Miller's death—"

"We had nothing to do with her death. We don't have the luxury of time, Gerry. When we're fully operational, Breakwater Security will provide a necessary, legitimate service. Everything we've done or plan to do not only complies with the law but exceeds industry standards. Once people see for themselves, I think we'll allay any community concerns. We're trying to be as open and as sensitive as possible."

Gerard couldn't help but chuckle. "Damn, Ollie, you should be working in a government public information office. You can spin with the best of them."

"I'm just telling the truth." He seemed offended. "Will you come tomorrow?"

"Of course."

"Invite Quinn Harlowe to join you."

"Ollie—"

"You need to know who your friends are, Gerry. And your enemies. I can help."

"Quinn's a friend," Gerard said. "I have no doubts."

"Good. Then you'll bring her tomorrow."

His car had arrived at the restaurant where his meeting was being held. Gerard had to hang up, but when he said goodbye, he felt a crawling sensation that he couldn't quite describe or understand. The kidnapping in December had been a brutal ordeal for his old college buddy, and Alicia's accidental drowning almost two weeks ago, coupled with her bizarre behavior, had been an unexpected blow for everyone. For Oliver Crawford, a multimillionaire businessman who liked control, Alicia's death alone would have been cause for him to retrench. Add in an intense, inquisitive Quinn Harlowe, the events of the past few months had to have rubbed raw every fear and insecurity he had.

A spring-weekend afternoon party at beautiful Breakwater could just be what the doctor ordered—for all of us, Gerard thought.

"One moment," he told his driver, dialing Quinn's cell phone.

Ollie's warning was pure drama and post-trauma edginess, Gerard decided, dismissing it from his mind.

He trusted no one more than he did Quinn Harlowe.

26

When Lubec, Rochester and Glover picked Huck up near the quirky American Society for the Study of Plants and Animals, he told them he was taking the afternoon off and would find his own way back to Breakwater. He didn't offer any explanations. Lubec didn't like it, but he had a helicopter waiting—no time to argue with a low-level employee like Huck Boone.

Diego Clemente, who, as Huck had expected, had just arrived in Washington, picked him up in front of the White House and took him out to Arlington and the historic northern Virginia house where Nate Winter lived with his wife and the ghosts of Abraham Lincoln and Robert E. Lee.

"Find another ride back to the Neck," Diego said. "I'm going to check on Harlowe."

"You're still ticked off at her because she made you."

Diego had made his opinion plain about Quinn Harlowe turning her research and analysis talents onto the two of them. He scowled. "Ever think she could have hooked up with these vigilante pukes and be playing us?"

"No."

"Historians," he said, as if that explained everything.

The second Huck shut the truck door, Clemente backed out, as if he'd seen ghosts coming out of the old house's chimney. Most likely, he just didn't want anyone making him stick around for a high-level meeting. Diego hated meetings. Huck had called Nate Winter an hour ago and said he was on the way. He didn't know who Winter had managed to get out to the house in the meantime.

He walked around to the back of the pre–Civil War house. Sarah Dunnemore, Winter's wife, was in charge of getting it ready to open to the public. They'd bought their own place. Huck noticed the boxes on the back porch and wondered what it was like to be that settled, moving into a home of his own.

Winter stood at the top of the porch steps. A tall, rangy, naturally impatient man with an unusual family background, he was fast becoming a legend in the Marshals Service. Last spring, he had survived a sniper-style shooting in Central Park. The incident had, however, led him to Sarah Dunnemore of Night's Landing, Tennessee, surrogate daughter to John Wesley Poe, former Tennessee governor and now the U.S. president. That had to complicate Nate's life, Huck thought.

As he mounted the steps and shook Winter's hand, Huck considered how much his own life had just been complicated by Quinn Harlowe.

"Where's Clemente?" Winter asked.

"On his way back to Yorkville."

Winter didn't seem surprised. "No point in risking anyone from town seeing the two of you together. Juliet Longstreet and Ethan Brooker are here."

"I don't mean to disturb you at home. Your wife—"

"She's out with my sister and brother-in-law." Winter's voice had tightened slightly. "It was my suggestion we meet here. It's safer for you. The U.S. attorney working with us wanted to be here but couldn't make it on such short notice."

"FBI?"

"No."

Nothing had been said, but Huck didn't doubt the FBI would have preferred to have one of their own working undercover with the vigilantes, not some deputy marshal from California who'd pretty much stumbled on them. He shrugged. "Good."

Juliet Longstreet—it had to be her, since she was the only woman on the porch—got up from the porch rail and introduced herself, then introduced a man in a dark suit, Ethan Brooker, a Special Forces officer who was now a presidential adviser. Diego's pal from his own Special Forces days.

Huck could feel their misgivings about him. He understood.

At least they didn't ask him if he'd been followed, a minor nod to his abilities.

"Have a seat," Winter said.

Huck shook his head. "That's okay."

A small table was set with a stainless-steel urn of coffee, white mugs, a matching sugar pot and creamer, a stack of pansy-decorated cocktail napkins and a plate of quartered pimiento-cheese sandwiches. Not Winter's doing, for sure, Huck thought, helping himself to a couple of the pimiento-cheese triangles. No one else was eating. Longstreet watched him with the kind of frank skepticism he could appreciate. Brooker was harder to read. The two of them supposedly were an item, but Huck hadn't heard anything about wedding bells.

"Steve Eisenhardt," he said to the assembled group. "What do we know about him?"

Winter sat next to the food table. "He works under Gerard Lattimore."

"I know that much. He turned up at Harlowe's office after I was dispatched to keep her occupied." He inhaled, impatient with himself. "I miscalculated. I thought they wanted me to find out how much she knew about their operation."

"You think they had Eisenhardt search her office?" Longstreet asked, dubious. "Middle of the day, building full of people—why take that risk?"

"What, as opposed to breaking in with crowbars and triggering alarms?"

She shrugged. "I suppose that's one way of looking at it."

Brooker had loosened his tie. He was dark-haired, dark-eyed, quiet—Diego had said he had attitude, especially after his wife's murder almost two years ago. "Did he take anything?" he asked.

"I don't know. Her laptop was still there." And stacks of books, notebooks, files, mail and letters, the one on top asking her if she would be interested in speaking with a certain congressman about her perspective on transnational crime. Her work before, during and since she was at the Department of Justice had brought her credibility and respect. "Harlowe took a quick look but didn't notice anything missing."

"If she finds out something is missing—"

"She'll call Kowalski."

Winter didn't react to what was said. "Kowalski's up to speed on the task force and the investigation. It's safer that way."

"I like to know who's aware of my status and who isn't."

"Now you know. Kowalski doesn't like Alicia Miller showing up at Breakwater the morning before she drowned or the mysterious black sedan that picked her up in Washington. Then there's the timing—she's agitated and upset, and yet soon after she arrives back in Yorkville, she goes kayaking?"

"She was obsessed with ospreys. There are nests all along the Yorkville waterfront."

"One right in front of the cottage she was borrowing," Winter said. "Why not put her kayak in there? Why take it two miles up the road?"

"She wasn't thinking straight. I don't have any answers, either. I wish I'd gotten to Breakwater sooner. I might have a better fix on what kind of relationship she had with Crawford and his crowd. I don't know, though. If it looks like a duck, walks like a duck..." He ate the pimiento-cheese triangle in two bites, although he wasn't hungry. "Usually it's a duck."

Brooker spoke, his tone mild. "You believe her death was an accident or suicide as a result of her agitated mental state."

"I don't believe anything. I just can't see someone killing her by getting her into a kayak and then knocking her out of it. It's possible someone took advantage of the situation and let her drown. The weather was bad that day. Worse than expected."

"If someone did seize the moment, so to speak," Juliet Longstreet said, "who?"

"Lubec." Huck didn't hesitate. "He and Sharon Riccardi have worked for Crawford longer than the rest of us at Breakwater. Something's bothering Joe Riccardi. He's not obvious about it, but there's no question he's on alert."

"Does he trust you?" Juliet asked.

"I'm not sure he trusts any of us. He's ex-military. He's in a job now that plays by different rules. He might do better with the ex-military and ex–law enforcement guys. I think he regards the rest of us as a bunch of thugs."

Longstreet poured herself a cup of coffee. "You *are* a bunch of thugs."

Huck didn't disagree. "I've been spewing the vigilante line since I got to Breakwater. Joe Riccardi doesn't bite. He says he wants Breakwater to be an elite, legitimate, respectable security firm with highly trained personnel. That's his mantra. If there's a thug quotient early on, he'll stamp it out in training, get rid of people who don't belong."

"'Elite' usually means small," Longstreet said.

"That's right. Both Riccardis say they're not looking to be one of the big players in the security field."

"This Joe Riccardi has a lot of responsibility," Brooker said. "Breakwater is a start-up with no reputation—he's building it from the ground up. One mistake—a training accident, anything—and they're out of business. He'll be living off his military pension."

Winter looked out at the landscape, at the height of its spring beauty. He seemed preoccupied. "The network we're trying to penetrate is loosely coordinated, which makes the people involved more difficult to track. When they act, they're brazen."

"It's their arrogance." Brooker stood, his eyes on Huck. "I ran into some of these guys in Afghanistan. They set up their own torture chamber to interrogate people they detained, under no authority whatsoever but their own. They were so convinced they were right that they assumed we would applaud their efforts and give them carte blanche. They were surprised and outraged when we turned them over to the Afghan government. Too bad we weren't able to break open their entire network then."

"They're not total whack jobs," Huck said. "If I'm on the right track, they're rational and very deliberate. They believe they're preventing, not sowing, chaos and self-destruction."

Nate turned from the view of the yard he'd be leaving within hours. "What about Quinn Harlowe?"

Huck didn't mince words. "She's made me. And Diego."

Winter had no visible reaction, but Juliet Longstreet threw up her hands and groaned. "How? If she—"

"She was focused on me. She has access to information the Breakwater guys don't. She's an expert on this sort of thing. She's a natural bird dog. Once she's got the scent, she won't let go." Huck realized he didn't like being in the position of defending her, or vouching for her. "She still has a high-level security clearance."

"You trust her?" Nate asked.

"It's not a question of trust. My first instinct was to pull her off the street. But if we shut her down now, these guys will crawl back under their rocks just as they're starting to come out into the light. If they blame her for upsetting their plans, she'll be worse off. I'm willing to keep going. Clemente is, too. A couple Californians like us—we went to a lot of trouble to make ourselves fit in out here."

"We're not risking this woman—"

"It's safer for her if we don't interfere with her." Huck picked up a couple more pimiento-cheese triangles; nobody else seemed interested. "She's not on the government payroll anymore. She answers to herself. What she does is up to her."

"I don't like it," Nate said.

"I'm not worried about me—or Diego. And we're not going to do anything to endanger Harlowe. Last thing we need is to have to put on the brakes to rescue her."

Juliet stirred. "I'll bet having you rescue her is right there with having her fingernails plucked out with pliers. My take? Quinn Harlowe's asking questions because she's trying to get used to her friend's tragic death. She'll settle down."

Ethan Brooker and Nate Winter didn't look as optimistic.

Finally, Winter sighed. "I'll pull you out in a heartbeat, McCabe, if I think you're taking unnecessary risks."

Huck finished off his pimiento-cheese triangles. Winter, Longstreet, Brooker. He had to trust them.

And they had to trust him.

"Relax. I can do my job."

27

Quinn splashed more champagne into Thelma's glass, an antique crystal flute that, according to legend, the first Quinn Harlowe had used to drink a toast in celebration of the discovery of a triceratops fossil in South Dakota.

After her close call in keeping herself out of Huck Boone/McCabe's trunk, Quinn decided she was in the mood to think about dinosaurs. The fiercer the better.

It was early afternoon, but the Society, in keeping with long-standing tradition, shut down at 2:00 p.m. on Fridays from mid-April through Labor Day weekend. A little early in the day for an end-of-the-week drink, but Thelma didn't seem to mind. She tipped her champagne glass to Quinn. "May your sanity return. Cheers."

"I'm going to the Breakwater open house, Thelma." Quinn had taken Gerard's call with

Thelma next to her, opening the champagne, not bothering to disguise the fact that she was eavesdropping. As a result, Quinn now had no plausible deniability. "I'm a neighbor."

"Lattimore's going to think you're his date."

"No, he's not. I'm meeting him there. You're being very old-fashioned, you know. He and I are colleagues. There's *nothing* romantic between us. Zip. Zero."

"You're both attractive and available."

"Available." Quinn wrinkled up her face, trying to keep the conversation lighthearted, which was not even close to how she felt. "I'm not sure I like that word. Think about the layers of different meaning."

Thelma settled deeper into the slouchy modern chair that Quinn had insisted on adding to her office, although it went with none of the stiff, late-nineteenth-century antiques. "Are you sure you don't want any of the champagne?"

"Positive. I'm my own designated driver, and a Friday afternoon in Washington in springtime— what are the odds I get to Yorkville in under four hours?"

"Slim to none." Thelma narrowed her eyes. "You'll need a champagne-free brain. Do you suppose Oliver Crawford knows Lattimore's invited you?"

"He says it was Crawford's idea."

"That doesn't make me feel better, Quinn. Why would he invite you to a party after he caught you trespassing?"

"Maybe he understands the emotional state I was in at the time."

And still am, Quinn thought. Her grief wasn't as raw and volatile as in the first hours after finding Alicia, and the shock had eased. Digging into Oliver Crawford and Breakwater Security had helped occupy her mind as she'd processed what had happened.

Of course, now she was in hot water with the marshals. Were they discussing, even now, what to do about her?

"You'll notice Lattimore keeps inviting you to parties," Thelma went on. "The marina party in March, and now this one. And you keep going."

Quinn changed the subject. "What are you doing this weekend?"

"Several friends and I are going birding in the mountains."

"That sounds like fun. You've never married, have you, Thelma?"

"No, I haven't." Her eyes sparkled. "Although I came close a few times. Why do you ask?"

"I have no idea. I suppose—" She thought of Huck, but didn't go there. She smiled at Thelma, who seemed not to have changed since Quinn's first memories of her as a child. "I suppose I'm just trying to distract you. Any regrets about not marrying?"

Thelma sipped her champagne. "Why, I wonder, do we never ask married women if they have any regrets?"

Quinn shrugged. "I'm not sure we don't. Isn't divorce a way of saying they regret having married?"

She sat back, eyeing Quinn. "I have a full life. I realize I have more days behind me than ahead, but that just makes me even more determined to live each one I have to its fullest."

"If you didn't have to work—"

"I love my work. This place." With a wave of one hand, she took in the Octagon Room, with its fireplace and oil portrait, its brass candlesticks, its worn wood floors. "I come to work, and I feel as if I've stepped back in time to my grandmother's day. She used to work here, too, you know. Some days, I swear I can hear her talking to me. It's very comforting."

Quinn looked up at her great-great-grandfather's dour face. "I'm not sure I'd want to hear him talking to me."

Thelma smiled. "He died before my time here, but in the early days, there were many people who remembered him. They said he wasn't at all a crazy adrenaline junkie. He was thoughtful, *very* intelligent. He had a purpose. He knew what he was here on earth to do, and he accepted the risks involved as part of the challenge." Her plain, frank eyes zeroed in on Quinn. "He didn't shrink from his duties and responsibilities, whether he'd had them foisted upon him or took them on by choice."

"Thelma…"

Quinn breathed out, setting the champagne bottle on a stack of cast-off files on her desk. She knew what the longtime receptionist—and adventurer—was trying to say, the point she was driving home in her own not particularly subtle way.

"Quinn, you know what you have to do."

"I can't say for sure that Steve was here to search my office. I can't say for sure he tried to access my laptop files." She watched the sweat from the champagne drip onto a dry, ancient file. "I don't want to make trouble for him."

"I saw him. I don't know him, of course, but I'd say he's already in trouble. It's not your job to save him from any mess he's gotten himself into. You can't help him by running from what you know." She finished off the last of her champagne. "That's another quality your great-great-grandfather had. He understood and respected his limits."

"Risk-takers think they have no limits."

Thelma snorted. "No, Quinn, grandiose idiots think they have no limits. You Harlowes are neither grandiose nor idiots."

"Just occasionally very unlucky," Quinn said dryly, getting to her feet.

She hadn't left anything out in the open in her office that provided any critical information—no names or numbers of her sources, none of her conclusions, especially about Huck. Nowhere had she typed or written a single word about her suspicions about who he was. If Steve had searched her office, he would only have seen cryptic notes, jotted questions to herself.

But there were enough, she thought, for even the most cursory search to confirm that she'd spent some time researching Oliver Crawford and Breakwater Security.

"I'll call T.J. Kowalski on my way to Yorkville," she said.

Thelma smiled knowingly. "You're afraid if you call him from here, you won't get to Yorkville. He'll stuff you into a hotel somewhere. I don't know what you've gotten yourself into this time, Quinn, but I can guess—" She tilted her empty flute up at the portrait. "I can guess your Harlowe genes are coming out in you."

"Special Agent Kowalski has his own ideas about what I should and shouldn't be doing."

"And you have yours," Thelma said, as if Quinn had just won her point for her about Harlowe genes.

Quinn ignored any reference to her crazy ancestors. "Thelma—I owe Alicia. My grandfather says I'm a catalyst. I make things happen."

"Spoken like a true Harlowe."

"I'm not about to do anything reckless. I want to make answers happen. I want to know why Alicia died. Why she came to me for help, talking about ospreys. Who was in the car that picked her up. Where they went."

"Understandable, but is any of that the responsibility of a friend?" Thelma's voice had gone quiet. "Be aware of who you are and why you're doing what you're doing. Don't delude yourself."

Quinn gave her a cheerfully stubborn look. "You're just telling me I've gone Harlowe because you don't want me going to that open house."

Thelma didn't relent. "I don't trust Gerard Lattimore. Or Oliver Crawford. You'll be all alone tomorrow."

Not alone, Quinn thought. Huck Boone/McCabe would be there.

But if he were here now, she had no doubt he'd be siding with Thelma. "It'll be fine, Thelma." Quinn picked up the champagne bottle and refilled her friend's glass. "Besides, I have to go now—I already know what I'm wearing."

Quinn had lied to Thelma. She had no idea what to wear to Oliver Crawford's open house. Choosing an outfit was the least of her concerns, but it gave her something inconsequential to focus on. What dress, what shoes, whether to go dramatic or natural with her makeup were all better than dwelling on undercover marshals and whatever Steve Eisenhardt was up to.

She decided on a simple champagne-colored silk dress with a 1930s shawl, strappy shoes and hot-pink lipstick.

If Huck Boone/McCabe was guarding bodies, she might as well be in hot-pink lipstick.

What a thought. She felt a rush of heat and quickly threw her open-house outfit and enough clothes for the weekend into a zippered bag.

In a few minutes, she was on the road, a stack of work next to her on the front seat. She rolled down the windows and opened the sunroof, letting in as much warm spring air as possible. She loved the freedom of being able to juggle her schedule and—often—work outside her office. Being her own boss had its downside, but not, she thought, today.

Once she cleared city traffic, she called Special Agent Kowalski on her cell phone. She hoped just to leave a message, but he picked up. "Where are you?" he asked her.

"In my car."

"In your car in Alaska, or in your car in front of FBI headquarters?"

"I'm on the Beltway."

"Going—"

"About sixty-five miles an hour."

He took an audible breath. "All right. What's up?"

"You all need to find Steve Eisenhardt and make sure he's not mixed up in—" She stopped herself. Did Kowalski know about the undercover marshals? Huck hadn't been specific with her. "I'm pretty sure he searched my office this afternoon. He just happened to stop by when I was out."

"Why should I care if he searched your office?"

"Because I had notes out on research I've been doing on Oliver Crawford and Breakwater Security."

Silence.

"Nothing I kept in the open would compromise me or anyone else in any way," Quinn added carefully. "No notes from conversations I had with sources, none of my conclusions—"

"What sources?"

"Just people I know from my work."

"What conclusions?"

"'Conclusions' is too strong a word. Thoughts, questions, speculations—none of that was in the open. Most of it's in my head or on a password-protected file on my laptop—"

"Which is where?"

"Right next to me on the front seat of my car. It was on my desk this afternoon. Steve could have grabbed it, but he didn't. He must have known Thelma would never have let him out of the building with it."

"Thelma's the receptionist," Kowalski said.

"I see you've been doing your homework, too."

"Any idea why this Steve character would care if you were researching Oliver Crawford and Breakwater Security?"

"No."

"Don't you lock your office?"

"I didn't think of it. Someone stopped by to see me, and we went out for coffee—I never went back upstairs."

Just a half beat's hesitation. "All right. Anything else?"

Quinn bit her lip, considering Kowalski's reaction. Why wasn't he asking her who'd stopped by her office? But she didn't pursue the subject. "Don't you want to know who Steve Eisenhardt is?"

"You told me you called him after Miss Miller took off in the black sedan."

"Good memory," Quinn said, tongue-in-cheek. He wasn't telling her everything—and he didn't care that she knew he was holding back. But she had no status herself in any investigation, whether it was Alicia's death or whatever—whoever— Huck McCabe was hunting in Yorkville.

"Thank you. I'll take that as a compliment." He didn't sound grateful for anything. "Where can I find you if I need to talk to you?"

"Yorkville."

"That's not a good idea. Why are you headed there?"

"I'm going to an open house at Breakwater tomorrow afternoon."

"You're joking, right?"

"Oliver Crawford asked Gerard Lattimore to invite me."

"You like playing with fire, don't you?"

"Actually, no, I like peace and quiet."

Kowalski grunted. "Then go pick lilacs and read a book tomorrow. Watch the birds."

"I had coffee with Huck Boone this afternoon," she said.

Another two-second silence.

He knows about Huck. Quinn felt her hand on the phone turn clammy. "I'm coming into traffic—I need to hang up."

She clicked off, tossing the phone onto the seat. Traffic was fine. She just didn't need another federal agent second-guessing her. If the FBI and the marshals had bad guys to catch, they could go catch them. She'd stay out of their way. In the meantime, Oliver Crawford was her neighbor, Breakwater Security wasn't going anywhere, and the best thing she could do—Huck had even said so—was to resume her normal routine.

In April, she'd spend the weekend at her cottage.

If invited to a party at the Crawford estate, she'd go in a heartbeat.

28

Although it wasn't yet dusk, tall white candles lit the elegantly set table in the formal dining room. Huck didn't want to be there. He had already refused Oliver Crawford's offer for him to sit at the long, antique table, with its high-backed upholstered chairs.

Everything was cream, crystal and silver. Tasteful. Crawford seemed to match his surroundings in his light-colored suit and tie, the candlelight flickering in his eyes. "Come, Boone," he said, "tell me about your work. I want to hear how we're doing from someone getting put through his paces. Are we ready for new trainees?"

"We will be," Huck said, telling the truth. As far as he could see, Breakwater Security was up and running, moving ahead fast with its plans to enter the high-stakes, competitive world of protective services and training.

Sharon Riccardi, who'd spotted Huck when he'd arrived back at the compound and all but ordered him inside, stood back, as if to give him space, room to show off before the boss. She'd dressed for dinner, wearing an ankle-length black skirt with a white wrap-top that plunged low. Huck was still in the clothes he wore to Washington. She raised her wineglass at him. "Mr. Boone seems to relish the physical challenges of our work here."

"I like to stay in shape." He didn't know what else to say.

Crawford seemed interested. "Joe Riccardi says you helped him design the training course here."

"The design was in place," Huck said. "I just worked with him to fine-tune it."

"I understand it's similar to what the feds put their special operatives through—the FBI Hostage Rescue Team, the U.S. Marshals Service's Special Operations Group." He paused, adding, as if it was some kind of secret he was letting Huck in on, "Others."

What Breakwater was setting up was good, and if it was a legit outfit, the training program would produce competent personnel. But Breakwater wasn't a legitimate outfit. Huck kept his tone even as he said, "So long as it's effective training, I guess it doesn't matter."

Joe Riccardi came in from the adjoining living room, dressed down in khakis and a Breakwater Security polo shirt. There didn't seem to be a place set for him at the table. "We're not trying to compete with HRT, SOG, Delta," Riccardi said. "They're who we call when we get into trouble. Our mission as private contractors is quite different from that of law enforcement. We just want capable people."

His wife concurred, her demeanor professional, low-key, almost as if she was trying to persuade Huck of the righteousness of their work. "Law enforcement doesn't have the same latitude we do. You'd think it was the other way around, but it's not."

"We can't break laws, of course," Crawford broke in. His tone was sincere, no hint of sarcasm, no wink and nod.

Huck, banking a surge of frustration at all the doublespeak in the room, picked up a glass of ice water. "Pay's better, too."

"That helps us recruit good people like yourself." Crawford sat back with his wine, his eyes on Huck. "Do you believe a private security firm like Breakwater should play by the rules? Or should we put our talents to use in a variety of ways, push the envelope—be creative?"

"You said yourself we can't break the law."

"But whose laws? So much happens these days transnationally. Look at my situation. I'm an American citizen who was kidnapped in the territorial waters of a small Caribbean island protectorate. My kidnappers were a variety of nationalities. They took me to another island nation."

"I see what you mean," Huck said.

Sharon Riccardi sipped her wine. "We're witnessing globalization on every level."

While her husband's expression remained neutral, Crawford immediately seemed more animated than he had earlier. "Politicians argue about legal infrastructure and nuances of interrogation techniques, and people like me—honest businessmen— are going about our business and trying to protect ourselves." His eyes shone. "I see nothing wrong with it."

Huck shrugged. "Me neither. I heard what happened to a couple of your kidnappers in Colombia. In my mind, they had it coming."

A distance came into Crawford's expression. When he didn't answer right away, Sharon Riccardi snatched a plate of cookies off the table and stepped forward, offering them to Huck. "They're linzer cookies. The raspberry filling's to die for."

"I guess I could die for worse," Huck said with a fake grin, taking a cookie.

She changed the subject. "I understand you found your own way back from Washington today."

"That's right."

"How?"

Ethan Brooker drove him. Even in a suit and tie, Brooker exuded competence. He would have taken Huck to Breakwater's front gate, but Huck had him drop him off in the village and walked out to the compound.

None of which he was telling Crawford and the Riccardis.

"I had Scotty beam me back down here," he said.

Joe took a sharp breath, not hiding his irritation, but Sharon smiled. "Did Quinn Harlowe give you a ride?"

"A friend," he said. "Most people have friends in Washington, don't they?"

"Where did you go after you left Travis?"

Huck bit into the cookie. "I got a pedicure."

Now she got frosty. "You're not used to answering to anyone, are you, Boone?"

He didn't respond. Crawford, who seemed more amused by the exchange than annoyed, collected himself. "But you did see Quinn Harlowe today?"

"We had coffee."

"That was Lubec's idea," Joe Riccardi said.

Crawford nodded. "Was it? I'm sure he had his reasons. Quinn's inquisitive—Gerry Lattimore thinks the world of her. I've invited them both to the open house here tomorrow."

Huck forced himself not to react. "You spoke to her?"

"No, I invited her through Gerry. He'll be here."

And so will Quinn. Huck had no illusions. If invited, she'd come. Hell, if she *wasn't* invited, she'd come—she'd paddle over in her kayak and jump over the barbed-wire fence, probably in her party dress.

"Quinn seems to have taken a liking to you," Crawford said.

"I wouldn't go that far. I was there right after she found her friend."

"A terrible tragedy. Gerry's very broken up about her death. Unfortunately—" Crawford set his wineglass down, pausing as he took a cookie from the plate Sharon had returned to the table. "Unfortunately, a rumor's come to my attention that the federal government might be interested in what we're doing here."

Huck bit into his cookie. "Interested as in suspicious?"

Sharon answered, her voice quiet, no edge to her tone. "I wouldn't go that far."

"We have nothing to hide," her husband said stiffly.

Sharon stood next to him. "That's right. If the FBI or anyone else wants to investigate us, fine. We're a legitimate operation. You've had a look at us from top to bottom, Huck. Wouldn't you agree?"

He shrugged. "Absolutely."

"However," she went on, "an open investigation is one thing. Spying is another. We don't want the federal government or anyone else infiltrating us, spying on us. No one would. If Quinn Harlowe is stirring the pot—"

"Then we need to know," Huck finished for her.

Crawford tilted his head back, his eyes half-closed as he studied Huck. "I'd like you to keep an eye on her, Boone. She seems to get along with you. Check in with her from time to time."

"That's not exactly the kind of mission I had in mind when I signed on—"

"Nor did I," Joe said quietly. He clearly didn't like the idea.

"It's not a mission," Crawford said. "It's an informal request. Quinn's absorbing a difficult blow with the loss of her friend, and given Alicia Miller's behavior in the hours, perhaps days, before she drowned, there are bound to be questions. I don't want them backfiring on us here. We're at a delicate stage."

Joe nodded, reluctant. "That's true. Bad publicity now could kill a start-up operation. We don't have a reputation years in the making to fall back on."

"That's right," his wife said. "If the first time people hear of Breakwater Security it involves the death of a Justice Department lawyer—well, that can't be good. We don't need Quinn Harlowe out there asking questions, spinning conspiracies, and turning what is clearly a tragic accidental drowning into something more sinister."

"If you're worried about Quinn Harlowe," Huck asked, "why invite her to the party tomorrow?"

Sharon Riccardi's eyes seemed to glow with intensity. Her husband was harder to read. Crawford ate his cookie, then answered. "It's a way to reassure her about us, at least indirectly."

"Okay," Huck said. "Your call."

"We'll enjoy ourselves tomorrow," Crawford added quietly. "I haven't hosted a social event since I was kidnapped. Many of my guests will be seeing me for the first time since my rescue. What do you think, Boone? Do I look normal to you?"

This struck him as a strange question, but Crawford seemed intent on getting an answer. "You look fine," Huck said.

Joe Riccardi excused himself and retreated through the living room. Huck couldn't tell if Breakwater's chief of operations approved or disapproved of the torture and execution of his boss's kidnappers. Was he a part of the vigilante network—or not? Whose side was he on?

After a few more seconds, Huck decided his presence was no longer required, and said something innocuous about seeing everyone in the morning, and left, heading through the living room, back to the kitchen and out a side door.

As he walked down a brick path, he had to bank his frustration. If Oliver Crawford and the Riccardis were building their own private vigilante army, they sure were doing a damn good job of keeping him on the fringes.

He needed more than glowing eyes, tight lips, cryptic questions and locked doors.

He reminded himself that his job—his real job— required patience as well as a willingness to act.

"If Quinn Harlowe is stirring the pot…"

She was more than stirring, Huck thought. Knowingly or unknowingly, she'd turned up the heat on all of them.

She could trust him. But could he trust her?

The air was warm, pleasant, laced with the salty, fishy tang of bay and marsh at low tide.

Huck wondered if Quinn was back in Yorkville, ready for her party tomorrow. Then he remembered he'd just been tasked to keep an eye on her.

No time like the present.

29

When Quinn parked in the driveway next to her cottage, for a split second everything seemed quiet and peaceful, as if she were arriving for a normal getaway weekend of work and relaxation.

But as she stepped out of her car, she saw an osprey soar above the bay and felt a pang of loss—and a surge of frustration. There were so many unanswered questions about why and how Alicia had died. Now one of her colleagues had maneuvered his way into Quinn's office, perhaps had searched it, and wasn't returning her calls. Quinn had left messages on every phone number she had for him—office, cell, apartment. She took his non-response as a confirmation of his culpability. He *had* looked through her stuff.

Quinn felt a gust of chilly air, the temperature on the bay much cooler than in the city. The lilacs, she noticed, had come into bloom, the breeze tinged with their soft, soothing fragrance.

Normally, she would tell herself she didn't mind being on the sidelines. By staying out of the center of the action, she could maintain a clear mind and a level of objectivity. She didn't have to plunge herself into the fray.

This is different.

Alicia had come to her for help, and Quinn still didn't know why, what she was supposed to have done to keep her friend from drowning in the bay.

Now there was Huck McCabe, the undercover federal agent. Quinn pictured his dark green eyes, not at all unreadable—he didn't like her knowing his status.

One of your brighter moves, Harlowe. Telling him.

He didn't like having her on the periphery, never mind in the middle, of his investigation, whatever it was. If she meddled, he wouldn't hesitate to put her under surveillance or arrest her or *something.*

Unless…

She didn't want to finish the thought, but it had hung around in the back of her mind for hours.

What if the feds were investigating *her?*

She knew Oliver Crawford. She'd let Alicia stay at her cottage. Alicia had come to her for help. Quinn had found her friend dead. Now, Steve Eisenhardt had searched her office. On his own? Or had someone put him up to it?

Did he believe she was involved in Alicia's death somehow—or was he acting on behalf of someone else? Someone at Breakwater? Lattimore? The FBI?

As unsettling as any of those prospects were, Quinn knew exactly what she'd done and hadn't done.

Maybe, she thought, worrying about staying on the sidelines was a moot point.

She grabbed her backpack of work and tote bag of clothes out of the car and carted them into the cottage, dumping them onto her bed, then headed back to the kitchen. Evening was coming fast. Hungry, distracted, edgy, she put on a kettle for tea, hoping to clear her head. She dug out a mismatched teacup and saucer and a white linen napkin, all at least fifty years old, and set her small table.

As she waited for the water to come to a boil, she fought back an unwelcome sense of loneliness. She'd never meant for the cottage to be an isolated retreat. She'd always pictured friends, family, joining her, if not all the time—a lot of the time. But who would want to visit now?

She looked out at her cove, gray-blue with the fading sunlight, and thought she saw baby ospreys in the sprawling nest.

"The osprey will kill me."

Her throat tightened. "Oh, Alicia. What were you up to here in Yorkville?"

But no answer came, just the wash of the tide and the cry of seagulls out on the open bay.

After her tea, Quinn resisted taking an evening walk. She didn't want to run into Diego Clemente. If she said something she shouldn't, who knew what he'd do. She had no desire to end up in the bottom of his boat, out of circulation. As much as she tried to tell herself she was being dramatic, she didn't know how Clemente had reacted to the news she'd made him and Huck. Surely Huck would have told him by now. Clemente was Huck's backup—his eyes and ears in the village. It was his job to protect Huck and their investigation.

Drama, Quinn thought, heading for the shower.

An hour later, her skin was still pink from her shower. She'd turned the water up as hot as she could stand it. She shook out her dress for Oliver Crawford's open house and tried to remember when she'd last worn it. She'd attended social functions at least once a week when she was at Justice, but, more often than not, would end up wearing whatever she'd had on at work, running from office to cocktail party.

Since leaving Justice, she'd felt more pressure, not less, to join the Beltway cocktail circuit. There'd been no shortage of invitations. Although she liked parties and recognized the importance of networking, lately she'd find herself digging around in the Society's musty, cluttered attic, glancing at her watch as party time approached, and ending up just not going—or hitting the road to Yorkville, a list of local weekend yard sales in hand.

Quinn slipped into the silky champagne dress. At least it still fit, although she didn't remember the neckline having such a deep V.

The silk brocade of her 1930s shawl reminded her of the blues of the bay, with a thread of champagne that matched her dress. She wrapped it over her bare shoulders, its long fringe tickling her arms, and spun out into the living room, pretending she had nothing more serious on her mind than an upper-crust open house in a beautiful bayside location.

She didn't think about armed bodyguards and undercover federal agents and kidnapping survivors and a troubled friend who was dead.

Opening her porch door, she welcomed the fresh breeze coming in through the screen, the smell of the water—and more than a hint of lilac. She put aside her questions and her ghosts, her fears, and danced barefoot out to the kitchen.

When she danced back into the living room, she stopped abruptly, noticing a figure in the doorway, and recognized Huck Boone/McCabe just in time to stifle a startled yell.

He wore a work shirt and jeans, and he shook his head at her. "You must have nerves of steel, Harlowe, dancing by yourself out here in a skimpy cocktail dress, your front door wide open."

"My dress is not skimpy, and my door—I was letting in the evening air." The shawl fell off her shoulders, landing in the crook of her arms. "How long have you been standing there?"

"Not long enough." He smiled. "I was hoping you'd do a couple dips before you saw me."

"No dips. I'm not that good a dancer."

He made no move to come inside. "You're not that bad, either."

She took a breath, her heart pounding from exertion and the start he'd given her, showing up on her front porch. "What are you doing here?"

"I was driving past and saw your door open. Thought I'd stop and say hi."

"You didn't walk—"

"I'm in my Rover."

"It's a dead-end road."

He shrugged. "I needed to turn around."

Quinn stood on the other side of the screen door, giving him a skeptical look, but she noticed that nothing about him was relaxed. The humor—the ir-reverence—was just a facade. But she tried not to re-act, and said, "I think you're checking up on me."

"Do you?"

"Did you follow me here?"

"If I did, you'd never know it."

She managed a smile. "Cocky, aren't you?"

"You're in your own little world here. You're not even playing music, but you didn't hear me walk up onto your porch." He tapped the screen, in front of her nose. "A screen door's not much protection."

"It's locked."

He just raised his eyebrows.

"I keep the doors and windows open as much as possible." She slipped the near-useless lock on the screen door and pushed it open, stepping out onto the porch. The floorboards were cool under her bare feet. "Otherwise, I might as well stay in Washing-ton. I like the bay breeze."

Some of the guardedness in his eyes receded, al-though he didn't relax. "Kind of cool tonight, isn't it?"

With a rush of heat, Quinn remembered she'd tried on her dress straight from the shower and hadn't bothered with undergarments. The filmy fabric and cold air left little to the imagination. And Huck had noticed—he couldn't not have noticed, even if he hadn't been trained to take in everything around him.

"Maybe it's cool by California standards," she said. "I think it's gorgeous. I was just trying on my dress for the open house tomorrow—"

"You're not going to the open house," he said.

"No? Did Oliver Crawford rescind his invitation?"

"Quinn—"

"Because I can call him and ask." Without giving Huck a chance to respond, she took a step back, resisting the urge to cross her arms over her breasts. "I think my outfit works okay. If it didn't—well, then I might not go."

His gaze drifted from her head to toes and back as he smiled. "I don't know about the bare feet."

"I've got strappy heels."

"Ah. Thank God."

She lifted her shawl back over her shoulders, subtly covering her breasts. "Gerard Lattimore's going to be at the party tomorrow. It'll be fine."

"Your buddy Special Agent Kowalski says you like to play with fire."

"So, you two have talked. I see." She tried to keep her tone neutral. "And Clemente?"

"Quinn, we've had one body wash up onto shore—"

"I'm aware of that." She tried to ignore the rush of images of the gulls at Alicia's body, the sudden jolt of mixed emotions. "I think it's best for me to do what I would normally do. If I don't—that would just draw more attention to me."

"You have plenty of attention on you as it is."

"Then all the more reason for you not to interfere."

He shook his head. "Don't even think you can help me. You're a historian. You might like playing with fire, but it's not real to you—"

"Did I say I could help you? If I do something wrong, you guys in the field can get hurt. I'm aware of my responsibilities, as well as my limitations."

"I'm not belittling you." His tone didn't soften. "I'm saying—"

"Anyone in my position would jump at the chance to go to a Crawford social function." Quinn tightened her shawl around her. "It'd look more suspicious if I didn't go tomorrow."

Huck sighed suddenly. "You must be hell in a meeting. Do you ever let yourself get sidetracked?"

"Not when I know I'm right. I listen, of course."

"Ha."

"I'm not arrogant, if that's what you're thinking."

"It's not." He smiled, and, with one finger, touched her shawl, just below her collarbone. "You've got a moth hole."

"Only a tiny one. It adds character." She felt a little breathless, and self-conscious, as if she'd just exposed too much of herself to this man—too many of her weaknesses. "Our grandmothers might have worn a shawl like this one to a pre–World War Two dinner dance. Have you ever been to a dinner dance?"

"Several."

"Not in your present line of work—"

"As a kid. My parents like that sort of thing."

"It sounds fun—I think. I'd wear a shiny, elegant dress—long, with a wide skirt so I wouldn't trip when I danced." She couldn't believe she was talking about dinner dances, but it was better than arguing about tomorrow's open house, having him probe her motives. "But then, I'd have to learn to dance."

"You've never taken lessons?"

"Not in my family. If I wasn't wandering through Civil War battlefields and hiding in musty corners of the Society headquarters with a book, I was supposed to be learning to dive, climb mountains, whitewater kayak, navigate, fly planes—not dance." She tilted her head back at him. "What about you? Did you ever learn to dance?"

"You bet." Without warning, he draped a muscular arm around her middle and swept her across the porch. "Follow my lead." He spoke softly into her ear. "A simple waltz step. One, two, three, one, two, three—"

"Should I ignore your holster and gun?"

"Sure. I'm not in a shooting mood."

Huck seemed to hold her closer, or she'd leaned into him without realizing it. He picked up his pace just enough that she tightened her hold on him, her shawl trailing down her arms and back. "I'm not all that coordinated…"

"You can do it." Settling his arm low on her back, he moved more smoothly than she'd have imagined for a man of his build and profession. "There you go. Easy, isn't it?"

"I'm going to step on your toes—"

"So long as I don't step on yours. I'd break a few."

Somehow, he managed to get the screen door open and waltz her into the living room, gracefully, nothing about him self-conscious or awkward or stiff. Her head seemed to spin, and yet she didn't falter, didn't trip over her shawl—and she only stepped on his toes twice.

In a low, sexy voice, he hummed a waltz tune into her ear, almost as if he were in another world.

"Huck…"

"It's okay. I'm not wired. Your cottage isn't bugged. No one will catch me singing and waltzing."

With a final swoop, he lifted her off her feet and dropped her effortlessly onto the couch.

Quinn gulped in air. "Where did you learn to dance like that?"

"My mother tried to make a gentleman out of me. She said I can never go wrong being a gentleman. I know how to tie a bow tie, do six different ballroom dances, eat with the right utensils, make small talk. And I learned not to drink the finger bowl." He sat beside her. "I don't look that civilized, do I?"

"Well, let's just say the small talk's a surprise. I don't imagine you suffer fools gladly—" She stopped, not knowing what to call him.

He looked at her. "Huck."

"That *is* your real name, yes? And these stories about your family—"

"All real. Think I'd make up learning how to waltz?"

She hesitated. "I'm not sure I know what you'd do."

"Probably just as well. My parents are open-minded by conviction and nature. Not a mean bone in their bodies. I, on the other hand—" He lifted Quinn's shawl back onto her shoulders. "Mean as hell."

"I don't know about that." She sat up straight, feeling a little light-headed now, and more than a little self-conscious. "I haven't had dinner, and I don't have anything here except tea. Lots of tea. I was thinking about crab cakes at the local marina. There's not much time before they close. Would you care to join me?"

"Only if you put on shoes."

"And take off the dress—I mean—" *Oh, hell.* "I'll change into jeans."

But as she jumped up, she got tangled up in her shawl and ended up whipping fringe into his face. When she tried to yank it back and apologize, she tripped on his feet, and fell onto his lap.

"I told you," she said. "I'm not that coordinated."

"An expert in international crime, and here you are in a moth-eaten shawl and bare feet, sprawled on the lap of a bodyguard—"

"An armed bodyguard."

He smiled, settling his arms around her. "I don't think you're as risk-avoidant as you like to pretend."

His mouth lowered to hers, but it was her idea to put her arms around his neck, their kiss, she thought, not so much sudden as inevitable. From the moment she'd seen him on her porch tonight, Quinn had known, on some level, that this would happen. She relished the feel of his mouth on hers, the taste of him as she let her palms travel up his arms, feeling the hard muscles under his denim jacket.

As she fell back against the couch, her shawl dropped to the floor and her dress rode up to her thighs. With a little jolt of panic, she remembered that she had absolutely nothing on under her dress.

Her mouth opened to the kiss, his hands coursing up her legs, then along the bare skin of her hips. She thought she heard his breath catch. He lowered one hand, parting her legs ever so slightly, teasing her with his fingers. She responded to his touch with a small gasp of her own, and a flood of wet heat.

"I want to make love to you," he whispered. "Now, tonight."

She brought one hand back down his arm, and, ignoring his holster and gun, down to his hip, her fingers drifting across his pants to his zipper. In a few swift moves, she could have him exposed. They could make love on the couch, in the bay breeze, keeping each other warm.

You are out of your mind...

The thought did nothing to stop her. With a feathery touch, she outlined the length and breadth of his erection, even as he slipped two fingers into her, his mouth finding hers again as he thrust tongue and fingers in the same erotic rhythm. Now she could barely breathe at all.

She placed her palm against him, pushing firmly, imagining his hardness inside her as they indulged the sexual tension that had sparked between them. She imagined herself naked under him. Finding his belt, she undid the buckle, fumbling, then lowered his zipper. Her dress was up to her waist now. He withdrew his fingers, cupping her with his palm.

"Quinn..." His voice was ragged, his eyes dark on her.

With a boldness that surprised her, she wrapped her hand around him, his erection thick and hot, so close to her she had only to guide him a few inches.

"We're not—" She couldn't believe what she was saying. "Huck, this is just nerves."

He pulled back so fast she almost landed on the floor. "Damn. I'm sorry."

"Sorry?"

He gave her a ragged smile. "Well, not that sorry."

He swept her shawl up and gently tossed it over her, and when she got up, this time she didn't trip. She fled back to the bedroom and stripped off her dress, threw it and her shawl onto the bed, and pulled on underwear, jeans, a cotton sweater, thick socks and running shoes. The marina was casual. She took a moment to dab on lipstick, using her bureau mirror, noticing that her cheeks were flushed. *What has gotten into you?* She had no idea, but doubted Huck had come there to dance with her, or make love to her, or do anything except his job.

Which job?

Who was he tonight, Huck Boone of Breakwater Security—or Huck McCabe of the U.S. Marshals Service?

Quinn pushed back her doubts but didn't chastise herself for them. Staying on guard made sense. Asking questions. Being analytical, objective. She could even rationalize dinner with a man she was almost certain hadn't told her even half the truth about himself and his reasons for being in Yorkville.

But she liked the idea of not having dinner alone.

30

Huck didn't know what was going on with him, but it sure as hell wasn't nerves. As he and Quinn walked along the dock of Yorkville's small marina, tucked in an inlet just off the loop road, he imagined a different kind of night, one where Quinn wasn't tortured by a friend's death and he wasn't working, torn by his responsibilities and sense of duty—and the sense of danger he felt. Hanging out with paranoid vigilantes and private security types was bad enough, but his uneasiness had more to do with what the network he was supposed to penetrate had planned. These weren't people who liked to stay idle for long.

Walking with Quinn Harlowe on a beautiful spring night only heightened his awareness of the stakes.

"That's Gerard Lattimore's boat," she said, pointing to a yacht at a slip about thirty yards down along the main dock. "Yorkville's a bit quiet for his tastes. When he was married, his wife almost never came down here with him. She doesn't like boats. I think he comes more because of his friendship with Oliver Crawford."

"Not because of you?"

"No." She didn't elaborate. "It doesn't look as if he's here yet. Maybe he'll come in the morning. He was on his way to a meeting when he called to invite me to the open house. I left town early—I have more flexibility than he does now that I'm out on my own."

"Lattimore wants you back at Justice," Huck said.

She shrugged. "I suppose that's better than breathing a sigh of relief that I quit."

"Why did you quit?"

"Flexibility, opportunity, the chance to be my own boss." She smiled. "I had illusions of having a life."

They stopped at a spot along the dock where there were no boats, the water black under the night sky, reflecting here and there the gleam of lights from boats and the rustic restaurant. A variety of pleasure boats and fishing boats bobbed in the low tide.

A quiet night in Yorkville, Huck thought.

Quinn stood next to him. Her hair seemed blacker, her skin paler, almost translucent, but her eyes had taken on some of the darkness around her. "Lattimore doesn't know anything about you, does he?" she asked.

"The fewer people who know about me, the better I like it."

"I'm not going to give you away. I can be discreet."

Huck let her comment go. After dancing and nearly making love in her cottage, he figured neither of them could claim discretion.

"I was still at Justice when Oliver Crawford was kidnapped," she went on quietly.

"Lattimore must have gone apeshit."

"It was a tense time. I left not long after Crawford was rescued. The FBI was investigating—I assume they still are." She looked back out at the water. "They must have briefed you."

"Quinn—"

"I'm not asking. I'm just saying." She paused, squinting down the dock, toward the marina, then touched Huck's wrist. "That's Lattimore there."

Huck, who'd only seen pictures of the deputy assistant AG, saw a good-looking, gray-haired man in a dark suit get out of a Breakwater SUV and shut the door, waving to the driver. The SUV backed out. Vern? Lubec? One of the Riccardis? Perhaps Oliver Crawford himself, Huck thought, watching Lattimore, caught in a dim streetlight, spot Quinn and smile, then join them out on the dock.

"Hello, Quinn." He nodded to Huck. "Who's your friend?"

Before she could answer, Huck said, "Huck Boone, sir. I work at Breakwater Security."

"Huck was on a run when I found Alicia," Quinn said, then introduced him. "Huck, this is Gerard

Lattimore, my former boss at the Justice Department."

"Good to meet you," Lattimore said, shaking hands with Huck. "I'm sorry you and Quinn met under such difficult circumstances. We're all still grappling with the tragedy. Alicia was a wonderful person, a very talented attorney."

"I'm sorry for your loss," Huck said.

He nodded his thanks, but said nothing.

Quinn deftly changed the subject. "Was that a Breakwater SUV? Were you out there?"

"Only for a few minutes. Ollie offered me a lift from Washington aboard one of his helicopters. He'd gone on ahead of me, but a few of his people were still in town. I just got here—a couple of Ollie's meats dropped me off." He sputtered into embarrassed laughter. "Boone, sorry. I didn't mean to impugn the work you do. I've been in situations where I've required a private protective detail, and it's very comforting to know how well trained you people are."

"No offense taken," Huck said.

"I'm afraid I shouldn't have had that one drink with Ollie. It went right to my head."

"How will you get back to Washington?" Quinn asked her former boss.

"Same way. Helicopter." He recovered himself somewhat. "I didn't use to like helicopters, but when you sail above snarled Beltway traffic—suddenly you don't think it's such a bad way to travel. Not that I'm in Ollie's league when it comes to private helicopters ferrying me around. I'm just a government employee."

"Huck and I are on our way to dinner. Would you care to join us?"

"Oh, thanks, but no—please, don't let me keep you." Lattimore made a broad gesture toward his boat. "I'm going to settle in for the rest of the evening. Enjoy yourselves. Boone—I'll see you tomorrow?"

"Yes, sir, I'm sure you will."

"Ollie's first social event since he was kidnapped, you know."

Huck nodded. "So I've been told."

But Lattimore turned his attention back to Quinn, started to say something, then abandoned the effort and, without another word, headed for his boat. He wasn't staggering, but he was obviously not entirely sober, either.

"Guess he's had a long day," Huck said. "I'll say it again—I think he has a crush on you. Threw him to see you out here with me."

Quinn scowled at him. "That's ridiculous. Gerard's only recently divorced—"

"Gerard, huh?"

"Oh, stop." But she smiled. "You're not even that funny, you know."

"I'm very funny."

"Well, Gerard is obviously under a lot of stress. I'm sure he's hardly even thought about dating again, never mind striking up any kind of relationship with me. I have an interesting family background, but the Harlowes have always been more eccentric than well connected."

"Seeing you wouldn't do him any good."

"I don't mean to make him sound crass—"

"A guy in his position, with his ambitions, needs to be strategic about who he lets himself fall for." Huck winked at her. "Unlike those of us who exercise no sense whatsoever."

"And which describes you? Are you the strategic type or the no-sense type?"

"Me? I'm not supposed to be falling for anyone, for any reason, strategic or stupid." He started back along the dock with her, the cool night air or the lights—he couldn't tell which—turning Quinn's lips blue. "And you?"

"None of the above."

"Meaning?"

"I don't want to be strategic or stupid. I just want to fall in love." She looked at him, her directness, her bright smile, catching him off guard. "I do try to stay away from heartbreakers."

"I can't see anyone wanting to break your heart, Quinn."

Although she must have heard him, she pretended not to, shooting out ahead of him. "The restaurant will be closing soon," she said, glancing over her shoulder. "We should get a table."

Once they were inside the small restaurant, a middle-aged man Quinn knew by name showed them to a table overlooking the water, with blue cloth napkins, fresh daisies in a flowered vase and a white votive candle flickering in a clear-glass holder.

Quinn ordered wine with her crab cakes, but Huck stayed away from alcohol. Gun or no gun, he wasn't drinking tonight.

Across the room, Joe Riccardi was drinking alone at the bar, no sign of his wife or their mutual boss, or any of his Breakwater crew. He carried his drink over to their table. "I thought I saw you head out earlier, Boone." He nodded politely at Quinn. "Nice to see you, Ms. Harlowe."

"You, too, Colonel Riccardi," she said smoothly. "Huck's keeping me from getting stuck having dinner alone."

"I understand Mr. Crawford invited you to the open house tomorrow." Riccardi spoke in his usual neutral tone. "I'd be glad to give you a personal tour of our training facility."

In other words, Huck thought, no sneaking around. Quinn didn't seem to take offense. "Thanks."

"We want to be as open as possible about what we're doing." Riccardi sipped his drink, an amber-colored liquid. "We don't want people creating fantasies about what we do."

"Not even good fantasies?"

Riccardi smiled at her, but not warmly. "We play by the rules."

"Whose rules?" She gave him a sharp look. "Oliver Crawford isn't known for his patience. He's known for pushing himself and everyone else. I'll bet he wants a state-of-the-art, high-quality security firm up and running with the snap of his fingers."

"He understands the importance of laying the proper foundation. We're dealing with people's safety. Their lives. Integrity and competence matter in this business more than all the bells and whistles." Riccardi's gaze bore into Quinn, but she didn't flinch. "I didn't realize you knew Mr. Crawford that well."

"We're neighbors, more or less." She raised her water glass. "I've been doing a little research on my own, talking to my contacts, checking the public record. Makes sense, doesn't it? I just found a friend dead under unusual, if not criminal, circumstances. If you were in my position, wouldn't you look into the people who'd seen her last?"

And she says she doesn't like playing with fire. Huck debated hauling her out of there and dumping her with Diego.

Riccardi polished off the last of his drink. "From what I understand, Ms. Harlowe, that would be you."

She didn't give up. "Whoever picked her up in the black sedan saw her after I did. I wouldn't be surprised if we all traipsed out to Ollie's place in the suburbs, we'd find shiny black Lincoln Town Cars—"

Huck broke in. "Drink's on me, Joe. I'll see you back at Breakwater."

Riccardi set his empty glass on the table, muttered a good-night and stalked out of the restaurant.

"He seems lonely," Quinn said, unrepentant.

Huck shook his head at her. "You're a pain in the ass, Harlowe. If he'd decided to throttle you, I'd have helped him."

She shrugged. "I'm sure that would have enhanced your reputation with your Breakwater buddies."

"You had to let him know you've been doing your homework on them, didn't you?"

Her wine arrived. When she picked up her glass, Huck saw the spots of pink in her cheeks, the sparkle in her eyes. She'd stayed cool, but she wasn't unaffected by her encounter with his retired army colonel boss.

She sipped her wine. "Think Joe Riccardi's the one who put Steve up to searching my office?"

"Uh-uh, Quinn. I'm not going there." Huck kept his voice low and calm, not because she'd care if he shook his finger in her face and yelled, but because he didn't want the few stragglers around them to notice he was on his last nerve. "You're done. You have a nice dinner. Then I take you back to your cottage, and you lock all your doors and windows, and I get my friend Diego to watch you. And in the morning, you get a coffee-to-go at the local gas station and you drive back to Washington."

She drank more of her wine. "Now that I think about it, I have no idea what you did after you left me at my office."

"Quinn—"

"Did your guys put Steve up to sneaking into my office?" She didn't wait for an answer. "I told Special Agent Kowalski about him. Do you suppose he'd tell me if Steve turned up?"

"I wouldn't," Huck said.

She smiled. "Relax. Quit worrying about me. I promise—" She leaned over the table, her eyes shining. "I'll do up my hair and wear makeup and underwear and everything tomorrow. I'll blend in. I'll behave. I'll dazzle. I'll do whatever one does at an Oliver Crawford party, but I'll definitely stay out of your way."

Their meals arrived, and she dug into her crab cakes as if she hadn't eaten in days—or just needed something to do besides argue with him. "Do you think Riccardi is in over his head at Breakwater?" she asked.

"No. I think *you're* in over your head."

She waved her fork. "By Harlowe standards, I'm not even close."

"Keep it up, Quinn. Diego's out there." He nodded toward the water out their window. "He's not as patient as I am. He doesn't have a sense of humor."

"He's also very protective of you."

"That's his job."

"I'm glad." She sat back in her chair. "It must be good to know someone you trust is out there."

"You can trust him, too, Quinn. And you can trust me. Stop, okay? Take a step back. Let us do our jobs."

She didn't respond. Her mood had darkened. Huck studied her, realized that she wasn't easily pegged. He remembered the feel of her mouth, her soft skin, her hand on him, exploring, tempting. He wondered how far they'd have gotten if she hadn't brought up that bit about nerves. Would he have made love to her?

In a heartbeat, he thought, not feeling any better.

Suddenly, everything about his assignment seemed crazy and so unorthodox that he was tempted to drive back to Nate Winter's house and give it up. Help the Winters move. Talk to the ghosts.

But he was hungry, and he wasn't about to walk out and leave her to Gerard Lattimore.

31

Quinn figured she had two choices. Either she had to get back into the Rover with Huck, in the dark, and let him drive her back to her cottage, or she had to walk the two miles by herself—also in the dark.

"I can call you a cab," he said, as if he'd been reading her thoughts.

"All the cabs in this town smell like dead fish."

He didn't answer right away. "Hell, Quinn." He spoke almost in a growl, slipping both arms around her waist, kissing her softly, gently. "I keep thinking I'll come to my senses, but I'm not even close. Must be this East Coast climate. It's not nerves. That's for damn sure."

"That's why you can do the work you do." She smiled. "Nerves of steel."

He pulled back, ripping open the passenger door. "Nothing about kissing you makes me nervous."

Quinn stepped past him and climbed into the Rover, and when Huck sat next to her in the driver's seat, he kept his eyes forward. He drove out the loop road, along the waterfront. Quinn rolled down her window and let in the night air, the smells of low tide.

By the time they reached her cottage, she was in a pensive mood. "There's a difference between strong emotions and recklessness," she said, almost to herself.

He leaned toward her, touched her hair, her mouth. "You lost a friend. You don't know what's happening on the other side of the marsh. You don't like sitting on the sidelines." His gentle tone took her by surprise, but with an abrupt sigh, he sat back. "And you know you're out of your mind to have spent so much time with me today."

"Who's the one who keeps popping up? Are you keeping an eye on me for the Breakwater guys—or for the marshals?"

"Does it matter? Maybe a certain amount of recklessness goes with strong emotions."

"All the more reason to beware."

His eyes seemed almost black. "Yes. All the more reason. Stop asking questions. Stop sticking your thumb in people's eyes." He didn't smile. "Quinn, you didn't fail Alicia. She's not dead because of you."

Feeling the sudden sting of tears, Quinn fumbled for the door latch. "She came to me for help."

"Help her by standing back. No more calling up sources in Venezuela, okay?"

"I suppose I could go to Fredericksburg in the morning and do battlefield tours with my grandfather."

"Quinn, if I could, I'd go with you. I'd like nothing better."

She gave him a sceptical smile. "Except finding your bad guys. If I hear from Steve I'm going to ask him what he was doing in my office."

"If you hear from him, call Kowalski. If you're still here, there's always Clemente."

"Don't worry about me, okay?" She turned to him, made herself smile. "Go do your thing. Track down your bad guys."

"What if my bad guys are fixated on you?"

"I'll lock my doors."

Huck tensed, looking past her out the passenger window. He put his hand at the base of her neck. "Get down." Almost as a reflex, Quinn spun around, but he shoved her head down, reaching for his weapon. "Stay put."

"Boone?" The voice outside, toward the road, was more of a croak.

He swore under his breath. "It's Sharon Riccardi," he said to Quinn. "*Don't* move until I say so."

She nodded, staying low. There was no car on the dead-end road—how had Sharon Riccardi gotten out there?

Huck climbed out of the Rover, leaving his door open. "Mrs. Riccardi—"

"Sharon, Sharon, Sharon." She laughed awkwardly, sounding half-drunk. "How many times do I have to tell you?"

"Are you alone?"

"Yes, I walked through the marsh. There's a path. It winds all over the place. I'm afraid I stepped in water and mud. My God, I'm covered in mosquito bites."

Quinn edged up toward the window, staying out of sight as she peered in the side-view mirror. She could see Sharon Riccardi, unsteady on her feet, wobbling behind the Land Rover, waving her arms as if swatting at mosquitoes. She wore an ankle-length skirt and sandals that were totally inappropriate for a night walk through a salt marsh.

"My husband used to run this way before he got too busy with you all. Before that girl was found dead." Her tone was angry, accusatory, but then she gave a sudden, harsh laugh. "That takes the bloom off, doesn't it? Finding a dead woman out here, in such a beautiful spot."

"It's dark," Huck said. "Must have been a rough hike—"

"Your eyes adjust. And the moon—did you notice there's a half-moon? You'd be surprised what a difference it makes." She thrust her hands onto her hips. "Where's your Quinn Harlowe?"

"She's here. I had her duck in case—"

Sharon snorted. "What, did you think I was some kind of wild animal or worse?"

He didn't answer. Quinn pushed open her door and stepped out onto the driveway, noticing now that Sharon Riccardi was shivering from the chilly evening air. "Hello, Mrs. Riccardi. Huck kept me from having to eat dinner alone."

"Now, wasn't that nice?" She spoke with a sardonic edge, crossing her arms on her chest, as if to ward off the cool wind. "Boone's got quite the soft spot for you. You two must have bonded when you found your friend drowned…"

Huck moved in next to her, everything about him on alert. "I'll take you back to Breakwater, Sharon. The mosquitoes are eating you alive."

Her teeth chattering now, Sharon stayed focused on Quinn. "You're coming to the open house tomorrow, aren't you? Oliver's expecting you." She slapped a hand in Huck's direction, missing him. "I'm having Boone here park cars."

He didn't react. "I'll do whatever you need me to do. Come on. Let's go."

"Parking cars—" Sharon Riccardi staggered back a couple of steps. "It'll give you the chance to meet the kind of people who Oliver socializes with. His equals."

"Fine. I'll park cars. Guess you wouldn't want me pouring champagne or teaching the guests how to shoot."

She gave him a cool look. "You're a flip bastard, aren't you, Boone?" She swooped toward the Rover, hanging on to the door as Quinn stepped out of her way. "Miss Harlowe. You're prettier than I realized when you were at Breakwater the other day. You were in shock, of course, after your friend's death. But Oliver tells me you're very good at what you do."

"I appreciate that," Quinn said.

"Being out on your own—at least now you can think independently."

"I've always done my best to think independently, Mrs. Riccardi."

"Sharon." She smiled, visibly straining to stay upright. "Sharon, Sharon."

Before Quinn had a chance to respond, Huck pretty much shoved Sharon Riccardi into the Rover and shut the door. He turned to Quinn. "You'll be okay? I'll wait until you're inside—"

"That's not necessary."

"Give my best to your grandfather."

There was no undertone of humor in his words. They were, she realized, a strong recommendation—go to Fredericksburg in the morning. Skip the Breakwater open house.

Leave the Riccardis—and everything else—to him.

"Don't worry about me." Quinn gave him an irreverent smile. "Have fun parking cars."

Alone in her cottage, Quinn knew she wouldn't be able to sleep and set up her laptop and notes on the kitchen table. When she caught her reflection in the window, she winced and quickly pulled the curtains, remembering, with a jolt, how Alicia had approved of her choice of curtain fabric. *"Cute, but not cutesy."*

Forcing back more tears, Quinn opened a file on her laptop that included all the research she'd done in the days since Alicia's death on Breakwater Security and her neighbors across the marsh. She'd jotted down a list of key words and phrases, hoping that, together, a pattern would emerge—something.

The Caribbean. The Dominican Republic.

A kidnapped American entrepreneur with close ties to Alicia's former boss.

Venezuela. A kidnapping and rescue there.

Emerald smuggling.

Colombia. Mercenaries tortured and executed.

More emerald smuggling. The finest, most valuable emeralds in the world were found in the Colombian Andes.

"What am I missing?" Quinn asked aloud, pulling up a *Washington Post* article she'd stored in a separate file.

The piece detailed a sensational case last October involving vigilante mercenaries and a long list of crimes.

As she read the article, Quinn remembered more details of the case and the reaction within the halls of the Justice Department when people realized the vigilantes hadn't acted alone, but instead were part of a network.

Bingo.

Breakwater Security, isolated on Virginia's Northern Neck, funded by a traumatized wealthy entrepreneur, was the perfect setup for a violent anti-everything criminal network.

They could train new recruits—they could launch operations. They could do anything. A legitimate private security company run by a respected businessman gave them all the cover they needed. Did Oliver Crawford know? Shaken, Quinn closed all the files on her laptop and shut it down.

Now, at least, she knew what Huck Boone/Mc-

Cabe and Diego Clemente were doing in Yorkville, Virginia.

They were chasing a particularly violent, lawless, ideological bunch of vigilantes.

A stiff Joe Riccardi was out on the front porch when Huck returned. Without a word, Joe took his wife into the house. Sharon, too, was silent.

Huck turned to start back down the steps but the door opened behind him, and Oliver Crawford stepped out onto the porch. He'd changed into loose, casual clothes and looked older in the harsh mix of night and porch light. "A minute, Boone?" He didn't wait for an answer. "Sharon and Joe Riccardi are on the skids. I don't know if you've noticed."

"Maybe they're just feeling the pressure of getting Breakwater Security up and running." Huck kept any critical note out of his tone. "Everyone's worked hard, but they've worked the hardest."

"You could have a point." Crawford looked out into the darkness, the porch light casting long shadows onto the lush lawn. "Have you ever trusted someone and lived to regret it?"

"Haven't we all?"

"I suppose so. I don't like betrayals."

Huck studied the man, but couldn't tell what was on his mind. "No one does. Has someone betrayed you, Mr. Crawford?"

"I make the decisions here. I always have." His voice took on an icy edge. "Any failures and mistakes—ultimately, they're my responsibility."

"The captain of the ship."

Crawford didn't even seem to hear him. "I'm a risk-taker by nature. That's how I've gotten as far as I have. A small inheritance helped." He waved a hand, as if taking in his entire bayside estate, the breadth of his wealth. "You don't get to be where I am by sitting back and letting other people run ahead of you. You have to see the opportunities and seize them. Take action."

"Understood," Huck said. "Is there an opportunity you see now?"

But Crawford wasn't focused on future operations. He shook his head sorrowfully. "Ultimately, the kidnapping was my fault. I wasn't paying attention." He clapped a hand on Huck's shoulders. "Don't ever let people make decisions for you, Boone. Don't let them manipulate you. Even people you trust."

"What about teamwork?"

"Ah, yes. The 'there's no *I* in team' line. Always remember that a team is made up of individuals with their own personalities, their own agendas."

"Mr. Crawford…is Sharon Riccardi out of control?"

Crawford relaxed visibly, as if he'd wanted Huck to guess Sharon's name, then smiled. "She would think I'm the one out of control." He collected himself and started back toward the porch door. "Good night, Boone. Tomorrow should be interesting."

Conversation over. Huck knew if he pushed Crawford, he wouldn't get anything more out of him. "Uh-huh." He forced himself to grin. "I'm parking cars."

He waited until Crawford was back inside before he walked down to the converted barn. He wouldn't sleep tonight. Quinn, Steve Eishenhardt, Sharon Riccardi's night walk through the marsh, Joe's reaction—and Crawford, that remark about being out of control. Huck had the same feeling he'd had before Alicia Miller's death. It wasn't a premonition—it was instinct.

Something was wrong. This time, he meant to find out what *before* another body turned up.

32

Steve parked his borrowed car in a far corner of the Yorkville marina parking lot and tried to act as if he belonged there. He didn't want anyone looking for him—feds, goons, whoever—to spot him. He'd dressed in a baseball cap and bubba overalls, but doubted he'd pass for a redneck fisherman. If he was lucky, people would think he was some kind of boat hand, although he didn't know a thing about boats.

Most of the fishing boats were already long on the Chesapeake. It was midmorning, bright and sunny, the cool wind gusting hard, as he trotted onto the wooden dock. He was ragged and stiff, frayed at the edges from lack of sleep and fear. He'd spent the night in the car, moving from place to place to keep cops from shining a flashlight in his window.

He wanted a hot shower, food. Pancakes would be nice.

Gerard Lattimore was up, Steve could see now, dressed in battered canvas pants and a long-sleeved polo as he stood on the small outdoor deck of his yacht playing a rich guy roughing it in the sticks.

Without waiting for an invitation, Steve jumped aboard.

The deputy assistant AG gaped at him and instantly went pale. "Steve, what are you doing here?"

"I really don't look like a redneck fisherman, do I?"

"Are you trying to?"

"Not really." Steve decided he didn't have time to waste. "I like you, man. You did what you could to help Alicia. You're a stand-up guy. I'm not. I'm pond scum."

Lattimore lowered his voice. "Steve, the FBI wants to talk to you—"

"I know." He glanced around. "You're not under surveillance, are you?"

"What? No, of course not. I'd know—"

"Don't be so sure."

Some of Lattimore's legendary self-control slipped. "What do you mean?"

"You really don't know, do you? Shit." Steve didn't remember ever having sworn in front of his boss. "Your pal Ollie Crawford is under investigation."

"That's ridiculous. Start making sense or get out."

"The feds think Breakwater Security might be a front for vigilante mercenaries. Real psychos."

Lattimore was white now. He said nothing.

"Either your pal Ollie is involved with them or he's being used by them."

"That's absurd."

"No, it's not. You know it isn't, or you'd be screaming for the cops right now. Has Ollie talked vigilante crap to you?"

"No."

"But you suspect something's off about him, don't you?" Steve didn't relent, just stuck to what he'd come there to say. "You've been kept in the dark. Deliberately. In case you're involved—voluntarily or involuntarily."

"I won't be manipulated by you, Steve. You're obviously upset and desperate." Lattimore was so tight, he hissed when he spoke. "What's your role in this so-called investigation?"

"Weasel. That's my role."

Lattimore made a small choking sound. "Get off my boat."

"If I were you, Gerry, I'd hide my money and make sure my family's safe." Steve paused a moment, watching his boss's nostrils flare. "You've got daughters, right?"

"You bastard. Don't you even mention my daughters."

"I am a bastard. I have no illusions. Everything about me confirms Crawford's Nazis worst prejudices about lawyers and federal law enforcement."

"What the hell—"

"I'm trying to help you. I have my own selfish reasons, but most people do. Alicia's dead because

I couldn't help her—she wouldn't let me. The lunatics who work with Ollie—protect him, use him—thought she might be part of a federal investigation into their activities. Kind of an undercover agent."

"Steve, for the love of God—" Lattimore's voice held a note of panic. "I don't know what you're talking about. Did you kill Alicia? Is that what you're trying to tell me?"

"I might as well have." Steve could feel the regret well up in him. His compulsions, his desire to protect himself—he felt his throat constrict with fear and self-loathing and half wished he'd just have a stroke and drop dead on the spot. "I was in the car. The black sedan Quinn's been going on about. Alicia saw me—she was supposed to see me. I was someone she trusted."

"Dear God."

"A couple of Ollie's Nazis were up front. I didn't know at the time who they were. They slipped up yesterday and told their names, except—except I don't think it was a mistake. They wanted me to know. I haven't figured out why."

"Steve, you're not making any sense—"

"Quinn's been researching them. You know what she's like—she's got the mind for this sort of thing. They sent me to collect what I could from her office. Now they want me to get names."

"What names?" Lattimore twisted his hands together in controlled frustration. "Slow down. Start making sense."

"I told you—you've been kept in the dark.

There's a task force investigating these wing nuts. Your pal Ollie."

"Good God."

"Gerry, my friend, you're screwed. You're out here on your boat, expecting to go to a nice party—and the shit's hitting the fan all around you."

"What do these people have on you?" Gerard asked abruptly.

Steve felt his head spin, but he couldn't turn back now. "Don't think about me right now. Think about yourself. Think about whether you've done anything—told Ollie anything—that you'll live to regret. Decide whose side you're on."

"Steve, are you wired?" Lattimore dropped his hands to his sides in a kind of sad resignation. "Are you waiting for me to betray myself somehow?"

"I only wish I were working for the feds."

"If what you say is true, you took a hell of a risk to come here. Why?"

"Because you're innocent."

"Bullshit, Eisenhardt." Lattimore's voice croaked now. "You're trying to save your own skin. You need to talk to the FBI. Tell them everything."

"Not without a deal."

"So that's it." Lattimore seemed almost relieved that Steve had finally said something he could understand. "You want my help to cut a deal."

Steve gulped, hating himself—hating the position he was in. "My only chance is to disappear or turn state's evidence. The more I have to offer, the better. I'm not as big a creep as these guys think."

"My God, Steve. You think I *am* involved with

these vigilantes. You want me to give you something you can use to save yourself." He inhaled sharply, maintaining his self-control now. "I'm calling the FBI."

But Steve was already onto the dock, running. He knew Gerard Lattimore wouldn't follow him—and if he was smart, he wouldn't call the feds. Instead, Gerry Lattimore would find his own way of running.

Quinn shoved her hands into the pockets of her oversize sweatshirt, the hood protecting her head against a stiff, cold wind as she walked up her narrow dead-end road. The wind had whipped up whitecaps on the water, even in her quiet cove, but it was supposed to calm down by midday and turn warm.

If the undercover marshals in town had their way, she'd be up on Lee's Hill by then, talking Civil War history with her grandfather. But it wasn't going to be that way.

Over her morning tea, she'd opened up the small spiral pad in which she'd jotted notes and found the top three pages missing.

The shock of her discovery was still fresh. "Steve," she whispered, shoving her hands even deeper into her sweatshirt pockets. "The bastard."

He *had* searched her office. She had confirmation now. She spotted Maura Scanlon on her hands and knees in her side yard, pulling weeds in her vegetable garden, obviously absorbed in her work. But she sat back on her heels, wiping her brow with the back of her wrist. "I saw you coming up the road." She peeled off bright orange garden gloves that matched her bright orange overshirt, then got up stiffly.

"I'm trying to give everything a good weeding before we leave for North Carolina. Don's packing. We're off to visit our daughter for a few days."

"Is this a spur-of-the-moment trip?"

She averted her eyes. "We're not having an easy time putting Alicia's death behind us."

"It's been difficult, I know." Quinn gestured at the small, tidy garden. "Your peas look great."

"Don't they?" Maura concurred, but there seemed to be no pleasure in her response. "They'll be ready by the time we get back. I've been working in the garden day in and day out since last week. There's nothing quite like gardening to soothe the soul."

"I haven't touched my garden at all this spring."

"Well, that's understandable. Alicia was a beautiful young woman taken from us too soon." A gust of wind whipped her gray hair. "How are you managing?"

"Better."

"I don't mean to bring up a difficult subject…"

"No, it's okay. Actually, I'm here because I wanted to talk to you about Alicia. I've had the impression that you and Don know something that you didn't want to talk about. Maybe you thought it was inappropriate under the circumstances."

Maura looked away. "Sometimes neighbors see and hear things. It happens. Don and I don't pry—"

"Nosy neighbors you are not," Quinn said with a quick smile.

"Alicia was sweet. She tried to pretend she loved it here, but we never thought she did. At first, she seemed just to want to keep to herself. She was obviously unhappy…depressed."

"A lot of people thought she was burned out at work."

"I think it was more than that." Maura clearly was reluctant to say too much. "She became more animated in the past couple weekends here. I'm not sure I'd say she was any happier. Oh, Quinn. I hate to gossip about someone who's passed on."

"I understand. Alicia came to me before she died. She was very upset—anxious, frightened. I couldn't make sense of much of what she said." Quinn squatted and plucked up a dandelion, then stood up, tossing it into the pile Maura had made of her weeds. "I can't help but feel I could have done more to save her."

"I wonder if there's anything Don and I could have done too."

"Please, Maura. I knew Alicia for a long time. I won't pretend we didn't have our problems in recent months." Quinn brushed the dirt off her hands. "It's possible there's more going on here than any of us wants to believe. I think that's why you and Don are heading to North Carolina."

Maura sighed, nodding. "It's as if things are bubbling under the surface." She stared out at the water a moment. "We suspect that Alicia and Oliver Crawford were having an affair."

"Alicia and Crawford?"

"Well, we can't be sure, of course, but we saw him here several times. He came alone, without his usual entourage."

Quinn tried to picture Alicia and Oliver Crawford as a couple. Alicia had always gone for powerful men—but Crawford? Quinn couldn't see it.

"We could be wrong," Maura added quickly. "But he did come here alone—we were surprised he was alone, especially after what happened to him over the winter. The kidnapping and everything."

"Maybe he just feels safe in Yorkville. Do you know if he ever stayed overnight?"

"Oh, no. I'm sure he didn't. Perhaps *affair* is too strong a word."

"Did Alicia ever meet him at Breakwater?"

"We think she would kayak over there. She'd pretend to go into the marsh, but you know Alicia had no interest in bird-watching or nature walks." Maura's face had reddened. "I'm not condemning either of them. If she found some happiness in the weeks before her death, then that's a good thing."

"When did you first see Crawford over here?" Quinn asked.

"Mid-March. The second or third weekend Alicia started to stay out here." She smiled faintly, her color subsiding somewhat. "Truly, Quinn, we don't like to spy on our neighbors."

"You don't? That's no fun." Quinn tried to lighten the mood. "I spy on you and your husband all the time. One morning, you'll be having coffee on your porch. Another morning, he'll be watering the garden and you'll be taking a walk—"

Maura laughed, finally relaxing again. "We worked hard to be able to lead such boring lives in retirement." But she fumbled with her garden gloves, avoiding Quinn's eye. "We didn't tell Special Agent Kowalski or the local police any of this. If they'd asked, of course we'd have told them what we saw, but otherwise—" She shook her head. "It's just gossip among friends."

Kowalski and the locals would want to know, Quinn thought. So would the undercover marshals in town. "Maura, I can't keep this secret. I think you know that." She glanced at her friend and neighbor and smiled gently. "That's why you told me."

"Don and I have been fretting over what to do for days. It doesn't feel like such a betrayal of Alicia to tell you. We know you have to do what you feel is right." She shrugged, looking as if a burden had been lifted from her. "We see what we see."

"Alicia was burned out—"

"She was more than burned out, Quinn. I've been thinking about what we saw of her over that last weekend and what you say she was like when she came to you in Washington. It's pure speculation on my part." Maura hesitated. "Let me just say that I wouldn't be surprised if she was on something that didn't agree with her. When I was a nurse, I saw a lot of that sort of thing."

"What do you mean, Maura? When Alicia was in college, she was prescribed an antidepressant. She had a negative reaction. She told me about it when I first knew her. She said she'd never go on antidepressants again."

"Then I must be wrong. I should mind my own business."

But when Quinn pressed her, Maura explained in detail what she knew about antidepressants and the kind of reactions, although rare, she'd seen during her years as a nurse.

When she returned to her cottage, Quinn didn't call T.J. Kowalski right away. She didn't flag down Diego Clemente's boat or charge up to the motel and have Buddy Jones go find him.

Instead, she dressed for the open house, again trying to imagine Alicia Miller and Oliver Crawford romantically involved—but she just couldn't do it.

Another question, another loose end, another problem.

She waited until she was in her car, on her way out of the village, before dialing Brian Castleton's cell-phone number; she hadn't bothered erasing it from her call list.

He picked up on the first ring. "Quinn, my God, it's good to hear your voice. How are you doing? I've been thinking about you."

"I'm okay."

"I'm really sorry about Alicia."

"I know—it's a tough one. Brian, Alicia told you about her reaction to the antidepressant she took in college, didn't she?"

"Yeah, I remember the whole story."

"Did you ever tell anyone?"

"Me? No, why would I? She repeated it not long ago. I think she was more matter-of-fact about it— not the reaction, but having suffered from clinical depression. She accepted it as a treatable illness, not an a sign of personal weakness. Attitudes have changed."

"Was anyone else there?"

"Yeah. Yeah, the new guy. Steve Eisenhardt." Brian, an experienced reporter, immediately turned suspicious. "Why? What's going on? Eisenhardt stopped by yesterday and asked to borrow a car. He said his was in the shop and he couldn't get a loaner. It was kind of weird, but what the hell."

"You loaned him a car?"

"Shouldn't I have? Am I never going to see it again?"

She gave him T.J. Kowalski's number and suggested Brian call him.

"That'll teach me to do anyone a good turn." He spoke with a touch of dry humor. "You want to tell me what's going on? You're more tight-lipped than the FBI, I swear, but I'm here to help."

"I'm attending an open house at the Crawford compound out here on the bay this afternoon."

"Oh, yeah? Call me if there's anything you need."

"Let's hope it's just a regular garden party. Thanks, Brian. If I hear anything about Steve, I'll let you know."

After she hung up, Quinn realized that any lingering animosity between them had dissipated— and so had any attraction. They'd both moved on.

She dialed T.J. Kowalski, and not surprisingly, he didn't like one thing she had to tell him.

"Special Agent Harlowe." His tone was mildly sarcastic, but not angry or mean-spirited.

"The Scanlons are leaving soon, so if you want to talk to them—"

"I'll handle it."

"Can you still check Alicia's blood for antidepressants?"

Kowalski ignored her. "Where are you right now?"

"In my car."

"On your way back to Washington?"

She came to a four-way stop and waited for two boys with a mutt on a leash to cross in front of her. *Normalcy.* "I'm on my way to the Crawford compound. I'll be one of dozens of guests. It'll be fine."

"That's probably what your great-grandfather said before the avalanche hit him."

Quinn smiled. The kids had reached the other side of the road. "I've got to go. You wouldn't want me to have an accident because I was talking to the FBI on my cell phone."

"I'm in Yorkville. Call me if you get into trouble."

"Thanks," she said, meaning it, and hung up, tossing her phone onto the seat.

She wondered if Kowalski would consider almost letting Huck Boone, aka Huck McCabe, undercover deputy U.S. marshal, make love to her, getting into trouble.

If he knew, Kowalski would find a reason to lock her up for sure.

33

Huck left a meeting with Joe Riccardi and Vern Glover to go over his car-parking duties—a serious matter, as far as his Breakwater colleagues were concerned—and spotted Cully O'Dell staggering out of the marsh, half falling over the barbed-wire fence.

With everyone else preparing for the arrival of guests, Huck moved in behind O'Dell and followed him to the indoor shooting range.

The kid had a swollen, bloody lip and left eye, and winced aloud as he walked, leaning to his right as if his ribs hurt. Huck had endured enough thrashings to recognize the signs of broken ribs in someone else.

Inside the range, O'Dell got out his gun box and set it on the counter. He was a dead shot, better than everyone Huck had seen at Breakwater, except himself.

"O'Dell?"

The kid didn't look at him, but mumbled, "These guys aren't about protection." He shoved a fresh magazine into his Glock 17. "They're a bunch of damn liars."

"What the hell happened to you?"

He wiped blood off his lip. "Leave me alone."

Huck stayed where he was. "Emptying a few mags into a target isn't going to get you stitches in that lip."

"I don't need stitches."

"At least come with me and get some ice."

"I'm okay. I just need to think."

"Cully, who pummeled you?"

"No one. I fell in the marsh."

The kid didn't even try to sound convincing. "What were you doing in the marsh?" Huck asked.

"Bird-watching."

"You've done well here the past couple weeks. Do you like this work?"

"Protective service work, yeah. Sure. I like it a lot. I'm good at it. But this place—" O'Dell glanced around, as if he was afraid someone might be eavesdropping, then pulled goggles out of his gear box. "This place has guys who are batshit insane."

Not something Huck was about to argue. "If someone I worked with beat me up, I'd quit."

"I told you—"

"You didn't get that cut lip bird-watching, O'Dell."

"I was jumped from behind. I wasn't paying attention and shouldn't have let it happen." He got out his ear protection. "I don't know if this place will ever get off the ground. The training's been good. Joe Riccardi seems like a stand-up guy…"

"Are you sure you didn't see who hit you?"

Cully shook his head, moaning in pain, as if he'd forgotten for a second how much he hurt. "If I saw anything, I don't remember. I went into the marsh. I was—I don't know what the hell I was doing. I saw Sharon Riccardi go in there last night. She was drunk."

"I ran into her in town and brought her back here."

"So I'm not crazy. She *was* out there. I was beginning to wonder. I had no idea what she was doing in the marsh, especially at night, so I thought I'd follow her. But I didn't see anything. Just tall grass, underbrush, birds. Next thing, I'm in the mud, covered with mosquitoes." He ran a surprisingly steady finger over the barrel of his gun. "I want out, Boone."

"Then go. Now. Pack up your gun and get out." Huck managed a smile. "I'll clean out your room and mail you your stuff."

Overwhelmed by emotion, the kid set his gun on the counter, the barrel pointed toward the targets. Even beat-up and clearly distraught, he put safety first. He was thorough—but, as Huck had suspected, not one of whatever was really going on at Breakwater.

"I hoped I'd fit in here," O'Dell said. "I thought I could make a go of it."

"There are other firms. They're more established, they've figured out how to screen out the crazies. You'll do fine."

O'Dell turned to him. "What about you?"

"I'm not a kid like you. I have a track record. It's not as easy for me to land somewhere else. I can hang here and draw a paycheck until things go south, and it won't come back to haunt me."

O'Dell tried to put on the goggles, but he smeared blood on them, and set them down, frustrated, the reality of the beating he'd taken finally sinking in. "Why do you care what I do?"

"I don't, except you remind me of myself when I was your age."

"How old are you now?"

Huck grinned. "Older than you."

"I don't want to turn into a Travis Lubec, mad at the world. It's no way to live."

"Go, O'Dell. Get out of here now. Just say you're not cut out for this work and leave. You have a cell phone?"

He nodded.

"Call me if you get into any trouble." Huck tore off the corner of a paper target and jotted down his cell number.

"Who are you?" O'Dell asked, taking the number.

Huck was willing to go only so far. He winked. "Be good, O'Dell."

The kid dismantled his Glock and put it back in the metal case, along with the goggles and ear protection. Then he left without another word. Huck followed him out the door and watched him walk sullenly back toward the converted barn. The kid would get out of there. Getting his head smashed in had put Cully over the edge, forced him to question what was going on at Breakwater Security.

Huck noticed Travis Lubec falling in behind O'Dell and called to him. "Hey, Lubec. What's up?"

Lubec hesitated, then abandoned O'Dell and joined Huck at the shooting range. "What are you doing?"

"Target practice. Want to join me before I have to go park cars?"

"O'Dell—"

"Looks like he had his face smacked against a tree." Huck shrugged, nonchalant. "I figure he had it coming."

Lubec didn't respond, just stepped past Huck into the range. He got ear protection out of a closet, pulled a Heckler & Koch USP out of his belt holster and started firing at a paper target. No vest, nothing on his eyes, his face as pale and expressionless as ever. One-handed, he put ten rounds into the target at twenty-five yards, hitting center mass with every shot.

"Bet the marines would love to have you," Huck said.

Travis shrugged. "Too old."

"The feds'll take you up to thirty-six."

"I don't see myself toeing that particular line, do you?"

Huck grinned. "No. Me neither."

Travis, almost as good a shot as O'Dell, seemed to take no pride in his skill. He peeled off his ear protection and put a fresh magazine into his H & K. "We need to get moving."

"Party time, huh?"

Lubec didn't take the bait and comment further. When he got outside, he headed for the main house, not inviting Huck to join him, not waiting for him.

As he headed for the barn, Huck risked using his cell phone to call Diego. "Cully O'Dell is on his way out of here. Pick him up." He squinted up at an osprey hunting over the marsh. "Quinn?"

"In her party clothes driving in your direction."

"She doesn't listen, does she?"

"That's why you like her."

Gerard finished getting dressed for the open house at Breakwater and told himself that Steve Eisenhardt was burned out, insane, paranoid or all of the above. Alicia's death must have affected him more than anyone had realized.

But Gerard couldn't ignore a gnawing feeling in his gut that told him that Eisenhardt was on the level. What if something was going on under the surface and he was being shut out? He'd been fighting a growing sense of uneasiness about Ollie ever since the kidnapping. Yet, over and over again, Gerard would tell himself that he needed to let any investigation take its course. Ollie Crawford was too high-profile, too wealthy, too invested in the system to do anything totally outlandish.

Denial.

Gerard climbed out onto the marina dock, the wind having finally died down. A dozen gulls had clustered around a small fishing boat. The sun glistened on the water. He loved this spot for its lack of

glamour, its simplicity, but often found himself restless here for the same reasons.

"You're never happy. You're always striving."

His wife's words. He could hear her voice, sad
more than angry, resigned more than accusatory.

What would happen to him if he lost everything?
He'd already lost his wife. He didn't see his children
nearly often enough. The family life he'd envi-
sioned for himself had been a myth. All he had now
was his work. His reputation. His ambitions.

If Ollie had gone over the edge in some way, if
trouble was brewing, Gerard knew that his own
name and reputation would be tarnished. Guilt by
association. He and Ollie had been friends for
twenty years. There was no way to downplay their
friendship.

He pushed back the glum thought. He hated the
fear that gripped him. What wasn't he being told?
What more did Steve know?

And Quinn, what did she know?

Gerard knew he had enemies. Rivals. People
who resented his access to power, his success. People who wanted his job. People who wanted the
jobs he would have *after* the Justice Department,
who'd slice and dice him now, just to get him out
of the way.

He had never imagined that Ollie would be his
downfall.

Out on the parking lot, a Breakwater Security
SUV waited to take him to the open house.

Before he headed across the parking lot to meet
his ride, Gerard took out his cell phone and dialed

the number he had for T.J. Kowalski. He'd tell the FBI agent about Steve's visit. Then truth would prevail.

But Gerard had no illusions.

If Oliver Crawford was under investigation, *he* was under investigation.

34

Huck half thought Quinn would change her mind and head back to Washington, or go visit her grandfather in her party dress, but he spotted her Saab coming toward him and directed her to a parking place.

She got out of her car, strappy high heels in hand. "I can't drive in these things," she said, kicking off a pair of water shoes. She scooped them up and dumped them on the back seat of her car, then put one hand on the driver's side door as she lifted a bare foot and slipped on the high-heeled sandal.

Huck noticed that somewhere between dancing with him last night and now, she'd painted her toenails a dark red.

"You don't want to lean against your car." He grabbed her hand as she balanced herself to put on her other sandal. "You'll get your dress dirty."

If she noticed his mix of irritation and pleasure

at seeing her, she pretended not to. She stood up straight and smiled. "Thanks." She adjusted her shawl over her shoulders, polite, as if last night hadn't happened. "I had to pop my trunk at the gate. No Uzi in back, no gate-crashers in the trunk."

"Why aren't you in Fredericksburg?"

She cocked her head. "Do I hear a string quartet?"

"It's for the party—"

"Well, then. That settles it. You have no reason to worry, Mr. Boone. Nothing can possibly happen at a party with a string quartet playing." She teetered a bit in her strappy shoes. "Whoa. I forgot how high these heels are. And skinny. I might sink in the grass. But, with all you security guys here—"

Something about her was off. Heady. She was on the verge of spinning out of control. "Quinn—"

"If you can…" She paused, obviously debating just what she wanted to say. "You might want to talk to Special Agent Kowalski."

Hell. "Quinn—what's happened?"

Before she could answer, Vern Glover arrived with Gerard Lattimore, who just about jumped out of the SUV before it came to a full stop. Quinn greeted her former boss warmly, and he slipped an arm over her shoulders, telling her that he needed to talk to her. He was intense, stiff.

"Sure. Now?"

He nodded and the two of them went off together, along the brick walk to the main house.

Huck listened to the string quartet and watched the gleam of Quinn's black hair in the sunlight, figuring he'd parked his last car. He had no intention of staying on the sidelines with Quinn and Lattimore there.

Vern got out of the SUV and shook his head, irritable. "Guy's a wreck. I couldn't wait to get here and dump him."

"What's wrong with him?"

"Must be that girl's death. Being in Yorkville must bring up all the emotion." Vern, however, wasn't one to discuss emotions. "Unless he's got something going on at work. He's a scumbag federal prosecutor—I don't know how he gets up in the morning."

"Vern—I want in," Huck said quietly.

Glover gave him a blank look. "What?"

"I'm not in this job just for a paycheck. Neither are you. If something's going down, I want to be a part of it."

"No, you don't. It's crazy—unless it works. Then we'll all look brilliant."

"Unless what works?"

But Vern nodded out at their boss's well-heeled guests. "Not the kind of crowd to start a food fight or get drunk and throw each other into the bay, is it?"

After months of dealing with Vernon Glover, Huck knew he'd pushed him as hard as he could for the moment. He shrugged. "With any luck, it'll be a boring afternoon."

Quinn could feel Gerard's tension as he swept a glass of champagne off a tray, smiling stiffly at the waiter before taking a gulp. "That man you were with—Boone," he said. "Has he been following you? You two seem to keep bumping into each other...when you found Alicia, last night at the marina, just now."

"He was parking cars."

"Not your type, then, is he?"

"I've got a lot on my mind right now," she said vaguely. "Have you heard from Steve Eisenhardt?"

Gerard tilted back his champagne glass. "Have you?"

She shook her head, noticing he hadn't answered her question.

"Quinn—" He finished off his champagne too quickly and switched his empty glass for a full one from another passing tray. "If you knew anything, you'd tell me, wouldn't you?"

"Anything about what?"

"Alicia's death. Her relationship with Oliver. She was out here, screaming at the front gate, before she came to you in Washington. If you knew why—"

"I don't. I'm not sure *she* knew why. She wasn't herself that day."

His gaze settled on her for a few seconds. "Quinn, what do you know?"

"Believe me, I've asked myself the same question over and over."

Not wanting to endure Gerard's glare any longer, she pretended to see someone she knew and excused herself, crossing the lawn to a minibar set up in the shade. The lawn was filled with tables and chairs and more waiters passing trays of hors d'oeuvres. Joe Riccardi had a small group clustered around him as he discussed the mission of Breakwater Security.

The pleasant music and surroundings—the soft laughter and beautifully dressed guests—reminded Quinn of Alicia and how much she'd have enjoyed such an event, but she felt edgy and out of place. With a glass of sparkling water in hand, she ambled toward a back entrance to the house and slipped inside, ducking into a short hall that led to the kitchen, its main work area out of sight. She could hear the rush of the caterers, the clatter of dishes, pots and silverware. She cut through a corner of the kitchen and down another hall, ending up in a sun-filled living room of soft yellows and blues, the furniture surprisingly informal. Two sofas faced each other, with chairs on either end and a tufted leather ottoman forming the main seating area. Along the walls were side tables, an antique grandfather clock, large-scale oil paintings and tall, immaculate windows that looked out across the lawn toward the water.

To her left was a dining room, more formal, quiet now. Quinn drifted toward a door in the right corner of the room. Another hall. She saw an open doorway just into the hall, another one farther down, and a graceful staircase. She wondered what she was doing, sneaking around Oliver Crawford's bayside house.

Suddenly, Oliver himself was standing in the doorway, inches from her. "Quinn!" He smiled. "I thought I heard someone. Come—join me. I just had a call I had to take."

"I don't want to keep you from your guests."

"And I don't want to keep you from your spying." With a chuckle, he stood back from the door and motioned her inside. "I can't say I blame you. It's a boring party."

"No, it's lovely—"

"'Lovely' is another way to say 'boring.'"

She stepped past him into the library, all dark leather and wood, with framed black-and-white photographs on the walls. A stuffed owl stared at her from a shelf of vintage books.

"The original owner of the house was an amateur bird-watcher," Crawford said behind her. "He left a number of stuffed birds here, but, fortunately, far more watercolors, many of which he painted himself."

"Any good?"

"Not particularly, but I enjoy them nonetheless. They have an honesty and simplicity that I can appreciate." He stood in front of a window overlooking a white lilac. "You and Gerry just got here, didn't you?"

"Yes—but we didn't come together."

"No, of course not."

Quinn heard the wry tone in his voice. "It's funny how rumors get started, isn't it? People get an idea in their heads, and suddenly they start thinking it's reality. For instance, what was your real relationship with Alicia Miller?" she asked candidly.

"So, you've obviously heard rumors." He dropped onto a leather club chair and crossed his legs, swinging one foot as he stared out the open window, the sounds of his party faint, the smell of the lilac in the air. "Alicia and I were friends. I was very fond of her. She was like a little sister to me. We got to know each other over the past month."

"You weren't having an affair?"

He didn't seem surprised or offended by the question. "I won't say it didn't cross my mind, especially at first. But, no, we were not having an affair. Since my kidnap and rescue, the thought of romance, frankly, hasn't appealed to me. I could feel normal around her. I like to think she could feel normal around me." He sighed heavily, but his expression didn't change. "But I couldn't save her."

"You knew she was troubled?"

"Yes. Yes, I knew."

Quinn heard footsteps in the hall and turned, just as Huck materialized in the doorway. His gaze fell on her, his jaw set hard. He shifted his attention to his boss. "I'm sorry, Mr. Crawford. None of us saw her come inside."

He held up a hand. "It's not a problem, Mr. Boone. Quinn and I are friends. Go ahead, Quinn. You can continue. I have nothing to hide from you or anyone else. As I told the FBI and local police, Alicia's moodiness started shortly before her death. She'd been unhappy for a while, of course, but the irrational talk—the kind of behavior you reported she exhibited when she came to you in Washington—" He paused as if in pain. "Let's just say she went downhill very fast."

"I think I know why," Quinn said, avoiding

Huck's eye. "Alicia had a very bad reaction to an antidepressant back in college. My neighbor here in Yorkville is a retired nurse. She's pretty sure she recognized the symptoms."

"Why would she take a medication when she'd already had a bad reaction to it? What doctor would prescribe that if he knew her history?"

"I'm not sure a doctor gave it to her. I told the FBI."

"Special Agent Kowalski?"

"I suggested they check their blood sample for antidepressants, in particular SSRIs."

"SSRI?"

"It stands for selective serotonin reuptake inhibitor." She smiled faintly. "I wrote it down. SSRIs are the most commonly prescribed antidepressants. According to Maura, my neighbor, tricyclics are more likely to be lethal in overdose, but SSRIs can produce a temporary increase in anxiety. Most of the time it's mild and goes away after a few days. In rare cases, the anxiety and agitation can be very severe and frightening."

"As with Alicia." Crawford sat forward, intent on what Quinn was saying. "This is all news to me."

"I'm not a doctor, and neither is Maura—she emphasized that to me. Most people do well on antidepressants and don't have this kind of severe, unpleasant reaction. Depression is a treatable illness."

"Alicia's bad reaction in college was to some kind of SSRI?"

Quinn nodded. Huck hadn't made a sound in the

doorway. "I don't know which one," she said. "Alicia told me that she had reacted very badly and refused to touch any kind of antidepressant. If depressed, she would try alternative therapies. Psychoanalysis, exercise, meditation—but not medication. She was adamant about it."

"Then you're suggesting she didn't know what she was taking."

"I'm not suggesting anything," Quinn said.

"Who else knew about her reaction? Presumably her doctor, and her family—any other friends, colleagues? Besides yourself, that is."

Quinn shifted in her chair. "I did not provide Alicia with any kind of medication, with or without her knowledge. Not even a vitamin. I don't know anyone who would."

"No, of course not." He exhaled, adding simply, "I miss her."

"Do you know anything about the car that picked her up in Washington?"

"It wasn't me."

"One of your security people?"

"Not that I'm aware of."

Quinn noticed his pained look. "I don't mean to sound as if I'm interrogating you. I understand you'd visit her at the cottage—"

"Mr. Crawford," Huck interrupted, "I can take Miss Harlowe out of here."

He shook his head. "No, no. It's all right. Quinn's been through a terrible ordeal herself, losing a friend." Crawford got to his feet, and took a few steps, as if he just needed to move. He had a lost quality about him. "I walked through the marsh to your cottage, without security. You'd think I wouldn't risk it, given my recent history. But Yorkville's so small—and I've been coming here for years. I couldn't imagine anything bad happening here. Maybe it's me. My fault she died, that is. I'm bad luck."

Quinn let her shawl fall off her shoulders. "Did she think of you as a brother?"

"She'd never say. She wasn't one to open herself up to that kind of emotion. She protected herself, hated to be vulnerable." He stopped pacing, looked at Quinn. "You believe we were having an affair, don't you?"

"Oh, God—Oliver!" Sharon Riccardi burst past Huck into the library, her bare arms red with mosquito bites from last night's trip through the marsh. If she was embarrassed over her behavior, she gave no indication. "I am so sorry. Boone, why didn't you get her out of here?"

"I asked her to stay," Crawford said. "It's all right, Sharon. Quinn and I have been having a nice chat."

"It's *not* all right." Hands on hips, Sharon swung around to face Quinn. "You were invited here today because we believed you needed a break after what happened to your friend—we all needed a break and some closure. We assumed you'd act appropriately, not sneak around in private areas."

Quinn thought Huck might say something in her defense, but he didn't. "One thing just led to another," she said.

Sharon Riccardi wasn't mollified. "You need to bury your friend and leave the rest of us in peace. Oliver, you trust me to make difficult decisions, and I'm making one now. It's time Miss Harlowe went home."

Joe Riccardi appeared in the doorway and stood next to Huck, who still hadn't moved or said anything. "What's going on?"

Sharon stiffened. "Miss Harlowe is leaving."

"I'll see to it she gets home." Huck calmly inserted himself between the Riccardis and Quinn and took her by the elbow. She felt the tickle of shawl fringe on her arm and remembered last night.

"I can find my own way out," she said quickly.

Shaking her head, Sharon addressed Huck. "Take her back to her cottage in her car. That way we know she gets there safely. I'll send Glover for you."

Oliver Crawford rose, sweeping Quinn's shawl up from where it had dragged on the floor. "I hope our discussion eases your mind."

"It doesn't, really, but thanks for your time."

Keeping one hand on her elbow, Huck ushered Quinn past a dumbfounded, almost ashen Joe Riccardi. She wondered if he'd take the hit for her sneaking into the house, and felt a pang of regret. Just because he was married to ice-cold Sharon didn't mean he'd escape her ire.

Huck picked up the pace as they walked back out to the kitchen. "Hey," Quinn said, "I'm in high heels."

"You're keeping up just fine."

He took her through the side door that she'd used to get in, skirting the edge of the party. But Gerard Lattimore waved from the shade of an oak. "Quinn! There you are. I've been looking for you." He walked over to her, but glanced at Huck, saw his tension and frowned. "What's going on?"

"I'm getting the boot," Quinn said.

"Why?"

"Poking my nose where I shouldn't."

Huck loosened his grip on her arm. "I'm escorting Miss Harlowe back to her cottage."

"I got caught talking to Oliver Crawford in the library," Quinn explained, not exactly mortified over getting tossed from Breakwater. "Big sin."

Gerard's mouth twitched with humor. "Well, perhaps I can redeem you."

"It's okay. Really. I just wanted to see the place."

"You're sure?"

"Quinn's leaving," Huck said.

Gerard frowned at him. "I was hoping she and I would have a chance to talk."

Quinn knew he would only grill her about what he hadn't told her, and she'd lost any desire to stay. "I promised my grandfather I'd visit him on my way back to Washington," she said. "I should get going."

"Honestly," Gerard said, "I can intervene and explain to Ollie that you're like a wandering two-year-old—"

Quinn grinned at him. "Oh, that's a big help."

Huck straightened, everything about him on edge. "I need to get a move on."

When they reached her car, he stood by the passenger door until she was inside, then shut it. If he'd had a dead bolt, he'd probably have used it to lock her in. He went around to the driver's side and climbed in.

Quinn sat back in her seat. "You Breakwater guys need more to do if you're getting all excited about me sneaking in through Crawford's kitchen."

"Crawford was exposed," Huck said. "The Riccardis will regard your little escapade as a major security breach."

"I should have knocked him on the head with a vase, just to give you all a rush." She snapped her seat belt into place. "*Relax.* It all worked out."

"Not by their standards."

"Look, go on, go back to work. I'll drive myself to my cottage. Kowalski's probably sitting on my front porch waiting for me."

Huck ignored her and started the engine.

"I did tell him about the rumor of an affair and the SSRIs first."

"How good of you."

"I'd have told you, but you were parking cars."

He shot her a look. "Quinn, this isn't a damn game."

"I know that." She spoke softly, just managing to maintain her composure. "At night—I wake up seeing the gulls at Alicia's body."

He gripped the wheel of her Saab. "I'm sorry."

"No, you have a right to be angry, and concerned. I came out here on impulse." She looked out the window at the beautiful setting. "This place is a viper pit."

"That's where guys like me get sent."

"Steve Eisenhardt stole notes out of one of my re-search notebooks. Nothing that would compromise your work." She continued to stare out the window as Huck backed out of her parking space. "My neighbors think Alicia and Oliver Crawford were having an affair, but he says they weren't. Their re-lationship was platonic. He could talk to her. Then there's the possible SSRI reaction—"

"That's why you need to step back."

"I didn't mean to cause any trouble."

He didn't respond. They drove to her cottage in silence, and when he pulled into her driveway, he turned off the ignition. "I don't want to leave you alone."

"If one of your guys is coming for you, I don't see that you have much of a choice."

"You've pissed off too many people this after-noon."

"I've never been thrown out of a party. I've never been thrown out of *anything*." She opened up her door and smiled over at him. "It's not as humiliat-ing as I thought it'd be."

But he didn't smile back. Instead, he got out of the car and walked behind her to her side door.

"You know, it's occurred to me—how do I know for sure you're who you say you are?" She gave him a cool look that was entirely fabricated. "What if this is a case of the wolf guarding the henhouse?"

He stepped in close to her. "If something goes wrong, sweet pea, you'd better hope I'm a wolf."

Her mouth went dry. As she unlocked the door,

Quinn noticed her hands were trembling. And not from fear, she realized, or even embarrassment over her removal from the Crawford party. From awareness. Pure, physical, *sexual* awareness.

Huck slipped his arms around her middle and turned her to him, gently, any irritation with her gone now. "You and I have unfinished business." He kissed her deeply, romantically, and whispered with a hint of a smile, "Get your butt back to D.C., Harlowe."

"Or I'll have a marshal on my tail?"

"You're on Diego's radar screen as it is. Showing up at Breakwater today and getting tossed out just caused you to be a brighter blip."

"What does kissing you do?"

He gave her a sudden grin. "Let's hope Diego didn't see that part."

"Kowalski—"

"The FBI's on your case too. Lucky you."

A black SUV pulled alongside her cottage, Vern Glover in the driver's seat. Huck winked at her. "See you, sweet pea. Be good."

But Quinn noticed the seriousness that had returned to his eyes, and by the time the SUV was out of sight, she was still on her doorstep, shivering, and, for the first time, afraid for him.

35

Gerard paced along the stone patio agitated beyond all reason in the forty-five minutes since Quinn had left. The party was winding down quickly. People seemed reassured, even excited, about Breakwater Security, as if somehow having it in Yorkville made them safer. Perhaps, he thought, it did, but he had always been skeptical about Ollie's new venture.

A sudden surge of loneliness caught him by surprise. He didn't like attending social functions alone, but he'd never considered bringing a date to Yorkville. He didn't know why. Quinn? He shook off the thought, as if temptation's long reach had struck out and knocked him for a loop. He needed to resist. Quinn Harlowe had nothing to offer him or his career, except a fascinating pedigree and the most beautiful hazel eyes.

He swore under his breath at his own calculated

thinking, but he had to do *something* to cut through his fears.

He finished another glass of champagne. He hadn't seen Ollie at all, perhaps just as well. In his current mood, Gerard didn't trust himself not to go over the line and say more than he should, accuse his longtime friend of playing him for a fool, accuse him of going overboard since his kidnapping.

Best to get the hell out of here.

He would let the FBI find Eisenhardt and talk to him.

Getting rid of his champagne glass, Gerard looked around for someone to drive him back to his boat. He'd collapse and sleep late, cleanse his thoughts, then hire himself an attorney, on the slim chance that Steve hadn't exaggerated or lied altogether. His warning had shaken Gerard more than he'd realized at first. It brushed too close to his life, his ambitions. As callous as that sounded, what else did he have? He would be irresponsible not to protect his interests.

"You look as if you're about to run screaming back to D.C."

Gerard turned, smiling, in spite of his mood, at his longtime friend. "Ollie. I was beginning to wonder if you'd given up on your own party and gone for a walk on the beach."

"What passes for a beach out here." He gave a short, awkward laugh, then turned to face the bay, glistening in the afternoon sun. "I never should have had this open house. It was a bad idea."

"Your guests all seemed to enjoy themselves. I

got the impression that being able to actually see what you're doing here won most of them over."

"That's good," Crawford replied, but he didn't sound pleased. He sighed, keeping his gaze on the water. "There was a scene earlier with Quinn Harlowe."

"I heard," Gerard said, surprised that Ollie didn't seem irritated with her. "I didn't get any details. What did she do?"

"She slipped into the house and found me in the library. No one noticed. Then she..." Pausing, Oliver turned to his old friend. "She's suspicious, Gerry. She's spinning conspiracies and fantasies where there are none. I'm afraid she's going to get burned."

"She's still upset over her friend's death."

"Gerry, perhaps you should remember that Quinn Harlowe isn't just a pretty face. She's a well-respected, very sharp expert in transnational criminal networks."

Gerard tried to smile. "Yes, but unless you're operating a criminal network out of your dining room, you have nothing to worry about."

"Sharon was very angry with her. One of the new guys, Huck Boone, escorted Quinn out of there. Joe Riccardi went pale. I think he was worried about what his wife would do, actually."

"From what I've seen of her, she's one tough cookie." Gerard frowned at his friend, who suddenly looked as if he wanted to cry. "Ollie? Are you okay?"

"Alicia's death has affected me more than I realized." He cleared his throat, rallying. "I don't mind saying so."

"But you hardly knew her…"

"I got to know her over the last month. We became close—not romantically. I've never met anyone I could talk to the way I could her."

Gerard felt his spine straighten. "Oliver, you might not want to divulge more."

"You're right. I'm just—" He clapped a hand on Gerard's shoulder. "I'm just contemplating what might have been. Come in for a drink before you leave."

"I shouldn't. I've had too much to drink as it is."

"Gerry…I had nothing to do with Alicia Miller's death."

"If I thought you did, I wouldn't have come near this place today."

"Stay, Gerry. Let's talk."

But a stiff-backed Travis Lubec was waiting just off the patio to take him back to his boat. Gerard wanted to go back to Washington, but wondered what would happen if he said no. He told himself he was being ridiculous, he was getting paranoid—thanks to Steve Eisenhardt.

"Of course, Ollie. We've known each other a long time." He met his friend's gaze. "I'd be happy to stay and talk."

Quinn ducked into the bedroom and changed into jeans, a sweatshirt and water shoes, wondering what had possessed her to fall so hard for Huck, because that was what she'd done. If Vern Glover hadn't shown up, she had no doubt she and her undercover marshal would be in bed right now.

She hoped she wasn't responding to some need to remind herself that she was alive and had done her best by Alicia—that kissing Huck Boone/McCabe on her doorstep wasn't just about the risk, the adrenaline rush of being around him. He was sexy, confident, irreverent. She *liked* him.

On the other hand, he was pretending to be a bodyguard. She'd never seen his badge. She'd never seen him off duty. She couldn't picture where he lived, didn't know who his friends were, what he liked to do when he wasn't working undercover.

Basically, she didn't know much about the man at all, she thought, tying back her hair. But as she finished up and shut the bureau drawer, she caught the reflection of her bed in the mirror and saw that the bed linens were askew. She'd been too preoccupied to notice sooner.

She felt a crawling sensation and, grabbing an antique wooden canoe paddle she'd meant to stick on a wall, returned to the kitchen.

Her silverware drawer was partially open, but she was positive she hadn't left it that way.

Quinn walked into the bathroom and found an entire drawer dumped into the sink. Bottles of aspirin, antihistamine, antacid tablets. Her first-aid kit.

She checked the guest room. It was torn apart— bureau drawers, bed linens, closet.

Heart pounding, Quinn grabbed her cell phone

and dialed Kowalski's number. She didn't reach him and left a message, then called his pager number.

While she waited for him to call her back, she headed outside, half hoping to find Huck or Diego Clemente on her doorstep.

An osprey circled over the salt marsh.

Alicia had tried to tell her something.

"The osprey will kill me."

Quinn unlocked the shed and dragged her green kayak down to the water. She figured she was just as safe—safer, actually—on the water.

Although she had mastered a quick entry into her kayak, she nonetheless always managed to get wet, especially since her cove wasn't the best spot for launching. At least she was more appropriately dressed for the conditions than the last time she'd paddled, when the initial shock of Alicia's death still had her in its grip.

But as she paddled out to the mouth of the cove, Quinn felt a range of emotions, none of them simple.

There were babies in the osprey nest. It was high up—no way could Alicia have left some kind of message in the nest itself.

Quinn placed her paddle across the cockpit and let her kayak bob in the water. Maybe there was no meaning to any of Alicia's ramblings at the coffee shop, and she'd been focused on ospreys just because she had them in her head.

A coincidence, not a message.

Sitting quietly in the kayak, Quinn looked at the shore and saw more osprey nests. She counted five without even trying.

And Alicia, she remembered, had launched down the shore—where there were *more* nests.

So many.

The kayak bumped against the buoy pole, hitting a dark blue line tied just under the water. Quinn couldn't recall ever having seen it before. Careful not to tip too far in one direction and capsize, she dipped her hand into the cold water and pulled on the line, feeling a weight on the other end.

"What on earth?" she said aloud, splashing water from the line onto her boat, her sweater and jeans, but ignoring the cold, the discomfort as she continued to reel up the line.

In another few seconds, she heaved a small, black waterproof bag, hooked securely to the line, onto her lap in the cockpit.

Her fingers cold and wet, she managed to open the bag.

Inside were a clear plastic bag and a prescription bottle.

Quinn dried off one hand as best she could and pulled out the bottle, gasping when she saw that it was leftover prescription-strength ibuprofen from an old knee injury. She thought she'd left it in her bedroom nightstand.

Ten to one, she thought, it didn't contain ibuprofen.

She held the bottle up to the light and saw blue pills…different pills.

Whatever they were, Alicia had taken them, thinking they were ibuprofen.

But who'd switched the pills?

Steve. He knew about Alicia's reaction to antidepressants. Brian had said Steve was there when she'd talked about it.

Quinn didn't dare open the bottle and risk accidentally spilling the contents into the bay. She carefully returned the bottle to the bag and checked the clear bag, just peeking inside at the contents.

Pictures, printed off a digital camera.

Two color photos were clearly visible on the top sheet. Rocking in her kayak, she focused on them.

The top photo was of two crates of weapons. Grenades, mortars. Very illegal.

Beneath it was a photo of a small, rustic hut.

On its roof was an osprey nest.

Quinn quickly closed up the clear plastic bag and tucked it back into the waterproof bag. She hadn't taken her cell phone out onto the water with her. She hoped Diego Clemente had seen her and was on his way—that Kowalski was just around the corner.

Where had Alicia gotten such pictures?

When?

Quinn made sure the black bag was secured and dropped it back into the water.

Alicia had tried to tell her. Agitated, frightened, out of her head—she'd done what she could to tell everyone.

Including the wrong people.

The mama osprey dive-bombed toward her nest and Quinn, the intruder.

Moving fast, out of the angry bird's path, she paddled straight for shore, using the wind to her favor. The closest, easiest spot to reach was the stretch of marsh where she'd found Alicia.

No wonder she ended up here, Quinn thought, leaping out of the kayak into the water and dragging it ashore.

"Quinn...help me."

She thought she'd imagined the voice. *Alicia?*

"Quinn!"

Quinn picked up her kayak paddle. "Who is it?"

"It's me, Steve." He was on his hands and knees in a snarl of brush and small trees, blood dripping down his left arm. "Please—Quinn, I need your help."

Paddle in hand, Quinn shook her head. "FBI's on the way. You need to tell them everything, Steve— you hear me? Everything."

"I know, I know." He staggered to his feet, half sobbing. "Just help me..."

Quinn couldn't work up any pity for him. "You're a son of a bitch, Steve. You switched my prescription ibuprofen for some kind of antidepressant. You knew Alicia would react—"

"I didn't make the switch. I just told them about her reaction. If it'd been me—I never would have left any pills behind after she died."

"It was you in my cottage—"

"They wanted to know what she was up to— how much she knew about them." His voice croaked, more blood dripping down his arm, the shirt sleeve red with blood. He seemed to be in genuine agony. "I told them nothing, only that she wasn't spying on them. They wouldn't believe me.

I had to tell them about her reaction to antidepressants. I hoped it'd just give them room to maneuver. I thought the pills would make her weird, not suicidal."

"She didn't kill herself. You killed her."

"Her shoulders hurt from kayaking." He stopped, bending over as if he had a stomach cramp and couldn't take another step. "She told me she found your old prescription."

"And you told—who?"

"The Nazi. The SS guard. That's what I call him. Travis Lubec."

Lubec, Quinn remembered, had engineered his boss's rescue in the Dominican Republic and was instrumental in converting Crawford's Chesapeake Bay compound into Breakwater Security.

She thought of Huck, wondered how much he knew, how she could get this information to him. "Damn it, Steve. Why?"

"Quinn, I'm not like you. I'm weak." He stood up straight, leveling a pistol at her. He must have had it tucked in his pants—Quinn hadn't seen it. "I'm sorry, but Crawford's guys have me by the short hairs."

"Damn, Steve. Look what you've done…"

"Lattimore didn't listen. I tried to warn him. They'll either convert him or kill him as an example of their power and purity."

"They're true believers in their cause."

"Oh, yeah. Big time. They're going to save us from ourselves."

Quinn nodded to the gun. "You don't need to

keep that pointed at me. I'll do what you want me to do."

He motioned halfheartedly for her to go ahead of him, onto a narrow footpath. "Just walk."

The path wound through the buggy, marshy wetland, and Quinn hoped they'd startle a snake, and Steve would drop his gun. She thought of the ospreys and the gulls, soaring above the coastline, seeing everything.

She came to an abandoned hut.

The hut in Alicia's pictures.

Quinn felt her throat catch. "Steve—what's going on?"

He pushed open the door, but there was no sign of any crates. Any illegal weapons and explosives stored there when Alicia was alive had been moved out.

Travis Lubec stepped out of the hut with a sniper rifle, tapping Steve in the chest with it. "Nice work. Always can count on you to be a weasel."

White-faced, bleeding, Steve turned to Quinn. "My gun's empty. Lubec caught me searching your cottage. He'd have shot both of us if I didn't cooperate." He began to sob. "If it'd been just me, I'd have let him put a bullet in my head. I'm so sorry. I had no choice."

Quinn reined in her fear and tilted her chin up, eyeing Steve coldly. She had one chance to get out of this—convince Lubec she was on his side, at least long enough to buy herself time. "Lubec's right. You *are* a weasel. Even now, you're hoping the feds saw us and will come to your rescue." She shook her head. "But I took steps to prevent them from following me." Nonsense, of course, but she hoped Lubec would be confused or thrown off enough by her act to give herself a chance to alert Huck or Diego. Diego and Kowalski were hopefully en route—Diego must have seen her in her kayak, at the buoy, and realized she'd found something.

Steve's eyes widened. "What?"

Brazenly standing between the men, Quinn knew she couldn't stand there and let Travis Lubec shoot even a coward like Steve Eisenhardt in cold blood.

"How do you think Sharon Riccardi found the thugs to snatch Crawford off his boat in December?" Quinn asked.

Lubec stared at her. "What are you talking about?"

"I know—you must be confused. You weren't in the loop. I helped Sharon. I have contacts all over the world. She needed expendable mercenaries—thugs—and I found them for her." Quinn sighed, glancing at Steve, who was applying pressure to his injured upper arm with the palm of the opposite hand. Blood oozed between his fingers. She turned back to Lubec. "I'm not your enemy. I'm on your side. I've been working quietly, anonymously, on your behalf for months. Why do you think I left Justice? I needed the autonomy. I'm the one who told Steve about Alicia's reaction to antidepressants."

"Pills for the weak."

"I agree."

Lubec clearly wasn't entirely convinced by her performance. "Who knows about you?"

"No one. I've been more subtle than that. I've covered my tracks. You want to know what I know, don't you?" She narrowed her eyes on him and went still deep inside herself. "Then take me to Oliver Crawford. I tried to get to him at the party this afternoon, but I was interrupted. I've spent a lot of time and exerted a great deal of effort to lay the proper groundwork."

"You're one of us, huh?" Lubec pointed his rifle at her. "I don't believe it."

"I don't care what you believe or don't believe. You're not going to kill me when you don't know for certain whose side I'm on and whether or not I have information you need. And you're not going to complicate our situation by killing Steve right now."

Lubec rifle-butted him in the head and the gut, sending him down in a heap, and turned to Quinn, even as she pushed back her revulsion. "Let's go."

Vern Glover couldn't stop moving. Huck kept up with him on the walkway to the converted barn. Glover had rattled the steering wheel all the way back from Quinn's cottage, and now he was moving fast, agitated, on some kind of adrenaline rush. The party-goers and caterers had left Breakwater, an almost strange silence overtaking the sprawling property.

"Something's going down, Vern," Huck said. "I'm not stupid. I can tell. I want in."

Vern shook his head, not slackening his pace. "It's crazy. It's too much, too soon."

"What is, Vern?"

"Lubec licks Crawford's boots. The guy's rich, but he's reckless—half-crazy." Breaking his stride slightly, Glover glared at Huck. "Quote me, and I'll kill you."

"I don't like recklessness. That's what gets people killed." Huck kept his tone calm, focused, knowing Vern would respond to self-control. "What about the Riccardis?"

"Sharon's trying to run damage control. Joe, he's in the dark. Like you."

"I don't want to stay in the dark. Can you get me in?"

Vern took a sharp breath. "I don't know, Boone. I don't trust anyone. The feds grabbed my best buddy right from under my nose. Some undercover fed fuck."

At your service, Huck thought. "The feds don't play by the rules. Any of them."

"That girl who drowned was one of them."

"A federal agent? I thought she was a lawyer—"

"I wasn't here for a lot of what went on. Lubec says she played on Crawford's insecurities after the kidnapping. He trusted her, and she betrayed him." Vern hissed through his teeth. "She had pictures."

Vern obviously wanted to talk, maybe just to keep his mind off whatever was bothering him. At the same time, his instincts would tell him to shut up if Huck pushed too hard. He stayed casual. "Pictures of what?"

"Some weapons we brought through here. Stuff the government doesn't want us to have."

"Such as?"

"Things that go boom."

Huck could see himself reporting that one to the task force. "Where did the stuff end up?"

He'd gone too far. Glover gave him a sharp look. "I don't know. I don't ask questions. Neither should you." They came to the back door of the converted barn. Vern opened it, pausing a half beat. "You've been spending a lot of time with Harlowe. She get you fired up to ask all these questions?"

"She's just upset about her friend."

"She fancies herself an expert in international crime—"

Huck shrugged. "Not much of an expert, if you ask me. At least she's pretty." He followed Vern inside. "Come on, Glover. What gives? You're like a worm in hot ashes."

Vern relaxed marginally. "The feds are still investigating Crawford's kidnapping and rescue. In my opinion, we should have bided our time a few more months. Let things cool off before we launched a big operation."

"You used the past tense, Vern. Something's going down. I want to know what."

"Yeah, well, too bad. Not my call." He got out the keys to his room. "I don't make the decisions around here. I just do what I'm told. I saw what happened last fall when some of our guys got ahead of themselves."

"Juliet Longstreet's and Ethan Brooker's vigilantes. They had a set of principles they believed in and were willing to die for. They took risks."

Vern shook his head. "They were good guys, but they were reckless. They went too far. They exposed the movement to even more federal scrutiny." He walked down the hall to his room, sticking his key in the door. "I'm afraid Crawford's doing the same thing."

Huck followed him into the neat, dorm-style room. "Vern, talk to me, okay? I can help."

"Crawford was on the periphery of the movement until he was kidnapped. It goosed him into serious action." Vern opened his closet door and pulled out a gun box, setting it on his bed. "I don't know the whole story behind the kidnapping. I wasn't a part of that deal. Sharon Riccardi and Lubec were."

"Nick Rochester?"

"No."

"The guys who turned up tortured and executed—"

Vern grunted. "They got what they deserved."

"Yeah, but who was responsible?"

"CYA time. Cover Your Ass." Using a small key, he opened up the metal box. "Crawford wants to make a big splash. Let's just hope we don't get drowned in the process."

"Vern—"

"The less you know, Boone, the happier you'll be."

Every instinct Huck had told him that Vern Glover was on the verge of snapping. "Vern, something's happening today, isn't it?"

"Crawford thinks the feds are investigating us all right now." He lifted a loaded clip out of his gun box. "He's going after them. Making a statement. It's crazy."

"He's going after federal agents?"

"Nate Winter, Juliet Longstreet—they're marshals. Ethan Brooker. He's a former Special Forces officer. He and Longstreet killed one of our guys last fall." Vern sighed, his misgivings obvious. "It won't be easy to take them out. They're pros."

"Simultaneous attacks by multiple teams?" Huck asked. "Or sequential attacks, one team?"

"Two teams. One team for Longstreet and Brooker. One for Winter—and his wife."

"His wife?"

"She and President Poe are close personal friends. She's like a daughter to him." Vern stood up straight, his nostrils flared, nothing about this mission going down well with him. "It'd be a feather in Crawford's cap to get her."

Hell. Huck stayed focused. "What about Gerard Lattimore? Is he on his way back to D.C.?"

"That creep's not going anywhere today. He cooperates or he's dead."

"You're the one who'd have to take him out?"

Vern didn't answer.

Huck couldn't leave Glover to kill Gerard Lattimore or anyone else, and he had to warn Winter, Longstreet and Brooker.

He drew his Glock and pointed it at Vern. "You're done, Vern."

"You, Boone? Fuck."

"It's Deputy U.S. Marshal Huck McCabe."

Vern's shoulders slumped. "I should have known."

"Well, you didn't. Do you want to die for the cause?"

Glover didn't answer.

"Vern?"

"No."

"Then do exactly as I say."

36

Steve vomited onto a sandy, rough wooden floor. He had no idea where he was. He was light-headed, his stomach cramping. He rose up onto his hands and knees, dry-heaving, moaning. Hot needles seemed to stab into his chest and head, down his left arm. Blood dripped out of his mouth.

His hands were covered in blood.

I'm dying.

A sudden bright light pierced his eyes, and he fell back onto his side, his bowels loosening. *What the hell?*

A creaking sound—a door opening.

The hut.

He remembered now and sobbed. "Quinn…"

"Uh-uh, pal." A tall, dark man squatted next to him, patting him down. "Diego Clemente."

Big, firm hands picked him up by the waist and set him down against the hut wall, away from his puddle of barf. Steve squinted, focusing on the handsome man in front of him. *A Yankees sweatshirt.*

"I love the Yankees," Steve said.

"I don't. I'm from California. Where's Quinn?"

"Lubec…" Unable to continue, Steve dry-heaved, as if his stomach muscles couldn't stand the idea of what he'd done—couldn't stand him—and were trying to spit him out, get rid of him. Kill him.

Clemente stayed on task. "What about Lubec?"

"He has her. He was going to kill me. I had no choice." He remembered now, and started to cry. "I'm so sorry. I'm so damn sorry."

"Where did he take her?"

Steve held back another heave. "Up—up to the Crawford house. At gunpoint." He lifted his head. "She's pretending she's one of them. One of the vigilantes."

"Lubec believe her?"

"These fucking Nazis don't believe anyone. They're paranoid."

Another man arrived. Steve squinted at him in the bright afternoon light, recognized the spit-and-polished FBI agent.

Special Agent Kowalski.

"Steve Eisenhardt," Kowalski said coldly. "We found the car you borrowed at the marina."

Steve tried to stand up. "I want to cut a deal."

The FBI agent and Clemente both laughed, without humor. "You're a lawyer, Eisenhardt," Clemente said. "What do you think your odds are?"

Shit. This Clemente's another fed.

Steve wished Quinn had just let Travis Lubec shoot him.

Using Vern's cell phone, Huck called Nate. "Unless Glover's lying through his teeth or has bad information, you're in danger. You, your wife, Longstreet, Brooker. Oliver Crawford has two teams coming for you."

Winter wasn't one to waste words. "You?"

"Don't worry about me right now. I'm good."

Huck disconnected and dialed Diego's number. "Where are you?"

"About to climb over a barbed-wire fence. O'Dell's with Kowalski's partner. We've got Eisenhardt. We're on our way."

"Quinn?"

A half beat's hesitation. "She's with Lubec. I hit the alarm, Huck. We've got guys on the way. We're moving in."

Huck looked down at Vern, cuffed, glowering—yet refusing to incriminate himself further. He wasn't stupid. "It's not that simple," Huck told his partner.

He heard the familiar creak of the outer door and stuck his head out into the hall. Nick Rochester nodded to him.

"Rochester!" Vern yelled. "Boone's a fed!"

Huck tossed down the phone and eased into the hall, putting his Glock to the kid's temple. "Hands where I can see them, Nick." Huck patted him down, taking a nine-millimeter out of the kid's belt holster and a thirty-eight off his ankle. "Quinn Harlowe. Gerard Lattimore. Where are they?"

"Crawford's living room."

"Who's with them?"

"Crawford, Lubec, the Riccardis."

"You're caught between a rock and a hard place, Nick. What's it going to be? You want to cooperate?"

The kid inhaled sharply through his nose. "The creep from Justice. Eisenhardt. I was supposed to kill him." Hands up, he glanced at Huck. "I'm not a murderer."

"You chickenshit asshole," Vern said.

Rochester paid no attention to him. "Lubec would have killed me if I wasn't armed. I thought—" He choked up, the enormity of his situation obviously hitting him. "Too much of what's going down is personal. It's not smart. It's not going to help us win people over."

"Nick." Huck kept his tone even. "What's happening in Crawford's living room?"

"If Lattimore doesn't cooperate, he's dead. Lubec wired his boat with explosives. He'll take Lattimore back to the marina and—that'll be it." Rochester's tone stayed flat. "I saw Lubec take Harlowe up to the house. I don't know Eisenhardt's status."

"He's alive," Huck said.

Visibly relieved, Rochester's knees buckled under him, but he kept his hands up, didn't push his luck. "I didn't know what was going on with Alicia Miller. I thought she was sick. Lubec made sure she took the kayak up the loop road. He knew it was going to storm. I had nothing to do with it. I wasn't there. I'd have stopped it—" He broke off, swallowed. "I told you. I'm not a murderer."

"You guys have been funneling illegal weapons through here," Huck said. "Where are they now?"

"I don't know. That's the truth."

"The teams going after Nate Winter, Juliet Longstreet—"

"They're not going to waste a shoulder-fired missile on a fed," Rochester said. "We haven't had anything come through here since you and Glover arrived and Miller drowned. Too hot."

"Inside with Vern."

Rochester was reluctant. "He'll kill me—"

"He won't get that chance. I won't let him."

"That's supposed to make me feel better, a fed covering my ass? I hope you have backup, Boone."

"It's McCabe, actually."

"Lubec will kill you. Sharon's one bloodthirsty bitch, too. She approved all of us herself. Lubec, Glover, O'Dell. You." Rochester looked as if he'd smelled something awful. "She was distracted or she'd have sniffed you out sooner."

"She's been focused on stopping Crawford from going overboard."

"She blames herself."

Keeping his gun on Rochester, Huck found another pair of cuffs in Vern's gun box. Vern had lapsed into silence, but his eyes had taken on a piercing glow, as if he wanted to turn them into laser beams that could cut Huck in two or just set him on fire. Then, he'd start on Nick Rochester.

"Blames herself for what?" But even as he asked the question, Huck knew the answer. "Damn. She had Crawford kidnapped. Then she arranged his rescue. The torture and execution of the men she hired was her doing, wasn't it?" He shook his head. "Real nice."

"She wanted Crawford fully committed to the cause," Rochester said with no hint of irony.

"Sounds as if she got more than she bargained for."

Talk time was over, Huck thought. Diego Clemente, T.J. Kowalski and a haggard, bloody, barf-encrusted Steve Eisenhardt had arrived.

❦

37

Driving at breakneck speed, Nate Winter tried once more to get through by cell phone to his wife—nothing.

He told himself it could mean anything.

But Huck McCabe's words rang in his head, and although he'd called for backup, he knew he'd get to their house first.

As he pulled into his driveway, he saw the big moving van—then, Juliet Longstreet's truck. His relief was palpable. If anyone could handle a team of hired killers it was Longstreet. He got out of his car, ignoring the wobble in his knees as she ran onto the driveway waving to him.

"Sarah—" His voice cracked.

"She's safe. It's okay, Nate. We've got them—"

"How many?"

"A half-dozen. They were supposed to kill Brooker, you, me and—"

Sarah, his wife. Juliet didn't need to finish. Oliver Crawford had sent killers out for Sarah, too. Nate had to push back a surge of anger.

"I don't think these Special Ops types even needed me here. Brooker and your brother-in-law. Crawford's goons thought they were moving guys. Big mistake." The tension of the past hour brought out Juliet's natural irreverence. "I like your sister's husband. He can think in a crisis, that's for sure. Of course, Sarah threw up all over the damn place."

"Sarah threw up?"

"Yeah. Who could blame her, all these assholes coming to kill us. For a tough guy, PJ North doesn't like vomit."

Nate's mind was turning to fuzz, which wasn't like him. "Why did Sarah throw up? The fear—"

"I don't think it was fear." Juliet looked uncomfortable. "Talk to her about it. FBI and God knows who else will be here any sec."

She returned to the house, and Tyler North, compact, superfit, joined his brother-in-law on the driveway. He'd performed Special Ops missions as an air force search-and-rescue specialist under the most grueling, dangerous conditions imaginable. But, right now, he was grimacing. "Man, Nate. I hate barf."

"What about the guys who came to kill you all?"

"Piece of cake. Brooker's watching them until all you law enforcement types relieve him."

Sarah, pale but okay, appeared behind her brother-in-law. "It wasn't the bad guys trying to kill us that made me sick to my stomach."

Nate tried to smile through his own tension. Since the call from Huck, he'd been on autopilot, doing what he needed to do, relying on his training, his experience. "Some new casserole recipe?"

"I only have my grandmother's casserole recipes."

"Come on, Nate," North said. "You have two sisters."

He felt his knees going out from under him.

A baby.

He looked at his beautiful wife, at the moving van—his younger sister, Carine, coming off the porch with her and North's little boy in her arms. His sister Antonia and her husband were joining them later, with their baby girl. Nate's head spun. Orphaned at seven with two little sisters, he'd never seen himself settling down this way. He'd never allowed himself to believe he could have this kind of happiness. The thought of a wife, children, a house used to scare the hell out of him.

Police cars streamed into the driveway. Local, state, FBI, marshals.

Ethan Brooker joined Juliet, car keys in hand. Juliet, who had a big family of her own, some of whom were endangered last fall because of her work, touched Nate's shoulder. "Shit's hitting the fan in Yorkville," she said. "Sarah and your sister and brother-in-law can answer questions here for the time being. We're on our way. What're you doing?"

Nate hesitated, but his wife shoved him. "Go, Nate. Do your job."

38

"It's a beautiful afternoon." Quinn gestured out the window of Oliver Crawford's cheery, restful living room, the decor a total contrast to the moods of the people around her. "I don't think you all will be sending me out kayaking and hoping I capsize and drown."

Gerard Lattimore had sunk onto the sofa facing the view. "Quinn, don't even say such a thing as a joke. No one's going to harm you. Ollie? What's going on here?"

Quinn didn't let him answer. She was standing near the end of the sofa Gerard was sitting on, with Crawford opposite her. Her only plan was to keep them talking for as long as she could. "Ollie's trying to figure out if I'm for real, or if I get to be made an example of," she said. "He knows, Gerard. So do you, if you'll just admit it. Traitors inside and outside the government will make our lives impossible in short order."

Even Lubec, whom she'd almost convinced on the way from the marsh, didn't look as if he believed her. He stayed near Crawford. Mosquito-bitten Sharon Riccardi was sipping champagne, not speaking. Her husband stood in the door to the front hall. Whether he was blocking an exit or making sure he was near one, she couldn't tell.

Unfortunately, Quinn had no idea where Huck was. Until he showed up, or she had no choice but to act, she'd keep spewing the vigilante line and see how far she got with it.

"Alicia didn't understand what you all are doing. What *we're* doing." Quinn let her voice harden, as if she had nothing to fear. "Killing her put you under the kind of scrutiny you don't want. I'm not sure it was one of your smarter moves."

"We didn't kill her—she drowned." Lubec's voice was toneless, his eyes flat. He was the most difficult person to read Quinn had ever encountered. "She kayaked in a thunderstorm."

Lattimore was ashen. "How can you be so cold?"

Lubec shrugged, as if it was nothing to him.

"My God, Ollie." Gerard seemed totally shocked. "What's happened to you?"

"I've come to my senses. I see the world and its dangers with a clarity I never have before. I'm willing to risk everything to save my freedoms. *Your* freedoms, Gerry." Crawford sat back on the sofa, looking smug, if also nervous, even agitated. "What are you willing to risk?"

"You need help, Ollie." Gerard shook his head sadly. "The kidnapping did something to you."

"It only galvanized me into action. I learned we can't have it both ways. I made a commitment. I've risked my fortune, my life. I operate outside of the rule of law only to save it. I have to violate the thing I love for the greater good. Do I sound insane to you?"

"No. You sound very rational."

"Help us, Gerry. Join us." Crawford sat forward, leaning over his knees. "Today we make our mark."

Sharon took a gulp of champagne. "Oliver, let's not scare anyone." Her smile was halfhearted, ragged. "We love to talk politics, even extreme politics, but we haven't broken any laws, no matter how much we disagree with them."

Quinn interrupted, remembering her research. "I think you all need to get your own house in order before you undertake any further operations. For instance, Oliver, you and your right-hand woman here need to work on your communication. Did she tell you that she's the one who arranged for you to be kidnapped?"

Sharon barely responded. "Don't be ridiculous."

"You're good, Quinn." Oliver Crawford sounded almost sympathetic. "Trying to turn us against each other—"

"I'm serious. How did the thugs know where to find you? Hasn't that little question been keeping you awake at night? I'll bet my green kayak that it has. And how did Lubec here know where to find you when he came to your rescue? And where to find these guys so they could be tortured and executed?" Quinn pointed a finger at Sharon Riccardi. "Right there. She arranged it all."

"Oliver, don't listen to her," Sharon urged. "You're the risk-taker. Look at what you're doing today. You know I'm against it. I think it's too much when we're just starting. You've said yourself that in many ways the kidnapping was the best thing that ever happened to you. It gave you clarity."

"That's what she wanted, for you to have 'clarity.'" Quinn kept her tone matter-of-fact. "You're scared witless, beaten, half starved, threatened with death, and she's pulling the strings on all of it."

"Travis," Sharon said coldly, "take Miss Harlowe—"

Oliver held up a hand. "Not just yet."

Quinn, her heart racing, faked a yawn. "You all are such amateurs. I thought you were real players. You have to get with the program here."

But the boss wasn't listening. He was staring at the woman he'd trusted with his life. "Sharon?"

She smashed her glass down onto a side table. "Oh, stop. Stop! I've been at this a lot longer than you have, Oliver. I know what's at stake. We were cash-strapped after that mess last fall. We had every law enforcement officer in the country looking for us. We needed you to get off the fence. I knew once you got a taste of what we were up against, you'd come through for us."

Oliver Crawford jumped to his feet and turned to the window, apparently trusting someone, Quinn thought, to keep Sharon Riccardi from shooting him in the back. At the hall door, Joe Riccardi was stiff and silent. Quinn suspected he was armed—and on her side.

Gerard Lattimore looked as if he was about to have a heart attack.

Sharon was near tears. "You give the orders, Oliver. You always have. Things are out of control. Call off the hits you ordered. We have to be patient. We have to pick our battles or we lose the war—"

"My God," Crawford whispered, "my kidnapping—it *was* your doing."

She spun to Lubec. "Travis?"

"Mr. Crawford gives the orders."

"Joe?" With a quivering lower lip, Sharon Riccardi turned to her husband. "You'll stand by me, won't you? I know you're not a part of our movement, not officially. In your heart—"

"No, Sharon." He shook his head. "I came here to do a legitimate job. I'm not some psycho making up the rules as I go along."

"Bastard."

He ducked into the hall. Travis started to follow him, but Quinn stepped in front of him, aware of Lattimore on the sofa, frozen, staring at her. She had no idea if he'd help keep everyone off balance, talking, instead of shooting—but she couldn't wait for him to make up his mind. "Travis, you didn't switch the meds, did you? My prescription-strength ibuprofen for an SSRI—"

"I don't know what you're talking about," Travis replied.

"No, that was Sharon, wasn't it?" Quinn pressed

on. "She wanted Alicia agitated and upset. Her husband—" Quinn turned, trying to keep both Lubec and Sharon in sight. "Sharon, you said he used to run through the marsh. You followed his same route last night. You'd had too much to drink—"

"I didn't follow *his* route. I followed a path through the marsh." She raised her chin, defiant. "Yes, I was a little drunk. I had a lot on my mind. Oliver—"

"You let Alicia take a medication to which she was allergic, thinking it was ibuprofen?" Oliver shouted. "*Why?* What was the point? She was so agitated, so out of control—" Crawford staggered toward Sharon, fighting a sob. "She wasn't a real danger to us until then. I couldn't risk—" He raked both hands through his hair. "Having her in that state was too great a risk. She knew too much."

"Not because of me," Sharon said, hoarse now. "Because of Joe."

"Oh, I get it." Quinn acted as if the realization had just hit her. "Alicia wasn't having an affair with your boss. She was sleeping with your husband."

Sharon took two steps forward and slapped Quinn across the face, a crisp smack that stung, then flew around to face Oliver. "You killed her?"

"We let her die," he confessed. "It had to be done."

"Oliver—" Gerard's voice was strangled. "You've gone off the edge."

His eyes shining with conviction, Crawford pleaded with him. "Help us, Gerry. Join us."

Lattimore looked away, as if he couldn't stand the sight of his longtime friend another second. "I have no intention of helping you or joining you."

"All right. Have it your way." Crawford stood up straight, deflated. "Travis, take Mr. Lattimore back to his yacht. I'll trust in our friendship and his own self-interest that he'll keep what we said here today private."

Quinn moved in front of her former boss. If he went off with Travis Lubec, Lattimore was dead. "Wait, let me try talking to him." She saw Huck enter the room from the same hall she had used earlier, his gun drawn. "Huck, why don't you and I take Gerard out of here and have a talk with him?"

His eyes connected with hers for half a second, just enough for her to know he understood the situation. "Vern and Rochester are on the way," he said, moving toward her. "Is everything okay in here?"

Sharon slumped with relief. "We've had something of a miscommunication here."

"I'll say." Quinn touched her cheek where Sharon had smacked her. "It seems Sharon and Oliver aren't on the same page. She had him kidnapped and tried to undermine her husband's affair with Alicia by making her crazy, but Oliver also went behind Sharon's back—"

"Sounds complicated," Huck said, easing toward Travis Lubec.

"Don't listen to her," Sharon said. "Oliver and I are a team. Oliver, call off the hits you ordered. The feds are fumbling in the dark, wondering who we are. Don't give them a reason to pursue us until we drop dead of old age."

Quinn could see Oliver losing patience. "How close do you think the feds are to figuring you out?"

Sharon scowled in disdain. "Not as close as they think."

Huck leveled his weapon on Lubec. "How about this close, princess? Lubec—hands where I can see them. I'm a federal agent. Another federal agent is behind Joe Riccardi, armed with an MP5. You do not want to make a move for your weapon."

"Fuck you both," Lubec said.

Sharon Riccardi turned white. "You son of a bitch, Boone. You *liar*."

Huck disarmed Lubec of a gun in a shoulder holster and an assault knife in a sheath on his ankle. On the sofa, Lattimore sat frozen, but Quinn could see he had a good grasp of the situation and didn't believe she'd turned into a vigilante.

From the hall door, Joe Riccardi said calmly, "Sharon wears a twenty-two on her ankle. Crawford isn't armed. He believes only his subordinates should have weapons."

Diego Clemente stepped past the retired army colonel and lifted the hem of Sharon Riccardi's long, rose-colored skirt. "I have the proper permits," she said coldly. "I've done nothing wrong."

Lattimore cleared his throat, staring at Huck. "Who are you?"

"Deputy U.S. Marshal Huck McCabe, sir." He nodded to his partner, who had moved to pat down

Oliver Crawford as a precaution. "That's Deputy Clemente."

"What about Kowalski?"

"He'll be here shortly."

Lattimore, who obviously had used up any reserves, collapsed against the back of the sofa, his face blank as he stared at his former college roommate.

"Thank God." Oliver Crawford's hands shook as he held them above his head. "Boone—whatever your name is. I knew you couldn't be on the same side as these crazy bastards. I had a vague idea what Sharon was up to, but no details. She had me *kidnapped*. I had to draw her out into the open. Quinn and I played along with her vigilante line—"

Before Crawford went any further, Diego arrested him and read him his rights.

"Quinn?" Huck kept his eyes on Lubec. "You okay?"

"Still smarting from Sharon's slap. I haven't been hit that hard, ever."

"You've been in the bay again?"

"Kayaking." She thought a moment, then continued, steadier. "Alicia sealed evidence in a waterproof bag and hid it in the water under the osprey nest out by my cottage. The medication she was taking. And pictures—pictures of illegal weapons and explosives." Quinn glanced at Joe Riccardi. "You gave them to her."

Riccardi's nostrils flared slightly. "Alicia said she'd get them to the right people. I didn't know—" His eyes filled with tears. "I never should have used her that way. I didn't want to tip off Sharon and Crawford I was onto them— I wanted to get as much evidence against them as I could. I only knew about the illegal weapons and their extreme views—not the rest of it. The kidnapping, the torture and murder."

"You thought you could help," Quinn said.

"We wanted to nail them, Alicia and I. They suspended shipments of illegal weapons. They knew someone was getting close. I thought if I bided my time..." He sighed heavily, drained. "I never thought they'd kill Alicia."

Kowalski arrived. In minutes the place was flooded with federal agents. Joe Riccardi sank onto a chair, buried his face in his hands and cried.

Sharon Riccardi spit on her husband as Huck placed handcuffs on her.

After he turned Sharon over to another federal agent, Huck stood next to Quinn and smiled. "You're still red where you got smacked."

"She's lucky I can't shoot. If I could—"

"You can't shoot, sweet pea, but you sure can talk." He winked at her. "You did great. You kept them off balance, and you kept yourself and Lattimore here. You isolated the situation as best you could."

Quinn nodded. "What about Nate Winter, Juliet Longstreet—the people Crawford sent his killers after—"

T.J. Kowalski answered. "They're fine." He smiled. "You okay, Special Agent Harlowe?"

She managed a smile. "What happened to Steve?"

"On his way to the hospital," Kowalski said. "He wants to cut a deal, but he doesn't know half of what you've figured out. Lubec has pictures of him and a congressman's fifteen-year-old daughter." The FBI agent made a face, disgusted. "Yeah. Can't wait to see those."

He pulled Huck away, and Quinn shivered, suddenly aware of how cold she was. Diego Clemente appeared at her side and put a blanket over her shoulders. "Cashmere," he said. "Ollie's going to have quite a comedown when he gets to prison."

"He and Gerard—"

"Not such good friends after all." Diego tilted his head back, eyeing her. "You and McCabe, huh?"

"I might just be a fling," Quinn said. "A stress reliever."

"Stress reliever? You, Harlowe?" He grinned. "I don't think so. Wait until you meet Huck's family. You two need to spend a few days at the McCabe family hotel. The towels are something."

Quinn tucked her hands under the blanket, trying to get warm. "I want my office and normalcy."

Huck joined them and gave her a skeptical look. "Sure you do."

39

Two weeks after he'd watched one of his longest friendships implode in front of him, Gerard Lattimore talked Thelma Worthington into letting him into the headquarters of the American Society for the Study of Plants and Animals. Thelma no longer trusted him, with good cause. Oliver Crawford, Alicia Miller, Steve Eisenhardt—Gerard was bad luck. If he hadn't had on blinders, he would have seen what was going on sooner, and Quinn wouldn't have almost been killed herself. For certain, she'd have been spared the trauma of the past month.

Quinn wasn't one to wear blinders.

Thelma sniffed at him. "Quinn's on her way down. She's just back from Quantico."

"How's she look?" He hadn't seen her since Breakwater.

"You can judge for yourself."

Ten seconds later, Quinn glided down the stairs,

wearing a suit, her hair shining. Gone were the strain and the intensity, the sheer determination he'd seen in her as she'd kept Oliver Crawford and Sharon Riccardi focused on each other, exposed the lies they'd been telling each other and everyone else. And kept him alive. If he'd gone back to his boat, Huck McCabe and his crew would have been scooping him out of the bay in pieces.

"Quinn," he whispered, kissing her on the cheek. "How are you?"

"Doing well." She smiled, standing back. "Almost back to normal."

"I'm not sure I know what normal is anymore."

"It's a word that has to be redefined from time to time. You? How are you doing?"

"All right. It's still a day at a time." He glanced at Thelma, who didn't pretend she wasn't listening in, then turned back to Quinn. "I've resigned from Justice. I'm taking a job at a law firm in Los Angeles. A fresh start."

"I hope it's a good one for you," Quinn said.

"My wife and daughters—" He broke off, collecting himself before he lost it completely. "They're coming with me."

"Gerard, that's wonderful!"

"I don't know if it'll work, but what happened in Yorkville woke me up. I wish I'd had an easier awakening, but at least I'm trying to make some positive changes in my life."

She took his hand and squeezed it. "Good luck."

"It was so easy to have a schoolboy crush on you, Quinn. I tried to deny it, even to myself, and I never wanted to pressure you...." He left it at that. "Be happy, okay?"

"I will—I am."

"Huck McCabe." Gerard smiled. "You'll have to keep him. Thelma likes him."

Quinn laughed, and Thelma scowled at him, and when he left, the Society's door shutting softly behind him, he felt as if he'd just crossed the threshold from one life to another, and truly did have a chance for a fresh start.

Quinn took a glass of iced tea down to the water's edge and gazed out at her quiet cove, her first day back in Yorkville since she'd ended up making international headlines.

The reporters were gone, the law enforcement officers were gone, Oliver Crawford and his people were locked up on a variety of charges and, for now, the wildlife of Virginia's Northern Neck once again had the run of Breakwater.

Diego Clemente had returned to California. "I'll never have to wear a Yankees shirt again," he'd told Quinn. "This is good."

But Diego had also wanted to give her and his partner space.

"Huck doesn't want to settle down." She'd had to fight for the right words.

"He wants to settle down with you. There's a difference."

Since the end of his undercover operation in Yorkville, Huck had stayed in Washington, tying up loose ends, helping Nate Winter and his wife get settled into their new home, arguing with Juliet

Longstreet—and listening to Diego and Ethan Brooker swap stories about their days together in the Special Forces. Quinn had joined him as much as she could, given his responsibilities and hers. Every minute she was with Huck, she found herself liking him more and more, enjoying his company, unable to imagine having him back in California and her in Washington.

But except for the occasional kiss, their encounters over the past two weeks were very chaste, and Quinn was going nuts.

She was, she mused, incredibly attracted to him.

"I pissed him off in Yorkville," she'd told Diego.

He'd grinned. "There's that."

"Hey, Quinn."

She spun around, spilling her tea, discovering Huck so close to her that some of the ice landed on his feet. "Do they teach you how to sneak up on people in fugitive-catching class?"

"Yeah, actually, they do."

"I didn't hear you. The wind, the tide coming in—" She looked around her. "It's such a beautiful spot."

"It is."

"Huck—"

He seemed to know what she was going to say. "It's okay. It can wait—"

"It can't wait. It's waited too long. I did what I did, took the risks I took that day because I had to. I'd failed Alicia. I didn't want to fail anyone else."

He smiled. "I should have locked you in the trunk from the start."

"Your Rover doesn't have a trunk. Neither does Diego's truck. You guys are just a lot of hot air."

"It was a figure of speech." He took the tea glass out of her hand and set it in the sand, returning to her, his eyes squinted against the wind and sun. "We took a risk in leaving you alone."

"I'm not an easy person, Huck. I never have been."

"That's why you're an expert in transnational crime at thirty-two. You push hard." He caught a few strands of hair that had escaped her ponytail and tucked them behind her ear. "You're also more of an adrenaline junkie than you want to admit."

"Kayak into the wind. That's my idea of an adrenaline rush. But you—"

"No more undercover work for me. That part of my life is over. I'm not doing it again."

"How much of the man I fell for in those weeks was Huck Boone, bodyguard, and how much was Huck McCabe, undercover federal agent?"

"I never lied to you." He thought a moment and shrugged. "Well, almost never."

"Are you going back to California?" she asked.

"After meeting your grandfather, I don't see you in California."

"You met my grandfather? When?"

He ignored her. "I want to be where you are, Quinn. I've got options. Nate Winter wants me in Washington. Hell, Thelma's working on a grant for me from the Society for Plants and Animals."

"The American Society for the Study of—"

"Right. She thinks I'm a born adventurer."

"You'll do what the USMS asks you to do," Quinn said. "Another task force, another assignment. You love your work."

"You? Have you done your workshop at Quantico? All those FBI guys."

"All very buff, I might add. They listened to my every word."

"That's because they knew I'd kick their butts if they didn't. And because you're good at what you do and everyone knows it. You're not a phony."

"I just work hard, and I have an insatiable curiosity."

"See? We're two peas in a pod. If you hadn't managed the situation, Lubec would have killed Steve Eisenhardt. Now, he's talking. You're independent, Quinn. You're courageous. You make things happen."

"But I'm not patient. *You're* patient."

"Only when I have to be. Right now, Quinn, I can't last another second without making love to you."

She smiled. "Oh, good."

By the time they reached her front porch, Huck scooped her up and carried her inside to the bedroom, clean and tidy, everything back in order after Steve's panicked search for the missing pills. Citalopram. That was what Alicia had taken, thanks to Steve, who was pressured by Travis Lubec, who'd believed he was acting on orders from Oliver Crawford through Sharon Riccardi. Only it was Sharon, not Crawford, who'd wanted Alicia dead.

It was all a mess, one still getting sorted out by local, state and federal authorities.

Huck laid her on the bed, easing on top of her. "Quinn?" He smoothed back her hair and touched the tears at the corners of her eyes. "I can tell you're thinking."

She smiled. "I'm always thinking."

"Stop."

He kissed her softly, briefly, then kept his mouth close to hers. She stared into his eyes, noticing how dark they were, how intent they were on her. He had such focus and control, and yet he was, she thought, one of the kindest men she'd ever known.

"Quinn?" He gave her a mock frown. "You're thinking, aren't you?"

This time she laughed. The afternoon sun filled the small room, the curtains fluttering in a warm breeze. She wrapped her arms around him and felt the weight of him on her, the hard muscles of his legs, his arms, his back. A wild mix of sensations made her head spin.

"Okay," she whispered, pressing him onto her, feeling his urgency. "No more thinking."

This time, their kiss was neither soft nor brief, deepening quickly, his hands sliding up her bare legs and over her hips to the waistband of her shorts. Quinn didn't try to stop or control her reaction, or hide it from him. She helped him slide down her shorts, dispatch with them, and then her shirt and bra. He rolled onto his back, pulling her on top of him, and, placing his strong hands just under her breasts, he held her up from him and gazed at her.

"You're so beautiful," he said. "Damn, Quinn—I'm the luckiest man in the world."

He smoothed his palms over her breasts, and she caught her breath, surprised at the sheer enormity of her reaction, until, finally, he drew her down to him, capturing one nipple in his mouth. She helped get him out of his clothes, and by the time they cast his jeans off, the anticipation of making love to him had her aching.

"I can't…wait anymore," she said.

He smiled. "Good."

She lay on her back, taking him with her, into her. For a moment, neither breathed. Then he moved, a slow, erotic thrust, and she clutched his arms, digging in her fingers, and lifted her hips to take in all of him, exulting in the feel of him inside her. It was all the cue he needed. He deepened, quickened his thrusts, and she responded, never having experienced such a powerful mix of emotions and sensations.

When she came, she cried out his name, but he was coming too, falling hard with her, until they were, exhausted, spent, clinging to each other in the afternoon breeze.

They made love again, taking their time, exploring each other at length, holding back nothing.

Quinn couldn't imagine not having him in her life.

Afterward, they drank iced tea on the porch, the tide out, dusk coming more slowly now that it was late spring.

"Now," Quinn said, "about Fredericksburg and my grandfather…"

Huck stretched out his thick legs. "You didn't tell me he dresses like Rhett Butler."

She laughed. "You're making that up."

His eyes glinted with humor. "Ah, the things your grandpapa's never told you."

"Who did you tell him you were?"

"The lawman in love with his granddaughter."

"Huck."

"He liked it that I'm a marshal. He's probably one of about a dozen people who knows that the Marshals Service is the oldest law enforcement agency in America."

"That's not what—"

He wasn't listening. "I told him that his granddaughter is a romantic adventurer at heart. He liked that, too, because it shows that I know you."

Unable to hold on to her tea glass, Quinn set it down. "Huck, my grandfather isn't an adventurer."

"I don't know. In some ways, he's the biggest adventurer of all you Harlowes. He's not afraid of asking questions, of seeing people in all their complexity. I told him I'm not a perfect man." Huck set down his own tea and got up. "I told him that I know I have to prove to you that you're the one for me. The only one."

"You don't have to prove anything to me."

"Quinn—"

This time, she was the one who didn't listen. "Diego says I should see the McCabe family hotel in San Francisco."

Huck grinned. "He likes the towels. I should get him a set."

"I've only been to San Francisco once," she said.

"All right. We'll stay at the McCabe family nuthouse—I mean, hotel—for a few days." He put his arms around her waist, his eyes serious now. "But we're not honeymooning there. No—don't talk. I love you, Quinn. I want to marry you and be with you for the rest of our lives."

"We fell hard for each other, didn't we? Damn, Huck, I'm starting to cry!"

"A hard-ass Harlowe like you?" He grinned. "We need to get a move on. Diego's waiting for us."

"But he went back to California."

"Nah. He had to come out here one last time. As himself. Without the Yankees shirt, not playing fisherman. Smoking one last cigarette." Huck winked at her. "He wants to take us out on his boat."

"I love you, Huck. I don't think I said that—"

"I kind of got that feeling." He tightened his hold on her. "We need to put some ghosts to rest, Quinn. You, me, Diego. We'll go out on the water and drink a toast to lost friends, and we'll make this place special again."

Quinn looked out at the water, mirrorlike under the blue-gray sky. "I was thinking I'd have to sell my cottage."

"Then I'd have to buy it. I can't think of a better spot for a honeymoon than right here."

She thought of Alicia, and knew somehow that her friend would approve.

An osprey circled out at the mouth of her cove.

When they'd gone back for Alicia's bag, the FBI evidence team had taken care not to disturb the nest. Now, there were osprey babies.

"Ospreys mate for life, you know," Quinn said.

"My kind of birds." He kissed the top of her head. "Let's take a walk and go find Diego."

The latest historical romance from

NAN RYAN

Kate Quinn arrives in Fortune, California, with little but a deed to a run-down Victorian mansion and a claim to an abandoned gold mine. But a beautiful woman on her own in a town of lonely, lusty miners also brings trouble.

Sheriff Travis McLoud has enough to handle in Fortune, where fast fists and faster guns keep the peace, without the stubbornly independent Miss Kate to look after. But when a dapper, sweet-talking stranger shows a suspicious interest in Kate, Travis feels it's his duty to protect her. And he's about to discover that there are no laws when it comes to love.

The Sheriff

"Nan Ryan is incomparable at building and maintaining sexual tension."
—*Romantic Times BOOKclub*

The latest sexy historical romance from

ANNE STUART

Christian Montcalm was a practical man, if a destitute scoundrel, but his plan to bed and wed the delectable Miss Hetty Chipple would take care of that sticky wicket. However, there was a most intriguing obstacle to his success.

Annelise Kempton desired nothing more than to come between the despicable rogue and the fortune (and virtue) of her young charge. Certainly, Annelise understood the desperation that came from hard times, but Montcalm would fail—she would personally see to it. But when you dance with the devil, you hold hands with temptation....

THE *Devil's* WALTZ

"Brilliant characterizations and a suitably moody ambience drive this dark tale of unlikely love."
—*Publishers Weekly* starred review on *Black Ice*

Available the first week of February 2006 wherever paperbacks are sold!

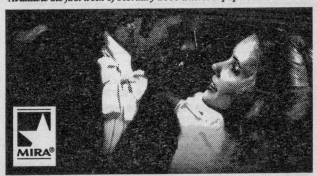

MIRA®

MAS2273

CARLA NEGGERS

32205	DARK SKY	___ $7.50 U.S.	___ $8.99 CAN.
32104	THE RAPIDS	___ $6.99 U.S.	___ $8.50 CAN.
32038	NIGHT'S LANDING	___ $6.99 U.S.	___ $8.50 CAN.
66972	THE CARRIAGE HOUSE	___ $6.50 U.S.	___ $7.99 CAN.
66971	THE WATERFALL	___ $6.50 U.S.	___ $7.99 CAN.
66970	ON FIRE	___ $6.50 U.S.	___ $7.99 CAN.
66969	KISS THE MOON	___ $6.50 U.S.	___ $7.99 CAN.
66923	STONEBROOK COTTAGE	___ $6.50 U.S.	___ $7.99 CAN.
66845	THE CABIN	___ $6.50 U.S.	___ $7.99 CAN.
66684	COLD RIDGE	___ $6.99 U.S.	___ $8.50 CAN.
66651	THE HARBOR	___ $6.99 U.S.	___ $8.50 CAN.

(limited quantities available)

TOTAL AMOUNT	$ _____
POSTAGE & HANDLING	$ _____
($1.00 FOR 1 BOOK, 50¢ for each additional)	
APPLICABLE TAXES*	$ _____
TOTAL PAYABLE	$ _____

(check or money order—please do not send cash)

To order, complete this form and send it, along with a check or money order for the total above, payable to MIRA Books, to: **In the U.S.:** 3010 Walden Avenue, P.O. Box 9077, Buffalo, NY 14269-9077; **In Canada:** P.O. Box 636, Fort Erie, Ontario, L2A 5X3.

Name: _____
Address: _____ City: _____
State/Prov.: _____ Zip/Postal Code: _____

MIRA®

www.MIRABooks.com

MCN0206BL